Simon & Audrey
Thanks for the support
& encouragement
enjoy the read !
Wendy May

RAE OF HOPE

The Chronicles of Kerrigan

W.J. MAY

MITCHELL-MORRIS PUBLISHING

MITCHELL-MORRIS PUBLISHING
Port Richey, Florida

Copyright © by W.J. May
ISBN-13: 9780983129790

Library of Congress Control Number: 2011940914

MITCHELL-MORRIS PUBLISHING , November 2011
http://www.mitchellmorrispublishinginc.com

Acknowledgements

Every book an author writes has a journey behind the story. (Author, ha! I still get a kick out of saying that). My life took a different route when I lost my father to cancer in 2008. This book is dedicated to him, for even in death he taught me how strong faith can lead you, and how much of an example to others we are (even when no one is watching). This book, and all my writing, is a result of his courage to chase after "the impossible" and follow your dreams. *Thanks Dad, I still miss you every day.*

I have so many individuals to thank for encouraging me, and pointing me in the right direction to show everyone Rae's potential:

My husband, who encourages me and makes me feel like the most important person in the world (I love you), and my three adorable kids (who even when they are sick of Mommy behind her computer, still love her). My extended family for their excitement – my mom, brothers and sisters (in and out laws :), and also my beta-reader nieces who read, and even wrote a book report on Rae before she became published!

My super-sincere and amazing agent, Dawn, who saw my potential when I had no clue it really existed.

Luci, my publishing editor, who "got" Rae, and knew exactly how to speak her thoughts.

Tracey, and everyone at Mitchell Morris Publishing – I still can't believe Rae is in print! Thank you!!

My GG crit crew: Tiffany, Chrissy, Holly, Trish, Marti, Jayde, June, Marva, Wendy, and anyone else I may have accidentally missed mentioning – you know who you are and I love you for it.

Extra note: special thanks to Ray – for letting me "borrow" his name.

Special thanks goes out to all the readers – you guys are fantastic!

CHAPTER 1
Guilder Boarding School

"YOU CAN'T UNDO THE PAST. THE SINS OF THE FATHER ARE THE SINS OF THE SON, OR IN THIS CASE, DAUGHTER."
Uncle Argyle's ominous words had echoed in Rae's head long after he dropped her off at the airport. "A proverb of truth" he had called it. Who spoke like that nowadays? *Some good-bye.* Tightening her ponytail and futilely trying to tuck her forever-escaping dark curls behind her ears, she looked at her watch, then out the bus window at the tree lined countryside. It seemed strange to see the sun. All she remembered was rain when she had lived in Britain nine years ago.

Trying to get comfortable, Rae tucked her foot up on the seat, and rested her head against her knee as she looked out at the scenery flashing by. A sign outside the window showed the miles before the bus reached Guilder. It'd be another twenty-five minutes. She popped her ear buds in, blew the bangs away from her forehead and stared out the window across the rolling farm fields, trying to let the music from her iPod distract her.

It didn't work. Just when she felt the tension begin to ease from her shoulders and she started to get into the song, something caught her eye. Black smoke billowed just near the top of a lush green hill. Rae stared, her heart fluttering as an old memory began to take hold. She knew what that smoke meant. She'd seen it before, long ago.

Someone's house was burning.

Crap, crap crap, no I don't want to go there. Her heart started racing and her stomach turned over, making her feel nauseous.

Dropping her knee, she gripped the seat in front of her, burying her face in her hands taking deep breathes, like the therapists taught her to do. She'd gone through years of therapy to treat what had been called "panic attacks". It didn't matter what other people called it. To her, it was simply hell; like being sucked back in time against her will, to a place she never wanted to revisit. So she breathed the way she'd been taught, slow breathe in, all the way, then slow breath out, all the time chanting *it's not real, it's not real* in her head.

It helped calm her racing heart and made her feel more in control, but it didn't erase the memory. Nothing on Earth could do that. Being back in England for the first time and seeing the strange smoke, Rae felt six years old all over again.

She'd been in the living room coloring with new markers before bed when her mother told her to take them to the tree house her dad had built for her and play there until she called her in. That call never came. The blaze bounced horrific shadows around the inside of the tree house. The stinky black smoke slithered in and scared her little six year old self in ways the monsters under her bed never had.

Rae shuddered and lurched upright, forcefully bringing herself back to the present. *Could this school be any further into the sticks?* Glancing around the now vacant bus, she wondered if the driver had purposely left her until last. She'd watched the last few people get off at a school about fifteen minutes ago, Roe-something or other. They all looked the same, all pretty girls with blonde hair, not one of them thin, pale, and tall like her. They hadn't been friendly. *Big surprise there...* She was used to it. She tended to fly under the radar at best. So she handled them the way she always handled the ones who instantly didn't like her for no reason she could come up with. Rae avoided making eye contact and tried to appear immersed in the Guilder Boarding School brochure. It wasn't that she didn't want to make friends. She'd just never really had any. Most kids her age either didn't like her or didn't notice her.

It bugged her that Uncle Argyle had pushed so hard for her to go when Guilder sent the letter. He'd been the one to move them all from Scotland to New York when she'd come to live with them, taking her away from the horrible tragedy of her parents' death, and now, he suddenly leapt at the chance for her to go back? It didn't make any sense. It sort of sucked to leave her current high school. She lacked close friends, but she also lacked enemies, which was a plus n her book. The girls there seemed just as stuck up as the ones who'd gotten off the bus earlier, but they'd simply ignored her. Rae always told herself it didn't matter anyway. Cliques were *so passé* in her opinion.

Another weird thing that she couldn't seem to find an answer to was why Guilder would choose her? How did they even know she existed? Her uncle boasted how big a deal it was for her to be selected, but he'd never once explained how they'd even come to know about her in the first place. She had the grades, the brain part always came

3

easy for her, but she didn't have any extra-curricular activities at all, nothing to make her stand out. So, how had this amazing school she'd never heard of before decide to take her on? It didn't make any sense. She tried a few times before she left to corner her uncle and get him to explain part or all of it, but he'd always seemed to be busy.

While this wasn't exactly abnormal behavior for him, it still left her with a sense of foreboding, something that had clung to her ever since she got the letter. She couldn't figure out why, but she had a strong sense that something big was coming. Whether it was good or bad, she didn't know.

A movement out of the corner of her eye caught her attention, pulling her mind out of the endless circle of questions in her head. She turned to look out the window, and was stunned to see the largest bird she'd ever seen in her life. *Maybe an eagle?* The thing flew parallel with the bus, right beside her. Pressing her face against the cool glass, her gaze focused intently on the curious sight. She jerked back when its large wings flapped, brushed the window, then veered away. She watched its graceful flight as it soared and then swooped to settle onto the limb of a large tree just ahead. As the bus passed by, the bird seemed to lock eyes with Rae and she was mesmerized. Rae had always wondered what it would feel like to be a bird, to fly so free, go anywhere the wind took her. She continued to watch the bird until she couldn't see it anymore, then slumped back into her seat as the bus sped onward down the long road.

Guilder Boarding School. She gnawed at the cuticle on her thumbnail a little too hard and ripped the skin, drawing a wince from her. She couldn't help it, she always did this when she was nervous, and she was certainly nervous now. She'd be the only American girl.

Well, not really American. She held a British passport but had been moved to New York after her parents died in the fire, leaving her orphaned. So...not really American, not really British; a little of both, but belonging to neither.

The bus cruised by an aged stone sign. *Guilder Boarding School, Founded 1520. One of Britain's Finest Educational Institutions.* Rae read the sign and wondered how a school could be that old and not be featured in stories or online. She found nothing when she tried researching it. They drove under an old, leaded window arch that connected two round, red-brick towers. The stream of people coming and going from the doors at the bottom made her think it must be some kind of office. She craned her neck to get a better view. The buildings were old but were well kept and held an almost magical aura of their original Tudor era. She half expected to see men in tights and codpieces strutting down the road, leading their horses, with corseted ladies perched delicately atop them. The mental picture amused her and she absent-mindedly smiled. Her eyes were drawn to the ornate, brick chimneys along the buildings' roofs. She glimpsed the other buildings beyond. *This place looks huge...hope I don't get lost.*

The driver pulled to a halt in front of a building with an embossed plaque that said "Aumbry House". The ancient building had ivy growing all over it. It looked like it was probably older than Henry VIII, leaving Rae with horrifying visions of chamber pots dancing in her head. *It better have indoor plumbing...*

The bus door slid open with a hiss. Rae gathered her two small suitcases and her book bag, clambered down the aisle and finally, blessedly, off the bus.

"Welcome to Guilder, Ms. Kerrigan." Rae awkwardly spun around to face the voice, finding that a tall, thin woman stood on the concrete steps of the building, her eyes darting left and right, pausing on Rae for barely more than a few seconds.

Rae stared, wondering where the lady had come from. *She wasn't there a moment ago.* Rae looked at the woman's long, wool skirt. *This might be England, but today is sweltering. How is she not melting in this heat?*

"I am Madame Elpis, your house mistress." The lady darted down the large concrete steps, pausing on the last step and, in one fluid motion, tucked her clip board under an armpit and extended her hand.

The woman's features reminded Rae of a bird – her jet-black hair, dark eyes, and especially the jutting nose. Rae nodded and dropped a suitcase so she could return the handshake, her fingers crushed by the woman's claw-like grip. *Ow, ow, ow! So you're freakishly strong, got it.*

"Come along. No time for dilly-dallying." She turned and marched up the steps, not checking to see if Rae followed or needed any help with her bags.

Huffing out a breath, Rae grabbed her things and clambered to follow, hearing the bus driver chuckle as he closed the door behind her. *I'm spending the next two years here? What joy. What freakin' bliss.*

Hammering and drilling noises from above greeted Rae as she came through the entrance. The clamor echoed throughout the building.

"Fifteen and sixteen-year-olds are on the second floor," Madame Elpis shouted above the noise. "Your room is the last door on the left." She checked the chart she'd been holding under her arm. "Molly Skye is your roommate. I assume you can find the way." The last part was more statement than question.

"Thank you," Rae replied uncertainly, not knowing what else to say.

Madame Elpis pointed to a door on her left. "The study hall's through there. The glass doors lead to the game room. The door to your right is to my living quarters. You are not permitted there." She led Rae to the winding staircase made of black and white marble. "Juniors are on the second floor, seniors on the third and fourth." She glanced at an old pocket watch hanging on a chain around her neck and, if possible, straightened even more. "Dinner is at five o'clock, sharp." She turned, her skirt swirling as she darted into her room, and with a kick of her boot, slammed the door.

Rae exhaled the breath she hadn't realize she'd been holding. The banging of hammers and screeching whine of electric saws reverberated through the hallway. She was so nervous, the hammering could have been coming from her heart and she wouldn't have been able to tell the difference.

Rae took her time up the marble stairs and, once on the landing, headed left to the end of the hall. Biting the inside of her cheek, she gave a light knock at the slightly open door and peered in. *Empty.* Rae cautiously pushed the door open and surveyed her new room.

Thick, lush brown carpet covered the floor. Two beds, with matching duvets and tan suede pillows, rested against the opposing walls, one of which already sat full of half-empty suitcases. Modern closets with ample space matched perfectly with the antique desks built into the wall by each oriel window. Rae inhaled deeply, taking in a mingled sense of fresh paint and the unique scent of antiques.

Finally! It'd been one helluva long day of traveling. Much of the tension ebbed from her shoulders and she cracked a smile for the first time in hours.

Rae dropped her suitcases on the uncluttered side of the room. Her roommate, Molly, must have stepped out halfway through unpacking. Her closet doors were spread open, with hangers already full of clothes and more shoes than Rae had owned in her entire life. She'd never been big on dressing up, but she still knew designer labels when she saw them and she saw an awful lot of them in that closet. Hopefully, her roommate didn't end up being superficial. Rae stood there wondering how she'd deal with it if she had to room with Guilder's Next Super

Model. Visions of her roommate stomping up and down the room in heels practicing her "walk" distracted her. She didn't hear the footsteps walking down the hall to the door.

"What are you doing in me room?" Rae jumped and dropped her purse. A fashionably dressed girl stood in the doorway. She had dark, mahogany red hair, the kind women paid insane amounts of money to try to copy. *Oh great...well, here we go.*

"Molly?" Rae swallowed. "I'm your new roommate."

Molly stared Rae up and down. "*You're* Rae Kerrigan? I pictured someone *totally* different. You're not scary at'all!" She laughed as if at some private joke. *Scary? Me? What is she talking about?*

"Name's Molly Skye. I'm from Cardiff, in Wales." She shoved one of her suitcases onto the floor and dropped into the small, open space on the bed.

Rae watched, confused. Why would anyone think of her as scary? Because she lived in New York? She had a terrible premonition of being the odd one out, and school hadn't even started yet.

"You're not sixteen, eh? No ta'too?" Molly pointedly dropped her gaze down to Rae's waist, as if she expected Rae to show her something.

Tattoo? Rae squinted, trying to listen closer to Molly's accent. The way she spoke, some of the words were hard to make out. *Why would she ask if I have a tattoo?*

"Me birthday's in three days. It's going to be so awesome!" Molly leaned back on her elbows. "When's yers?"

"My birthday? Uh...not 'til November." *Straight into the personal info. Okay, I think I know what my roommate is going to be like.*

"November? You do have a long wait." Molly grimaced and shook her head. "Poor you. You'll be the last one inked for sure." She jumped off the bed. Rae noted the strange comment, but Molly's motor-mouth went speeding on, so she filed it away for examination at a later time.

"What'd you think of our room? Pretty cool, eh? Aside from the construction on the floors above us." She shot the ceiling an annoyed look. "I just talked to one of the workers. He said they finish at four. They start again at like eight in the morning! Can you believe that? Who gets up at that time, anyway?"

Wow. Molly can talk without pausing for breath. Rae nodded and tried to keep up. She watched Molly roll from the balls of her feet to her heels, back and forth continually. It was a typically nervous gesture that Rae attributed to meeting new people. *Everybody has their issues, but it's still surprising, considering how fast she's talking.*

"Can you believe *we* got invited to Guilder? We're two of sixteen females within a landmass of rich, supposedly unattainable, handsome boys." When Rae didn't respond, Molly squinted at her. "You do know why you're here, right?"

Rae shrugged. Jet lag seemed to be eating her brain cells. "To be honest, I don't really know what you mean. I haven't been in England since I was six and I know nothing about Guilder." *Despite numerous Google searches at home and having my nose buried in the brochure for an hour on the ride here.*

"You're not slow or something, are you?" Rae shook her head slowly wondering if her talkative new roomie had just insulted her. Molly stared, scratching her head. "You really don't know, do you?" She looked up and to the left, obviously recalling something important. She straightened, as if quoting some bit of brochure from memory. "Guilder's a highly sought after educational institution, but it is primarily a school for the *gifted*. People who get to go to Guilder know why. The rest of the world has no idea!"

Rae curled her fingers tight, her nails digging into her

palms. She felt stupid and also irritated at herself for feeling stupid. It wasn't something she wanted to deal with, especially after such a long day of travel. "What makes us...gifted?"

Molly's eyes grew huge. She paced the room. "Oh, my... Me da's never going to believe this. You seriously don't know ANYTHING?!"

Rae felt her blood pressure rising. She knew she was tired, confused, and nervous. None of that it was helping her temper, but she was determined not to loose it on what amounted to a total stranger. She pressed her lips tight to stop any snappish comment that might escape. *Can't the ditz just answer a simple question with a straight answer?*

Molly swung around in front of Rae, dramatically squared her shoulders, and put on a serious face. "When we turn sixteen, we receive our ink blot."

"What?"

"A ta'too." She leaned forward and whispered, "It gives us special powers."

Pause...say what? "P-Powers?" Rae tried not to laugh. Had her uncle sent her to an institution for the insane? "You're kidding, right?" Uncle Argyle had told her the experience would change her life, but hadn't said how. Rae figured he meant she'd do some growing up – like a maturity thing. And, of course, there was that silly proverb. But perhaps he'd mistakenly sent her off to a giant rubber room.

Molly waved a hand. "I'm serious. The gift is passed down from generation to generation." She blew out an exaggerated breath. "Any guy around here who's sixteen has a ta'too on the inside of his forearm." She dragged Rae toward the window and pointed to the building across from them. "That's the boys' dorm. Let's go outside and walk around. I'll get one of them to show you what I mean."

Her eyes dropped down to Rae's clothes, her lips

pursed tight together. "Do you fancy a quick change before we go?"

Rae laughed, despite her roommate's serious expression. Molly definitely was crazy, but she had a point. She'd dressed comfortably for travel, and even though she wasn't big on fashion, even she drew the line at meeting her new classmates looking like a worked-over hag. She could use some freshening-up. "Yeah, give me a moment."

"I'm off downstairs to try and find some cute boys. Meet me outside when you're ready." Molly left, still chattering non-stop with no one in the hall to listen.

Rae opened the closest suitcase and grabbed the first pair of jeans and top within reach. She hesitated and dug a little deeper into her suitcase. The jeans were fine, they were new, but a white t-shirt seemed too plain. She found a pink Converse tank top with ONE STAR written in sparkles. She pulled out her hair tie, wishing her unruly black curls were straight like Molly's perfect hair. She never bothered with makeup because she had crazy-long eyelashes that mascara seemed to only want to clomp up against, and almost everything else just made her look kinda like a sloppy hooker. *Keep it simple,* that's what her aunt had always told her. She settled for lip gloss, and deodorant, and then grabbed a pair of sandals before tossing her purse under her pillow. *Now, time to find out what Molly's been babbling on about, or at least, maybe meet some cute guys.* She might be invisible most of the time, but eye-candy was eye-candy, no matter which side of the Atlantic it was seen on.

Once outside, she shaded her eyes against the bright sunlight with her hand and searched for her new roommate.

Molly stood further down the sidewalk, talking to a very hot guy with chestnut brown hair, dark eyes and a dimple on his right cheek. It disappeared when he stopped smiling and began talking again, making Rae a little sad. She wanted to see that dimple again. Rae bounded down the steps, then slowed down, trying not to appear too excited. She flinched and covered her head when a loud crashing noise sounded from above, and a large piece of debris flew down from the fourth floor and landed in the blue bin beside her. Face burning, she pretended it hadn't bothered her and continued walking. Molly and the boy turned to stare in her direction.

Rae heard someone holler from above, but couldn't make out what the guy said. Embarrassed by her reaction a moment before, she ignored the shout and kept walking.

Molly's eyes grew big, her hands flew to her cheeks and her mouth dropped open. She screamed. Rae stared as Molly frantically pointed above her head. Rae tipped her head up. She froze in horror when she saw a huge, severed piece of wood paneling balanced like a seesaw on the window ledge several floors above.

The wood scraped against the windowsill, and teetered as if undecided which way it should fall. *Oh crap!* A gust of hot, dry wind blew by, knocking the severed beam into final decent. It spun as it fell and all sound was just gone.

Fight or flight. Rae dropped her gaze, her eyes darted about. The guy beside Molly moved toward her frozen frame. Everything moved in slow motion except for the guy running like a freight train. He was greased lightning, moving faster than anything Rae had ever seen. It didn't seem possible for a person to move so fast. *And why am I focused on him when I'm about to be squashed like a bug?*

Chapter 2

Proverb of Truth

JUST as she was about to throw her hands over her head for what little protection she could offer herself, Rae's neck was jerked sideways, she went flying through the air and landed on dry dirt with a thump. Before she could react, warm arms wrapped around her body, forcing her head against a hard chest. They rolled together a bit and, and just as they stopped moving, Rae felt and heard the impact of the paneling hit the ground exactly where she'd been standing a moment before. Dropping her head back against the ground, trying to remember how to breathe after having the air squished out of her lungs, she opened her eyes and waited for them to focus. The cute guy lay on top of her, and the wooden beam had crashed down in the spot where she'd just been standing. The cute boy rolled off, but not before she got a thrill from the smell of his musky scent with a hint of delicious aftershave. *Wow…*

She stayed on the grass, unable to tell if being winded came from the fall or the boy. Rae spat some dirt out of her mouth and did a mental check. Nothing felt broken or even hurt too bad. Still dazed, she stared up at the building, trying to figure out if what had just happened was real. The shoulders and heads of two men in hard hats popped through the window.

"Everyone all right down there?" the one wearing a white hat shouted.

The boy glanced at Rae then called back up. "I think we're fine, but you guys are nuts!"

"Yeah, sorry about that. We're done for the day now, anyway." The men laughed and disappeared inside the window. Rae thought it seemed a bit rude of them, but had other more important things to focus on at the moment.

The boy dusted dirt and grass off his knees, then held his hands out to help her up. "I'm Devon Wardell."

Rae wiped her forehead, feeling dirt and grime mix into her skin. *Great first impression Rae.* She forced her attention back to the boy and nodded, her gaze drifting from his handsome face down his lean torso and along his bare arms. There, below the elbow of his right arm, lay a tattoo of a cute little fox with big ears. She blinked and sat straight up, silently pointing. Suddenly afraid all of Molly's crazy talk might be true, Rae didn't have the courage to ask.

"It's a Fennec fox. They're originally from the Sahara Desert." Devon's expression remained serious.

"You don't have long ears." Molly stated as she stepped over Rae to stand next to him. Rae could hardly believe the lack of concern for her well-being. *Gee, thanks roomie.*

Devon laughed. "No, I don't. Most of us don't actually take on the look of our ink." Shoving his hands in his pockets, he winked at Rae. He swallowed and then opened his mouth to speak, but Molly started before he had a chance.

"That's *so* cool! So, what's your gift? I mean, besides

14

the speed thing we just saw. Did you figure it out right away?" She moved in front of Rae, blocking her view.

Devon sighed and sat down on the grass and Molly followed suit, settling next to Rae and actually leaning into her, making Rae wonder what she'd done to deserve having her personal boundaries invaded. However, it wasn't of the utmost importance at the moment, since Devon was again talking, flashing that dimple her way. "No, I didn't. The morning I turned sixteen, I had no idea of the tatù's power. My father's got almost the same one, but we never talked about it." He stared up at the sky and snorted, then he smiled at the girls. "That night I figured it out quick." He gave a wry chuckle. "I got me some pretty cool nocturnal gifts."

"Awesome night vision?" Molly asked.

"Yeah, and incredible hearing. Plus, Fennec foxes can jump decently high, and are super fast."

Understatement, Rae thought. *Speeding-bullet fast...*

"Fantastic!" Molly dropped to the ground and sat close to Devon. "I can't wait! Only three more days for me. My father's got some zigzag line, which he uses at his jewelry shop and a few other places he owns. It's like he's got a pair of jumper cables instead of hands! Hopefully, I'll have something more girly for my power."

Rae finally found her voice around the same time her brain caught up to the conversation. "Wait. Your dad's got a tattoo?"

Molly gave her a funny look. "Of course. Your parents bo–"

"Are you sure you're all right?" Devon cut Molly off.

Rae didn't miss the move, wondering what it was about, but was unwilling to re-direct his attention back to the conversion. "I'm fine, I think." She stretched her back. "Just shocked, that's all." Which was putting it mildly. *I just narrowly avoided death, and am now surrounded by people obsessed with tattoos who also have superpowers.*

Fantastic...Sure...I'm great...

"Rae!" Molly turned, as if suddenly remembering the recent traumatic event. "Wow! You could've been killed! Glad Devon saved you, or I'd get stuck with some dolt of a roommate." She flipped her hair behind her shoulder. "What about you? Do you have any idea what yours is going to be? Any help from *your* dad? Or mom?"

Devon elbowed Molly in the ribs, but kept his concerned eyes on Rae.

"I...uh...my folks..." Rae didn't know what to say or think. Why would her parents have anything to do with this? Could what she was hearing even be remotely possible? Strange as it might seem, she knew it was true. It just seemed to make sense deep down inside, even though she couldn't pinpoint why. *Or...I could be going crazy...* Her stomach clenched and rolled. She suddenly felt woozy. "I...um...I think I need to walk around a bit and get some fresh air." She started to stand.

"Wait. I'll come with you. In case you pass out or something." Devon reached for her hand and helped her to her feet. Once she was up, he didn't let go, and Rae didn't want him to. "Molly, think you could grab Rae a bottle of water or something?" He smiled, and the cute dimple appeared again.

"Sure. I'll meet you guys on the front steps of Aumbry House."

Rae enjoyed the thrill from Devon's warm, strong hand in hers. She followed him down the sidewalk, concentrating on slowly breathing in and out. The dizziness began to disappear, but the dull pain of a headache beat at the back of her skull.

They passed a building marked Joist Hall. "I'm sorry Molly threw all of this on you. For the record, we aren't crazy. Headmaster Lanford told me you probably didn't know anything about our ink-art." He stared straight ahead. "The school isn't sure how much your uncle or father might've told you." He looked at her out of the corner of his eye. "Did you know they both attended Guilder?"

What? She planned to kill her uncle next time she saw him. She had obviously been owed a long conversation, stuffed with pertinent information, before he put her on the plane. *But all I got was a stupid proverb.* She shook her head. "Why do you know so much about me?"

Devon laughed and patted her shoulder. "You're quite the talk of Guilder at the moment — the English-American who convinced the headmaster, and dean, to open the college to girls." He coughed, as if trying to cover his words. "Or, uh...you know, open another college for females only...technically speaking that is...."

*Wait a sec...*Rae stopped in her tracks. "I didn't convince anyone! I haven't even spoken to the headmaster or the dean. One day I got a letter telling me I'd been accepted. I just assumed my uncle applied without asking me. He's originally from Scotland, so I thought maybe he knew about this place."

Devon waited a few paces ahead. "Weird." The puzzled look on his face turned to teasing. "Well, the faculty's pretty excited you came. You might not know them, but, trust me, they know all about you."

"What're you talking about?" She crossed her arms and felt the beginnings of annoyance emerge from her inner turmoil.

"You're special."

Rae's face burned. Giddy from his comment, she couldn't help but laugh. "No, I'm not. I'm just one of the average, quiet, sorta-smart girls. Though, at this moment, I feel pretty dumb." She tapped the toe of one sandal against the heel of the other. "Why in the world would the dean, headmaster, or anyone else think I'm special?"

"Because of *who* you are."

That didn't make sense. "'Cause I'm Rae Kerrigan?"

"Yes, silly, and because of your parents."

"What about my parents?" Rae could hardly remember anything about them. She'd been so little when they died in that terrible fire almost ten years before.

"I don't think it's my place to explain." Devon nervously shifted his weight from foot to foot. "Maybe you should talk to Headmaster Lanford."

"I plan to." She chewed on her nail, imagining some scary, crazy principal dressed in long, dirty robes who spoke in proverbs of truth like her uncle. "What's he...uh, like?"

"He's good. Big guy. Bad hair. You'll like him, and he'll answer all your questions." Devon absent-mindedly traced his tattoo with his fingers. "Don't pack your bags and jump on the first plane back to New York. Give Guilder a chance. It's even better than the brochures say." He grinned, showing his adorable dimple. "We'll grow on you. And trust me, when you get inked, you'll be glad you're here."

"On my sixteenth birthday, like Molly said? I'll get a tattoo on my arm?"

"Nah, yours is on your lower back." Devon's cheeks turned a light shade of pink. "It's way cooler on girls than guys."

Sexier was the word he didn't say, but Rae could read it on his face. She'd seen tattoos on girl's backs but never thought of them as anything more than ink. A tramp stamp. She needed to start taking notes if she planned to fit in at this school. "I guess I'll just have to wait three days and see Molly's." She had so many questions bubbling inside her. She wanted to ask if they got to choose their tattoo or if they were pre-selected for them. Maybe they had some kind of list. If there was, when did she get on it? She pressed her lips together, not wanting to appear denser than she was sure she already looked.

"Sure, or some of the older girls will show you." He

pointed toward Aumbry House. "Molly's talking to Haley and Maria. They're both sixteen. Want to go meet them?"

Butterflies bashed around inside Rae's gut. What if everyone knew about her like Devon did? What did that mean anyway? She let out a slow breath. "Sure." No sense in being shy in front of the hot, and probably senior, boy. For some reason, she wanted to impress him and being a recluse wouldn't accomplish that.

As they walked back to Aumbry House, Molly ran over to greet them. The other two girls followed at a slower pace.

"Rae, meet Haley and Maria!" Molly gushed the introduction in what Rae was beginning to see was her typical fashion.

"Hi," said the blonde-haired, brown-eyed girl. "I'm Haley."

A tiny, dark-haired girl peeked around Haley's shoulder. "Hello."

Rae blinked. She could've sworn Maria had just said "hi" but she hadn't seen the girl's lips move. She glanced at the others to see if they'd heard it as well, but she couldn't quite tell. *Maybe it's the jetlag in my brain playing tricks on me.*

Devon checked his watch. "Ladies, I'd love to stay and chat, but I've a football match. My housemates will be ticked if I don't show. I'm already late." He patted Rae on her shoulder.

As he jogged away, Rae noticed the others staring at his retreating figure. *No surprise there. He's part superhero.*

"He's so hot," Molly murmured.

"And sexy. Definitely worth watching," Haley said. "And chasing."

"No dating, remember?" Molly half-heartedly chided. "Guilder highly discourages that. It's taboo – not that I plan on paying attention to the that rule."

Molly walked behind Haley and reached for the back

of her shirt. Haley deftly stepped just out of reach.

Molly didn't even acknowledge the dodge. She just powered straight on into conversion. "Can we see your ink? Have you figured out how to use it?" *Molly, definitely not the shy type.*

Haley laughed. "I, by no means, have mastered my gift. But I'm sure I've figured out what I can do. Coming here is only going to make me stronger and better." She pulled her shirt up and turned around to show her back to both of them. Above her jeans was a stunning tattoo of a whirlwind or tornado.

"So, what all can you do?" Molly asked as she impatiently tapped her foot.

"I can make wind."

Molly snorted.

Haley shot her an annoyed look. "No, silly, not *that* kind of wind. I create wind. Big wind, or even just little gusts." Haley twittered a high-pitched laugh which Rae found annoying. "At my old school, I used to send small gusts to mess up my teacher's piles of papers, other stuff like that. Right now, though, if I try anything stronger, I end up flying backward."

Molly skipped ahead to the next subject, seemingly unimpressed with Haley's power. "What about yours, Maria? What's your ink?"

Rae felt sorry for the tiny girl. She looked like she wanted to disappear. Rae decided to come to the rescue and end Molly's little impromptu inquisition. "Hey, why don't we head over to where Devon's playing?"

"And meet more cute boys?" Molly gave a little kid-like bounce. "Let's go."

The girls headed off to the sports fields.

"Thanks." A soft voice spoke inside Rae's head, causing her to misstep, but she quickly caught herself. She glanced at Maria from the corner of her eye and nodded. When Maria smiled, Rae grinned. *Holy Cow! That really happened!*

She talked in my head! This school is going to be so amazing.
Molly suggested they head to the middle of the sidelines, so they could see both teams. They sat down on the bleachers to watch. It didn't take long for Rae to figure out Devon was easily the quickest and most talented on his team. The boys seemed oblivious to the girls sitting in the bleachers, which Rae didn't mind. It gave her time to calm the butterflies in her stomach.

A boy on the opposite team dribbled the ball near his goalkeeper. In the blink of an eye, he'd passed midfield and streaked around a defense player. He took a shot on the net, scoring easily. Rae blinked and rubbed her eyes, wondering if she was seeing things.

"No goal! No goal!" Devon waved his arms in the air. "Riley, you know the rules. Only natural play — *no* gifts!"

"Give me a break! I can't help if my slow running is faster than everyone else's," Riley shouted. His teammates cheered and slapped him on the shoulder.

"You're not faster than the speed of light without your gift! No way can you argue with the laws of physics." Devon tapped his head and the other boys laughed. "Trying to impress the girls?" The guys started walking over to where the girls sat.

"Whatever." Riley scowled at him.

Devon bowed dramatically to the girls.

"Hey, I'm Riley." He stepped in front of Devon.

Rae noticed a tattoo of a cheetah on his wrist. That explained his speed.

"Gals, this is my team. Our keeper is Nicholas, our two defensemen are ..." Riley's eyes and mouth stopped moving when they came to Rae. He simply froze, staring at her like he couldn't believe what he was seeing. *Is it my hair? Is there something on my face?* She suddenly wished she could hide behind Haley. But no matter how hard she wished, she could see by the look on his face, the something which had stunned him to silence, was her.

"You're Rae Kerrigan, aren't you?"

All laughter and jostling from the guys walking toward them stopped instantly. Rae swore all their jaws dropped open at the same time. Her temper flared from embarrassment and the stress of the day combined with the fact that she had no idea why everyone was acting so strange. Words rushed out of her mouth before she had a chance to think them through. "Yes, I'm Rae. I've no idea what you've been told about me, but let me assure you, I feel ten times more uncomfortable around you than you do around me." *You strange bunch of gifted people have no idea how terrifying you are.*

Devon came to her rescue. "Don't mind Riley. He may be fast as a cheetah, but he has the tact of a rat." Riley scowled at Devon's comment, but it broke the ice, and the boys laughed and relaxed. *They obviously trusted him. Hmm...cute, superhero, tactful and now, trustworthy...nice package.*

Molly piped up, "I'm not inked yet. My birthday's in three days. Rae doesn't turn until November fifteenth."

Rae stared at her roommate in shock. How did Molly know that? She hadn't told her. Molly had the date wrong. Due to a clerical error when she was born, her birth certificate showed the wrong date, but at this point Rae didn't really feel like correcting the mistake, since Molly shouldn't have known it in the first place. It suddenly seemed like a very good idea to make sure her true birth date remained a secret.

"So you're just normal 'til November?" one of the younger-looking boys asked. "Poor you for the next few months."

Rae just stared mutely at him. *Poor me?*

"That's Brady. He turned sixteen four months ago, but he's been here since he was thirteen," Devon said.

"Didn't help him learn any skills on how to control his gift," a different boy teased. Brady just smiled and pushed his fingers at the commenter, who went sprawling backward.

"Brady can control wind, like Haley." Devon ruffled Brady's hair. A tall boy with his dark, almost black, hair tied in a ponytail, rested his arm on Devon's shoulder. Rae noted the confident, comfortable gesture. This was obviously one of Devon's friends and Rae decided she wanted to know all of his friends. She'd need to start gathering information since everyone seemed to have the details on her already.

"Hiya. I'm Julian. My talent is by far the most interesting. I can draw the future." He tapped his long, artistic fingers on his wrist. "I've just had a vision telling me it's half past four and Lanford's getting hungry. If we want to eat, we'd better start heading back."

The guys collected their belongings. Rae stayed close to the girls as they headed back to the school buildings. She felt uncomfortable about the impact her name caused but she didn't know what to do about it, or even the reason behind it. She was glad that Devon walked beside them, along with Julian, who seemed unfazed about her identity. Anyone behaving like a normal person ranked high on her good list at the moment.

About half-way back, Devon interrupted what had become a comfortable silence. "We'll see you shortly, at the table." He let his shoulder rub against Rae's. "We'll save you a seat." The guys headed into Joist Hall, and the girls continued to Aumbry House.

"Don't you think they're all super hot?" Molly whispered as they headed up the steps.

"Dunno." She shrugged, caring more about information than boys at the moment. *The headmaster had better be at dinner tonight.* She wanted to get some answers to the millions of questions flying around in her head.

Chapter 3

Headmaster Lanford

BACK in their room, Molly did a quick hair check and make up refresher. Quick wasn't quite the right word exactly. She needed half an hour to *fix* what, in Rae's opinion, already looked perfect. Then they headed back down the stairs to meet the other girls.

"If we're the only four here so far, why the heck does Madame Elpis wanna meet downstairs? She makes it sound so...mandatory," Molly whined as they waited at the main entrance.

Rae ignored the childish tone of Molly's complaint. "Do you know what her i-ink is?" It felt funny trying to talk as if she understood everything.

"Madame Claws?" Molly laughed. "Not a clue. Each professor, as well as the headmaster and dean, is inked. So we know she has one, we just don't know what it is."

Rae grinned. Molly could switch moods faster than a light switch.

Haley, followed by Maria, came down the black and

white marble stairs. "'I heard Guilder won't hire anyone who isn't inked," Haley said. "My father says the school may seem like any other prestigious college, but everyone who graduates from here does big things. They're all successful and make loads and loads of money." She paused to flash a haughty smile. "My father does very well and has big plans for me." Haley finished with a snobbish smirk.

"What're you gonna do with wind power?" Molly asked flatly, rolling her eyes.

"I'll find something, and I'll be rich," Haley's expression transformed from snobby to terrifying, making Rae nervous.

What's the deal there? Rae wondered if Haley was any relation to the Wicked Witch of the West. *All she needs now is the cackle.* Rae could just picture Haley all done up in the witch's black dress saying "I'll get you my pretty!" and had to turn away from everyone to compose herself so she didn't laugh out loud.

"Um, okay...," Molly held her hands up. "How? I don't get how everyone here makes big money, if we're supposed to keep these abilities hidden from the rest of the world."

Haley smiled, all BFF again and Rae made a mental note to stay out of her way. She might switch moods as fast as Molly, but for some reason, it was creepier with Haley.

Haley linked her arm through Molly's. "Wait 'til you get your ink. Then you an' I'll figure out what we can do. We'll be rich and nab us some even richer hubbies."

Rae wanted to gag. *Real Housewives of Guilder?* How lame could they be?

"Haley's not that bad. Her father was real disappointed when Haley inherited the gift instead of her younger brother. Seems the gift gene is usually passed to males, and there has only been a shift in the past, like, forty years. Some people still would

prefer that boys get the gift rather than girls." Maria's quiet voice in Rae's head bore a hint of bitterness.

Rae shifted to dispel the shiver that crept down her spine. It felt incredibly strange to have someone else's voice inside her head. *Can she read my mind too?* She turned to Maria and half-smiled. The worried crease on Maria's face disappeared. *That's not a no...better find out the answer to that question.*

Before Rae figured out how to test the issue, Madame Elpis strode in from outside, her heels clicking on the marble tiles. "Ladies, one should not keep gentlemen waiting, especially at meal times." She turned and reached for a switch above the door. As she raised her arms, her blouse lifted revealing her ink. Rae strained to see over everyone's shoulders. It was a little bird, a magpie. Molly flapped her arms and made a sour face. The girls giggled, barely managing to suppress the laughter before Madame Elpis straightened and shot them a stern glance.

Molly straightened and whispered to Rae, "Madame Crow definitely has eyes in the back of her head." Rae thought to herself, *You ain't kiddin'.*

The girls followed Madame Elpis along the path, past Joist House to a smaller building set in the shadows. A plaque on the wall by the door proclaimed it Refectory Dining Hall. White with wooden beams throughout, topped with a thatched roof, it reminded Rae of a post card her aunt once got of a Cape Cod house.

The sound from inside the dining area was like a stadium full of screaming fans. But as they entered, all the noise and activity came to a standstill.

A very large man with an overgrown comb-over stood up from his seat at the front table. "Ladies, I'm Headmaster Lanford." He turned slightly and cleared his throat loudly. "Gentlemen, I'd like to introduce you to the new students at Guilder." He walked around the table and introduced the girls by name.

The boys clapped with each introduction, but hands froze midair at the mention of Rae's name. Boys leaned in toward each other; a murmur of whispers buzzed around the room.

Rae closed her eyes and wished the floor could swallow her up.

Headmaster Lanford seemed oblivious to the reaction. He simply told the girls to find empty seats. From the size of his belly, he seemed to be someone who didn't like to miss a meal and maybe had seconds and thirds to boot. *He probably pinches chips from other people's plates too.*

Devon's voice rang across the silent room. "We've got seats for all of you."

Rae was so relieved to see a familiar face, she nearly ran to him even with everyone staring. *Would hiding under the table be any less noticeable?* She settled beside Devon and stared at her empty plate.

"Hope you're hungry," the boy on her other side said. "I'm Andy." He reached for the water pitcher.

His sleeve slid up, showing Rae his ink. Dark ink detail in black, grays and browns displayed a wolf sitting on its haunches. Rae's natural curiosity over-ruled her discomfort with her surroundings. She couldn't stop herself from asking. "Do you have the characteristics of your tattoo? Like Devon does with his fox mark?" Rae dropped her gaze and scolded herself for sounding like Molly with the back-to-back questions. She worried she had probably just screwed up royally, and managed to make an already bad situation even worse. Surprised when Andy laughed, she looked up at him.

"No, I'm a shifter." He pulled his sleeve up all the way and traced the image with his fingertips, allowing Rae a better view. "Don't worry, I'm a good wolf. There's no need to be concerned for Little Red Riding Hood or the Three Little Pigs. They're all safe from me." He winked at her.

"Good to know." She laughed, liking his teasing banter. "Are there any other shapesters...I mean shiftsters...shape-shifters?" She cringed inwardly over her tongue-tied, stilted conversation. *Could I act any thicker?*

"One other." Andy pointed to a guy with a beak-like nose sitting further down at their table. "Rob. He shifts into an eagle. Lucky bugger gets to fly!"

"You're joking?" Rae glanced at Rob who sat across the table, disbelieving the long-armed boy could actually turn into an eagle. She thought back to the large bird on the bus ride and wondered if it could have been him.

"He's the only one at the school right now who can fly. It's pretty cool and unbelievable at the same time."

Rae smiled. "*Everything* seems pretty cool and unbelievable. Trust me."

Devon leaned across Rae and grabbed the basket of buns. "Pretty much all of us here knew about gifting before we started, at the age of twelve. Plus our dads usually explained things prior to coming." He chuckled. "Kinda like Dad's "'facts of life"' lecture."

Not me, thought Rae. *No dad to do that for me. And Uncle Argyle was certainly no help either..* But she planned on getting answers as soon as she could. Now wasn't the time to feel sorry for herself, so she pushed the emotion to the back of her mind.

Rae carefully schooled her expression to hide her feelings and focused on gathering information. "You've been here four years?"

Devon appeared happy to fill her in. "Yeah, the school's designed to give you three years to prepare for the gift and then another two to help educate you and train the gift. It helps you enter back into the 'real' world and do some good with what you've been given without revealing yourself."

"Quoting the school manual again, Dev?" Andy nudged Rae to show he was teasing.

Rae smiled and played along, but held her hand up, as if to try and stop her thoughts. "Wait a minute." she considered Devon's words. "So...you mean, you get this ability and the school helps you hone your talents," -- she waited to see Andy and Devon nod their heads -- "but then expects you to act like you're normal and hide it?" It didn't make sense.

Someone at their table coughed, and mumbled, "Like father, like daughter."

Rae gave a slight jerk to her head, trying to see who'd said it. She'd heard it loud and clear, even if they were trying to muffle the words. She glanced around, but no one seemed able to meet her gaze, all of them suddenly too interested in their plates to lift their heads. She didn't get the comparison, but knew it had to do with her. It sounded too similar to her uncle's last words.

"It's easier to hide it." Andy patted her forearm.

"Why? Wouldn't the government or the country want to know? They could stop bad guys, and surely, not everyone with this ink-stamp uses it for good."

A few more snickers erupted around the table. Rae glared. It ticked her off that people would think her dumb for not knowing any of this. They'd all been raised in this world, and she had only just been shoved into it today. *They know so much about me, don't they know that too?* She turned to Devon, wondering why his face had turned beet red.

Andy cleared his throat. "What would you do if someone shape-shifted right in front of you? Or while you were on a plane, you saw the stewardess boil water with no kettle, just her hand?" He shook his head.

Devon piped in, "If we let our secrets out, could you imagine how scientists or military people would treat us?

Andy replied before Rae had a chance to open her mouth. "Crap. They'd hunt us down, shoot first and ask questions later. We'd all be a bunch of lab rats." He grinned. "Or lab foxes and lab wolves."

Devon tossed a bunch of pasta on his plate and elbowed Rae. "Don't stress about it. These are really cool abilities to have at sixteen, but as we get older, they get strong --"

"-- And can become very scary," Andy added.

Rae shuddered. *Maybe that's the reason why Uncle Argyle didn't say a word about the real Guilder College. He didn't want to tell me that I'm a freak and I have to go to school with superkids.*

"Guilder just wants to teach you to appreciate the gift and use it to your own, and the world's, best advantage. Lots of famous people attended here. It's the reason King Henry VIII started this college in the first place," Andy said.

Rae sat back in surprise. *This goes THAT far back?* "He wasn't gifted, was he?" Nothing could shock her now.

Devon and Andy laughed before Devon replied, "No, he just wanted to find someone gifted to help get him a male heir."

Molly rolled her eyes from across the table. "He should've thought about not wearing those awful-looking tights, or maybe spoken to a doctor to learn it's the male who determines the sex of babies."

Rae glanced sideways at her, wondering if Molly realized yet that the science of genetics had not existed way back then. *If they had, good 'ol Henry wouldn't have needed a divorce, and England might still be part of the Roman Catholic Church.* She decided to ignore Molly's outburst. "I've got another question."

"Hit me." Devon slowly pulled his eyes away from Molly. The corners of his lips were twitching.

Obviously, he's thinking it too, but won't point it out. Handsome and nice...great combo. He just keeps getting better and better! He was looking expectantly now and Rae's mind snapped back to her question. "You said your dad told you. What about your mom?"

"She doesn't know."

Rae had been about to hit him with her next question, but hadn't expected that answer and got sidetracked by it. "Huh?"

"Dad's inked. He never told my mom. She just figures it's a tattoo from his teenage days. He told me the truth when I got the letter to come here."

Rae tried to absorb that, wondering which of her parents had a tattoo, or maybe if they hadn't died, if one of them would have told her about all this and sent her to Guilder three years earlier. The possibilities made her head spin, and it was only the continuation of the conversation that brought her back to the present.

Andy leaned forward, his voice slightly lower. "Only one parent's inked. Except in –"

"It's almost always the male." Devon shot Andy a look.

Rae didn't miss Devon's smooth attempt to cut Andy off and prevent him from saying something, and glanced back and forth at both of them. "What's the matter?" Her voice rose slightly and conversations around their table stopped. She turned her entire body to face Devon. "Why so secretive? Seriously, what could be weirder than what I've already found out today?"

He made no response. Everyone around them sat there with a wide-eyed deer-in-the-headlights look that people got when they were caught by surprise.

That's my look! I should be the one looking like that! Something doesn't add up. Something isn't being said and I have to know what it is. So she picked what she thought was a random response. "Does this have something to do with *my* dad?"

The entire hall became quiet. Everyone stopped eating. Rae felt hundreds of pairs of eyes focus on her. No one said a thing. Most expressions held dislike, others pity, which she couldn't stand. Devon's sympathetic face became too much to take. She stood, ready to go back to the dorm and pack her bags. *This is bullshit. All of it.*

"Getting a wee bit frustrated, Ms. Kerrigan?" Headmaster Lanford stood at the head of their table. He appeared calm, almost oblivious to the reaction of the other students. His eyes held understanding without pity. "Would you care to join me on a walkabout?"

Yeah, I have some questions for Mister Combover. "Fine, let's go," she snapped, and then hastily added, "Sir."

Chapter 4

Unwanted Answers

RAE and Lanford walked in silence. Rae grew more and more nervous with each step. She wanted answers, but now that they were outside, away from the expressions of strangers who knew more about her than she did, walking next to the one person who might have all the answers, the idea of asking seemed daunting, even scary. As they passed a sign marked Turret Hall, the headmaster started a seemingly pointless monologue about the campus, pointing at buildings with his cane.

"Turret Hall is the music and arts building. The Scriptorium is the English building and also includes the library with the history of our ink and gifts. Some of the gifts and ink stamps are documented on ancient scrolls dating prior to the Tudor era. Each dormitory is also equipped with a reference library and copies of the special ink charts and markings." His fingers drummed a rhythm on the silver head of his cane. "This path here will lead you to the Oratory. That's where students study their gifts and improve their skills."

Rae nodded but said nothing. At the moment, she didn't give a damn where classes would be.

They turned down the path, and Rae stopped to stare at the Oratory. Built in red brick similar to the other structures, this building was none-the-less distinctive. Ivy stretched across the tall, almost chapel-like octagon shaped building. The way the ivy grew, it seemed to emanate from the walls. She'd never seen anything so magnificent. The view belonged in the painting of a master artist. It was such a tranquil scene compared to the anger simmering inside of her.

"I've been wondering," the headmaster murmured. "Did your parents teach you about their tatùs?"

Rae froze, one foot dangling in the air. *He said parents, plural. That wasn't a mistake.* Both her parents had gifts? *Yet another thing about me I didn't know, told to me by a stranger. This isn't fair!* Why was she the only one who didn't know this stuff? With rage surging through her veins, it took an effort to speak without screaming. "My *parents* never had a chance to tell me anything." She shrugged, trying and failing to set her foot down on the ground normally rather than stomping it. "I was only six when they died in the fire, so I don't remember much." Most of her memories felt like dreams now.

Lanford stared pensively at the head of his cane and gave a slight nod. "Of course, the fire. How about Argyle? Has he explained anything to you?"

"Uncle Argyle?" *He'd better not be bloody marked as well.* "No, he never told me about any of this." *Plus, he likes talking in ridiculous proverbs.* "I think Guilder's made a mistake with me." Rae felt all the different emotions of the day rolling inside her. The fear and confusion, the suspicion and frustration, the wonder and disbelief...it all started to overwhelm her. And to top it off, she hadn't heard any of it from someone she actually knew. Anger began to override all the other emotions.

Lanford smiled and patted his combover down. "No, Ms. Kerrigan. You are, most definitely, the right person. Your mother only had one child, and that was you." He tapped his finger to his lips. "I'm not shocked your parents didn't have the chance to explain, but I'm quite surprised Argyle never took the time to enlighten you."

"Yeah, join the club." This seemed more important than a talk about the birds and the bees, which was, of course, another topic never broached.

The headmaster released a long, heavy breath. He pointed to a nearby bench with his cane. "Shall we sit? I think it's high time you learned a bit of your own history." Rae sat down heavily, realizing her posture, and most likely the expression on her face, made her look like a petulant child, but at the moment, she couldn't help herself. Despite everything, she noted that for his large frame, the headmaster settled easily, almost lightly, onto the bench. "It's time to shake that family tree up a bit, eh?"

Shake the family tree? That sounded like something her uncle would say. Rae gingerly balanced herself, paranoid the bench might topple over from his weight. It seemed likely. Having something other than her emotions to concentrate on allowed her to calm down. She needed answers. And apparently, Headmaster Lanford had them.

"Did you know your father and Argyle attended Guilder together twenty-three years ago?"

Rae shook her head so slightly she wasn't sure the headmaster even noticed. She planned on having quite the conversation with her dear uncle next time she saw him.

"Though your dad was a year older, they were best mates. From different ends of the country, your father from Manchester and Argyle from Edinburgh. Both started Guilder at the same time." Lanford sighed. "School was very easy for your uncle, so we put him in a higher level.

The two boys immediately became good friends. Both were extremely intelligent and promising young lads. The school couldn't have been more excited."

"So they were buddies." *Big deal.*

"We were concerned about your father. He quickly grasped the concepts, but also argued with our ideals." Lanford shifted and ironically, Rae didn't feel the bench move. "He vehemently disagreed with the idea that we should be unvoiced about our gifts. However, most of us – I was a young professor at the time – felt he'd outgrow his rebellious stage when he received his ink." The headmaster stared straight ahead, as if watching an old video replay.

"What happened?" Rae spoke in a quiet voice. The curiosity began to turn into dread as it settled in the pit of her stomach. *Not sure I want to hear what happens, but scared or not, I need to know.*

"Argyle influenced your father in a positive way. So it came as quite a shock when, a few months after Argyle's fourteenth birthday, he informed us he'd be leaving." Lanford smiled and patted Rae's arm. "I remember him as a young boy, always a mess -- clothes, hair, room...everything except his thought process. That always remained in perfect order. Brilliant lad. I'm sure he still is." Lanford cleared his throat. "Apparently, Argyle had an older sister who'd just turned sixteen and been gifted. His father wanted him back home to show her everything he'd learned." The headmaster smacked his cane across his knees. "Damn it! Such a good lad, and it was a shame to have to let him go."

"My mom? But how? If Guilder gives you the tattoo, how'd she get it?"

Lanford looked as surprised as Rae felt. "Guilder doesn't give you the tatù. It's inside of you and blossoms on your sixteenth birthday."

Her eyebrows shot up and she tilted her head. "Oh."

She didn't know what else to say. *So they just appear like magic? How does that work?* But Lanford was already talking so she kept quiet.

"Ink stamps tend to be patrilineal; passed down to the men of the family. Most gifted also will only have one child. It may sound silly to you at the moment, but with this power comes responsibility. It's simply easier this way. Some will try for a second child if their first offspring is a girl. Do you understand what I'm telling you?"

"I th-think so." Rae nodded. "Males are usually marked, but instead of Uncle Argyle, my mother got it." *You put the girl child out in the wilderness to be eaten by wolves.* Rae bit her tongue to keep from saying her thoughts out loud.

"Correct. Your grandfather had been such an asset to this country during the Second World War, we high hopes for Argyle. At the time, Guilder didn't allow girls into the school, so we were never able to work with your mother."

Rae couldn't believe her mom had a superpower...or her dad. *Oh yeah, Dad...* "What about my dad?"

"Your father, Simon, turned sixteen and received his ink – a unique one. Unfortunately, he continued to fight against the teachings of the school. It seemed that without Argyle here, he became more self-absorbed." The headmaster paused. "The summer Simon's father passed away, he went to stay with Argyle. He planned on returning to Guilder for his final year, but he met your mother, Bethney. I guess they fell in love. The school, your grandfather and your uncle all opposed their dating."

"Why?"

"It's...well...it is believed to be dangerous." Lanford fidgeted with his cane. "That's one of the reasons Guilder remained an all boys' school. It was thought best not to create challenges in our young adolescent boys' lives when they're challenged enough with what they have inside of them and gaining control over it."

What? How does that make sense? Rae itched to interrogate Lanford, but cautioned herself against it. *Skip it, don't ruin the talkative mood, Rae.*

"Until now." What about her mother? Couldn't she have benefited from the knowledge Guilder had to offer? Maybe she could've learned something and saved herself and Dad from the fire. They might still be here today if Guilder hadn't been so chauvinistic.

"Yes, until now." The headmaster smiled.

It set her off. Rae couldn't hold back; her temper flared, hands clenched, she pounded her knees. "What about us? You say you worry about the boys, but what about the females who could use help with their gifting?"

"My dear child, *that's* one of the reasons we've opened the school to young ladies such as yourself. We have high hopes it'll go well."

Still frustrated, Rae rubbed her hands down her thighs, squeezing with her fingers just above her knee, trying to relieve tension with a little self-massage. It didn't really help. "Devon said the reason Guilder opened its doors to females is because of me. Not some quantum shift in your chauvinistic thinking, but me specifically."

"Devon is a good lad, and it'll do you well to pay close attention to him. He'll help lead you in the right direction." Lanford's head bobbed up and down. "That boy has his head on straight and will do very well in life. His power is small compared to some, but his talent is immense. He's an example to us all – a natural leader the students follow." Lanford's chest puffed with pride.

Rae's eyebrows came together. She opened her mouth to ask her question again.

Lanford cleared his throat, cutting her off. "Now, be patient." He waited until she closed her mouth. "In truth, you are a big reason for the female enrollment. Your father and mother both possessed powerful gifts. If you inherited either or both of them, it would be unjust to have you learn on your own. What I don't understand is what your uncle Argyle was thinking by not mentioning anything to you." His cane pounded the ground, punctuating his words. "He's a smart man, I can't for the life of me figure out why he did not say anything to you. This is going to be a very challenging year for you, and I'm glad we've a few months before your birthday to help you prepare." He patted her knee and smiled.

She wasn't about to let it go that easily. The child deep inside who had been orphaned at a young age and had never quite healed from the experience, wanted answers. "If my parents' gifts were so strong and powerful, why'd they die? They should've been able to save themselves from the fire." Rae's eyes filled, but she refused to let any tears fall.

"My dear, there's so much you don't know yet. I promise you'll learn everything we can teach you, but not all of it tonight." He pressed his lips into a thin line. "I have matters I need to attend to, and I think you have enough information to absorb for today."

He rose quickly – faster than Rae thought his large frame should be able. She grabbed the arm of the bench, frightened it would topple backward, but was surprised when it didn't even rock. She checked to see if she could spot his ink, which was useless since his shirt and suit jacket covered his arms.

The headmaster walked a few paces and turned back around. "This is a school for learning and no question is the wrong one to ask. I've asked Devon to tutor and help mentor you for the upcoming year." He held up a hand to stop the question he knew she was going to ask. "It isn't because we feel you'll have trouble with your classes. I think, without your background knowledge of the powers, it'll make it easier for you to ask questions in a tête-à-tête setting.

Yeah, or if it has anything to do with my family, since I'm already a freak at this school. Rae ran her fingers through her hair in frustration as she tried to calm down. The headmaster did seem like he was trying his best to help her. The thought of hanging out with Devon a few evenings a week didn't sound too bad either. She took a deep breath and tried to let go of some of her tension.

Lanford straightened. "We want to help you understand how you can use your gift to its best advantage. How we can help make this world a better place for everyone. That is Guilder's quiet oath and the dream for all of its students."

Rae figured he spoke those words a lot. They sounded well-rehearsed. As she headed back to Aumbry House, she wondered what the big deal was about having both parents inked. Her chest tightened as she began to worry what the rest of her family's story was.

Chapter 5

Friends?

THE next day, the students sat in the dining hall eating breakfast. The tense atmosphere of the previous day seemed like a bad dream. Everyone appeared relaxed and informal, even jovial.

"Julian has a car?" Molly straightened in her chair, eyes bright.

Andy swigged the rest of his breakfast tea, then laughed. "Yeah, a few of us seniors do, actually. I've a feeling the school won't be allowing many of the girls to keep a car on campus – at least probably not in the near future." He tried, unsuccessfully, to wipe the smirk off his face.

"That's fine." Molly raised her eyebrows, a tight smile playing on her lips. "If boys have cars, why would I need one?"

"I think Andy's just teasing you, Molls." Rae laughed. It felt great to talk about normal things and forget about all the crap she was dealing with. Waking up, she had decided to leave all the confusing stuff under her pillow and not let anyone see it. She needed to fit in. Having people know so much about her when she didn't know them made her feel vulnerable, but there was no way she'd let anyone see it. In a weird way, it felt like her vulnerability was the last private thing she had.

"How's our American gal feeling today?" Andy looked at Rae. "You were...uh...you seemed kinda upset at dinner last night."

Rae swallowed an oversized bite of scrambled eggs, choking on it. "Yeah, about that...sorry." She paused, blinking. "I was really jet lagged, and I guess...everyone staring at me..." She let the sentence trail off, hoping someone would take up the conversation from there and not camp out on the one topic she didn't want to discuss.

"Don't worry." Andy nodded sympathetically. "The curiosity'll die down soon enough. You're a pretty girl, and there's a story behind your name. That's bound to turn some heads. On top of that, don't forget this has been an all-male school for a long time. It's an awesome thing to have girls here now."

Rae's cheeks pinked at the compliment. *Thank you Andy! My knight in shinning...fur...or something.*

"Are you up to anything this afternoon?" Andy asked.

Rae blinked, trying to forget her train of thought before she erupted into a fit of laughter. "Madam Cro— Elpis wants us to meet the new girls arriving. Wanna come?" Rae ignored Molly's giggles at her almost mix-up.

"Sure, but I'm pretty sure the interesting ones have already arrived." He quickly stood and turned, taking his tray to the collection area.

Molly leaned over to her and whispered, "I think somebody digs you."

Rae shrugged. "I think he was referring to you. You'd better watch out. He's hungry like a wolf!"

Molly stuck her tongue out, but put her poker face on

when Andy came back.

After eating, they headed to Aumbry House. They sat out front on the large concrete steps. Haley and Maria joined them, enjoying the bright sunshine. Andy came and sat between Molly and Rae, his leg touching Rae's. Rae shifted, moving just out of knee-knocking distance. She didn't seem to move far enough. Within minutes, Andy's warm leg brushed up against hers again. As she tried to figure a way to get away from Andy and his warm leg without making a scene, Riley and a younger, slightly-built boy came walking by.

"Hello, mates." Riley's eyes roamed over Haley's curvy figure. A small smile lifted his lips. "You're a senior, right? What's your gift, again?"

Molly spoke before Haley had a chance. "She can pass wind."

"I don't pass wind," Haley snapped, scowling at Molly. "I *create* it."

Rae rolled her eyes heavenward, embarrassed by both girls.

"Cool." He pointed at the sandy blond guy beside him. "This wee fellow's Nicholas. He's like an instructional guidebook. You name it, Nic can put it together without the manual."

"Handy. What does your ink look like?" Haley asked.

"Like an open book." Nicholas held his arm out. "The ink is kind of boring, actually, but the talent's totally useful." He sat down on the steps beside her.

"Especially when you're trying to get out of a tough situation," Riley bragged. "Nic can build a device out of a paper clip and a stick of chewing gum!"

"You sound like *MacGyver*," Rae said.

"Pardon?" Nicholas' eyes grew big and he began fidgeting. In fact, everyone stared strangely at her.

"You know, *MacGyver*?" Rae wondered what was up with the weird looks.

She got nothing but silence, followed by nudges and shrugs from the guys.

Rae sighed, wishing she'd just stayed in her dorm room. "It was a television show in America. About a guy who can get out of tough situations by using whatever's lying around. Kind of like a private eye – mystery series." She shrugged. "Maybe you never had it here in England."

"We've never heard of the show, but it sounds just like our Nicholas." Andy slapped Nic on the back. "The best part is Nic's last name is MacGyver."

"You're kidding me!" Rae glanced from Riley to Nicolas in disbelief. *Great.* Now Molly was going to tell everyone she was psychic. That's all she needed.

"No joke." A relieved-looking Nicholas let out a tentative laugh and started playing with his keychain. Rae noticed a Swiss army knife on it and held back a giggle.

"Maybe the show was invented by some distant relative who's getting a big kick out of the story line and the reality versus irony of the show!" Andy said.

Nic's face brightened, making him appear even younger than sixteen. "I'm checking it online tonight. I'll have to get the DVD for my dad for Christmas."

While they chatted about the upcoming school year, Riley made mention of a school dance in October and that Guilder always invited the nearby female college, Roe Hampton.

"Maybe they won't invite the girls this year since we're here," Molly said.

She sounded so hopeful, Rae felt a little twinge of compassion for her roomy.

"There are two dances held each year. One in the fall and the other in the spring. It's been tradition here for as long as the schools have been in existence. The dances are held like balls or masquerades – like they used to have in Tudor times with King Henry VIII. I doubt they'll stop it because sixteen girls are at Guilder now." His arm swept the school grounds. "We spend ten months of the year stuck here with all of us freaks, so it's nice to hang out for a bit with the rest of the world and act normal. You'll see for yourself. The fall dance is here at Guilder and the spring dance is at Roe Hampton."

Molly pouted and crossed her arms. "I prefer being around us *freaks* rather than those freakin' girls."

Andy laughed and grabbed Molly's hand to pull her up from her position lounging on the steps. "Come on. Wait until you've been here for a year. Then you'll be begging for some normal human interaction. We're not allowed to use our ink at the dances, but someone always plays the joker and stirs up some trouble." Andy winked at Molly. "It'll be right up your alley."

Molly's face turned red and Rae swore she could almost see steam coming out of her ears. Molly put her hands on her hips and squared off with Andy who had the good sense to look both sheepish and apologetic at the same time, for all the good it did him.

"And just what exactly do you mean by that?" Molly tilted her chin up, daring him to answer her. Andy sputtered, trying to come up with a good apology to get himself out of the tight spot he'd put himself into, all the while, Molly stood stabbing her finger into his chest and giving him what for in a tirade so non-stop Rae was seriously waiting for Molly to pass out from lack of oxygen. Everyone watched with rapt amusement and was only distracted by a new arrival.

Julian came toward them from Joist Hall. He walked with an air of confidence, with long, purposeful strides, his lanky artistic fingers constantly moving. Rae thought he tapped a rhythm, or, maybe, drew something in the air. But, she couldn't be sure because it seemed to be a sub-conscious kind of reaction, something he didn't really notice he was doing.

"Where's Devon?" Andy asked when he came within

earshot.

Rae said a silent thank you to Andy. She'd been thinking the same thing, but was too embarrassed to ask.

"Having lunch in town with Beth."

Rae choked on the water she was drinking.

"Are you all right?" Andy patted her back.

"Yeah. The water just went down the wrong pipe." She pretended to take another small sip. She heard Haley mumble something sounding like "faker".

"Bummer, Devon's got a girlfriend?" Molly shrugged and turned to Julian. "What kind of car do *you* drive?"

"A Jaguar." He said it as a matter of fact, and didn't appear to be bragging.

"Is it fast?"

Andy laughed. "Have you ever heard of a slow Jag?" Molly punched his arm hard enough to make him wince.

Riley snickered. "Julian comes from very old money, with a lot of new money on top of it."

"Shut up." Andy scowled at Riley. "Ignore him. He's just jealous. Julian's actually a very kind, gentle guy, not at all a snobbish rich kid." He looked at Haley when she snorted. "Don't start thinking I'm gay. I'm not. I definitely prefer girls." He glanced at Rae. "Julian's got an extremely big heart, which I'm sure some nasty gold-digging chick's going to take advantage of one day." Andy said the last bit while pointedly looking at Haley, who managed to look both innocent and evil at the same time.

I REALLY don't like her, Rae thought to herself. Since Andy didn't appear to like her either, Rae decided that put him on the positive side of her mental score card. She was trying to decide who might be trustworthy and who she should look out for. Haley was definitely on the negative side of the list. Andy just might be on the positive side.

"Awww...shucks," Riley taunted. "You watching out for your mates? You sound more like a dad than a friend." The jury was still out about Riley, but Rae was thinking so far he seemed to be leaning more towards the negative side.

"I'd quit now," Julian warned, his face turning from gentle to very hard – almost scary – making Rae wonder what was behind it. *What does he know that would make him give a look like that?* "I heard Andy's the leader of his wolf pack."

"Whatever." Andy replied petulantly. Riley's eyes slid sideways to Andy, but he kept his mouth shut. Rae filed the entire encounter away for later analysis. She knew there was something lying underneath the emotions and the words, and it might be important, but she had no idea what it was or how to go about finding out. However, if nothing else, it was information, and Uncle Argyle always said "information is power."

"Can you take us for a ride, Julian?" Molly asked.

Leave it to Molly to change the subject, Rae thought with a smile.

The rest of the afternoon flew by, even with her constant inner voice asking questions and making observations. Rae participated when asked a question, but spent most of the time listening to everyone else. By dinner, her ears couldn't handle anymore jokes, or warnings about which teacher to avoid, what which class you could slack off in, who smelled funny, and whose hands not to shake. She ate as fast as she could, without appearing rushed. All day, she'd felt like she'd been playing some twisted live action game, in which she didn't actually know who her opponent or opponents were, or what the goal was, or how to play, kind of like playing chess with a blindfold on. She'd been hyper-aware of every twitch, cough, laugh, side-long glance and comment made by anyone within ear shot and now she just wanted to go to bed.

Rae left dinner early, hoping no one followed her. She needed to clear her head and relax. Outside, as she walked the same path she had with Lanford the night before, the fresh air caressed her cheeks, cooling her. She inhaled the scent of fresh -cut grass and evergreen trees. In front of the Oratory, she settled on the cast iron bench. Resting her elbows on her knees, she dropped her head into her hands.

Could things get any crazier? She had so many questions. What was so important about her parents, and could their gifts have had something to do with the fire? Shoot, what were they marked with? Why hadn't her uncle told her anything before, not even when she received the scholarship from Guilder? And how could she get answers to all these questions?

Rae rubbed her temples. Thinking seemed to cause more confusion in her already chaotic brain.

"Everything all right?" Devon's concerned voice broke through the night.

Rae popped her head up and looked in the direction of the sound. She hadn't heard him approach and blinked in surprise to see him standing at the end of the bench.

"I'm fine… I guess." She didn't have the energy to lie and she needed to confide in someone. Could she trust him? Did she have a choice? *More questions, ugh!* She shook her head and decided to just go with it. "I'm just a little confused and very overwhelmed." Her brow furrowed as she rubbed her temples. "Or maybe very confused and a little overwhelmed."

He sat down beside her, but said nothing.

Rae sighed and dropped back against the bench. "My head's pretty messed up at the moment. And, crazy as this may sound, I'm glad my birthday isn't until November."

"November fifteenth is going to be a huge day for you. I think, actually, it will be for the entire college *and* our society."

Great, more cryptic and more pressure. On top of that, Rae didn't feel like explaining her birth certificate was wrong. Her mother had gone into labor early and had Rae at home. Two days later, she'd gone to the hospital to register the birth. The doctor had written the wrong date on the birth certificate. It had never been a big deal, even when she started school, and all the teachers constantly celebrated her birthday on the fifteenth. Rae never felt the need to correct it. Now, she felt that keeping it a secret might be a really good idea.

Devon stared at her, almost expectantly.

For what, she had no clue, so she tried another topic. "The headmaster said you'll be tutoring me two evenings a week." Rae wasn't sure how to turn the statement into a question and now wondered if Devon even wanted to tutor her. How embarrassing it would be if he didn't! She hoped it wasn't a chore for him.

"Yeah. He asked if I could help you with some of the beginning gift and skill classes. Offer an ear or mouth when needed." He smiled, showing off the cute dimple in his right cheek. She couldn't help but notice again.

The idea of borrowing his lips or ears made her face go hot. She stared at her hands, tracing the palm of one with a finger on the other. "Thanks. I appreciate that. I, um, I feel a bit lost at the moment."

"What's bothering you?" Devon tilted his head toward her.

"How long do you have? We'd be here for hours if I tried to answer that question." Rae tried to joke, but it came out sounding sarcastic. She cleared her throat and switched to a more serious tone. "I want to know what everyone knows about me. I'm obviously missing something here. What's so important about my past that makes everyone so quiet and makes me feel like a freak show?"

Devon ran his fingers through his short, dark hair. "I'm not sure I can answer you correctly. I only know what I've heard. Maybe Lanford's a better person to talk to."

I can't take this crap anymore. I need to know now. Rae

looked directly at him. "Can you tell me what you've heard? I spoke with Lanford last night, but I want someone my age explaining it in normal words."

Devon took a deep breath and leaned forward, resting his elbows on his knees. He paused a few moments. "Everyone knows who you are because of your past. You're the girl who survived the fire. To your hometown and the rest of the un-inked world, you were the little miracle girl who somehow walked out of the flames unharmed." He swallowed. "Nobody knows exactly what happened that day. If you don't remember..." He gave her a questioning look. Rae shook her head, not ready to share something so personal. "You do know both your parents were gifted, right?"

"Lanford said that last night. He also said people with the gift don't usually marry other gifted people. What's the big deal?"

"It's like some unwritten code or rule. I'm not one hundred percent sure why. No one really talks about it." He shrugged. "It just isn't done. I do remember your parents being the example often brought up if someone asked. I've also heard if two people with ink have children, it could possibly screw the gift up or change it. I'm not talking about making a unique ink. I'm talking about something darker...dangerous."

Rae straightened. "So the school's worried I might become some kind of monster because of my parents?"

"That's not what I meant." Devon put his hands up in a defensive, placating gesture. "Like I said, I don't know much about this. I just meant it can change the form of the gift. I don't know of any scientific studies or anything done on children from two inked parents. There aren't a lot of...you...them." He pinched the bridge of his nose. "Our society keeps our ink hidden from the rest of the world, even the ones we love."

Impossible. How could you keep this from someone you

really care about? "So what gifts did my parents have that might go haywire on me?" Rae couldn't believe something bad was going to happen to her. She'd lost her parents; what could be worse than that?

"You honestly don't remember anything about them?"

Rae sighed. "I remember stuff. Most of it's bits and pieces, like a dream from a long time ago. Or I see a photo my Uncle Argyle has and then I can remember the day the picture was taken." She shuddered, still able to vividly recall the stink of burning. "The fire happened about ten years ago, and I was only six."

"What do you remember about your mom?"

"My mom?" Rae smiled. A warm sense of longing filled her chest. She was glad Devon asked about her. Rae didn't spend enough time thinking about her mom nowadays. "I remember her as the sweetest person in the entire world. She doted on me, always protective and loving." Rae closed her eyes, trying to snatch a feeling or memory from her brain. "Whenever we were together, I felt warm, like it was always bright with her around." *I can feel that heat inside of me, just thinking about her.* She blinked and watched Devon.

He smiled. "Your mother's ink was the sun, so that might explain it."

"The sun?" Rae pictured a sun with squiggly lines coming out of it. "Probably a really cool tattoo." She wished she'd known and paid more attention as a kid.

Devon laughed, deep and husky, sending a shiver through her body. "A tattoo's just ink. What we have is tatù."

"Why do you say it so funny?" Rae'd heard the weird enunciation several times now.

"Tattoo is just what it means...a regular, boring mark someone paid to get. Taa – toe. You just say the first part long, the second part rhymes with shoe. It's the original Gaelic term."

Rae laughed. "Do you always pucker your mouth and scrunch your face when you try to pronounce words? You look like you just ate a lemon."

"I do?" His face pinched again. "Crap, I *do*."

They smiled at each other. She enjoyed the banter, but turned serious again when the moment passed. "I wonder what mine'll be."

"The ink's just a picture. It's what you do with it that makes you stronger and develop as an individual. The type of person you are...what you're good at, will be blended with the gift, as well. It usually doesn't come all at once, either. It grows with you as you mature."

"What could my mom do?" Rae asked.

"I'm not sure what her powers were. I just know her ink-art."

"Then why does everyone know about my past if people know my mom's ink but not what she could do?"

"They know about your mom 'cause of your...your dad." Devon suddenly seemed very interested in the night sky, the Oratory building, anywhere but looking at her. "It's because of him," he whispered.

"What about my dad?" She leaned forward so he had to face her. Her heart hammered, echoing inside her chest when she saw the fear in his eyes.

Chapter 6

Lessons of the Past

DEVON rubbed the stubble on his chin. "What do you remember about Simon Kerr – sorry, I mean, your dad?"

Rae stared at Devon. She couldn't figure how he'd hidden the scared look on his face so fast. One moment it was there, and the next...it was like he'd closed the shutters over his emotions. "He wasn't around much, to be honest. He always seemed to be gone for work, or whatever he did." Rae tried to think, cocking her head to one side as she sifted through her dreams and memories. She straightened when she realized they were the same – her dreams were actually her memories. It'd all been real.

Shifting slightly, Devon remained silent beside her.

"It's funny now," Rae murmured. "I've never noticed before, but it's like every memory I have of him seems to be about magic tricks or some sorta dream. One time, I remember being very little, maybe three or four at the time. It's one of my first memories, but I remember he made my toys float around the room. He could make my puppets dance without touching them. Another time, he made the rain go away when I wanted to play outside." She remembered sitting by the large bay window at the back of the house, one moment singing the old nursery song and the next, the sun burst through the clouds.

Rae coughed as another memory rushed forward. One she'd tried to suppress a long time ago. "When I was about five…he got mad at me one night. I'd been crying about monsters under my bed. He came into my room really pissed off, and told me the monsters that lived in our house didn't hide under beds or in closets. They were out in the open and fearless. I, of course, started screaming because what five year old isn't terrified of monsters? And now he'd just told me they weren't scared of anything and didn't have to hide. Basically, they were going to get me." *What kind of person would do that to a child?*

She exhaled, trying to calm the anxiety rising inside her that came with the memory. She tucked a long, Shirley Temple curl behind her ear and flipped her hand. "Anyway, my mom came running into the room. She was so ticked, and they started fighting, which only scared me more. In the end, she picked me up and carried me to her bed. I stayed there all night, and when I woke up in the morning, my dad had already left. *Not* like he was around much, anyway."

Devon reached out toward her, but Rae shifted so he couldn't touch her shoulder. She wasn't looking for pity. Staring straight ahead, she contemplated that night so long ago. It had always seemed more like a bad dream than a memory. She'd been terrified to sleep with the closet doors open and begged her mom to put stuff under her bed. She also slept with a night-light for years after she'd arrived in America. It seemed so long ago, nothing but little kid stuff. She brought her gaze back to Devon.

He sat, picking at his clean fingernails. "I think your

dad was right. There were monsters in your house... he was one of them."

Surprised, Rae's mouth dropped open. She didn't know what to say.

"He had one of the most powerful tatùs." He brought his head up and looked directly at her. "From what I've been told, he got greedy and began to use it for himself."

"Is that such a bad thing? It was his tatt—tatù. His ink."

"It goes against the code of our society. The more power he got, the more he wanted. He was insatiable. He didn't agree with the teachings at the school or helping humankind. He did as he pleased, at any cost. Your dad must've had some demons or monsters that took him to the dark side. He liked what they enabled him to do, and what he was able to gain. Others liked it as well and joined him; his ideas and philosophy were very convincing." Devon stopped talking and bit his lip. He seemed as if he wished he could take back some of the words he'd said.

The sins of the father are the sins of the son, or the daughter. Uncle Argyle's words hissed inside Rae's head. She kicked a small rock on the ground and it ricocheted off the brick wall of the Oratory.

Devon jumped, startled from the noise.

"What was my father's ink?" Rae whispered.

Devon kept silent for a moment. He let out a sigh and shifted in his seat to face her. He bounced his foot, his leg shaking the entire bench with its rhythm. "His looked like a Warlock or Sorcerer...something like that."

Rae hated the silence that followed. The quiet screamed the truth she didn't want to hear. Her eyes rounded in horror as she thought about the fire. She grabbed Devon's forearm.

"My father started the fire, didn't he? He wanted me and my mother out of the picture! He..." Rae tried to swallow the lump in her throat, unable to continue. Silent tears coursed down her cheeks, and her heart hammered out a funky, erratic rhythm. She covered her face with her hands. No wonder her uncle hated her dad. No wonder everyone stared at her like she was some sort of demon or monster.

"Rae, listen to me." Devon put his fingers on Rae's chin, turning her face so that she had to look at him. He wiped her tears away as he talked. "No one knows exactly what happened. A lot of people can speculate, but we don't actually know. You were there, and if you can't remember, no one can."

She shook her head. She was already deep in the memory of that horrible night when her parents had died. There was a fire. Her mother had told her in a calm voice to go to the tree house, but added that she needed to get out as fast as she could. Rae'd dashed out and climbed up the ladder as fast as her little legs could take her. Then she'd waited and waited. She'd gotten bored and started coloring with her new multi pack of markers. The burst of heat and flames from the house had hit like an explosion. Terrified, she'd stayed put until the fire no longer looked like it was reaching out to grab her. A nice fireman noticed her climbing down the ladder and brought her to an ambulance out front. People in uniforms, and suits, and gawkers swarmed her yard and she felt lost in a sea of strangers. Then her uncle arrived and took her away with him. He'd lived in Scotland at the time. They immigrated to the U.S. shortly after.

Devon quietly cleared his throat. "Don't get caught up in the past. You have your entire life in front of you. When you get inked, you'll be here, at Guilder, surrounded by people who care about you." He reached out and wiped away a tear trickling down her cheek.

"I'm sorry." She pushed his hands away as she stood up, angry at herself for crying in front of him, a stranger. "A lot of stuff I never realized suddenly makes sense now.

My dad wasn't such a great guy." It was no wonder her uncle had taken her to America -- away from this society of gifted people, away so the memories became dreams instead of reality, away to pretend that none of it was real. *But then why did he send me back here? Is he afraid of me? Afraid of what I might become?*

Devon stood up. He reached out as if to hold her, but then stuffed his hands into his pockets. He waited a few moments as Rae composed herself before he started talking again. "Hey, everything's going to be fine. I'm sorry I said too much tonight. I should've just let Headmaster Lanford tell you everything. I feel like an idiot opening my stupid mouth."

Rae turned, and walked to where Devon stood. She gave him a quick hug and instantly let go, slightly embarrassed. "Don't apologize. It's okay. It just shows me how much of a friend you're going to be. You hardly know me. Yet you know all about my past and never, for one moment, judged me the way the other students have."

Devon stared down at the ground for a moment, like he didn't want to see the look on her face. "There's more stuff you're gonna hear, and you might not like it. The truth doesn't always feel good, but it's the truth, and it's better than being misled. You'll handle it."

Rae thought about her uncle. He'd totally lied to her by not saying anything. Realizing she'd been lost in her own thoughts, she almost missed the rest of what Devon was saying.

"... Enjoy the next few months of learning, and when the day does come, you'll be ready. It's the best day in the entire world."

"My birthday?" She zoned into the conversation with Dumbo ears. Rae started pacing in front of the bench. "What's it like? Do you just wake up with some miraculous change and then start being all gifted and stuff?"

Devon laughed. "It doesn't quite work like that. Look, I've talked enough tonight. We can discuss more during one of our tutoring sessions, and you'll learn more in your classes. It's getting close to ten and the dorms get locked then. I don't think Madame Elpis would appreciate it if Rae Kerrigan's late."

Rae looked up to the night sky and heaved a sigh. "Great! I need to act like an angel or everyone's going to believe I'm some sort of demon." Devil's spawn from her father was what she wanted to say. "I'm going to have to be on my best behavior for the next three months."

"Don't worry. I'll make sure you still have fun. If I haven't mentioned it, I have some great connections to some very gifted people. Come on, I'll walk you back to your dorm. Why don't we plan on starting your tutoring next week? We can meet in the library at Aumbry House. Then you won't have to worry about getting in trouble with curfew."

"Sounds like a good idea to me. It's Molly's birthday tomorrow. I feel a little guilty. I didn't go out and buy her a gift, even something little. She is my roommate after all."

"She's already getting the best present anyone at sixteen could ever wish for." Devon laughed. "I can pull some strings in the kitchen for you. I'm sure I can get Sally, our chef, to make a cake at breakfast tomorrow. Molly might get a kick out of that."

"Awesome. I'll owe you big time." Despite the darkness, Rae still looked away so Devon couldn't see her blush. She was seriously developing a huge crush on him.

"Let's see what your tatù is. I might take you up on that." He elbowed her. "Just kidding."

Rae's watch beeped, reminding her of the time. Curfew. They both stood and walked back to Aumbry House. Rae started up the steps to the front door. She turned to wave good-bye, but he'd already gone.

She ran up the last few steps to the front door just as

Madame Elpis came walking out of her suite, big brass key in hand. Her brows came together as she stared down the length of her nose at Rae. Rae dropped her head, staring at the floor as she passed her, and ran toward the marble steps as fast as she could.

Halfway up to the first floor, she caught sight of the pay phone below her on the main floor. She turned and glanced around for Madame Elpis. The headmistress must've gone into her room already. Rae dashed over to the pay phone and dialed the overseas numbers for a collect call to her uncle. He had some explaining to do. She'd rather talk to him down here with no one around than argue with him in the room where Molly's ears would absorb every little word, and probably repeat it to anyone who would listen.

After ten rings, she hung up. She'd forgotten about the time change. Her aunt and uncle were probably out for dinner. She'd have to try again in the morning.

Rae trotted into her room, deep in thought. She glanced up to see Molly standing in front of the full-length mirror, trying to see her behind her. The girl had another mirror in her hand, trying to angle it so she could see if there was anything on her lower back.

When she noticed Rae, Molly grinned sheepishly. "I'm curious if there're any pre-ink, or if I'll just wake up tomorrow with it. Nobody will tell me what's going to happen."

"I wish I could help you. I have no idea." Rae walked over and squinted as she checked Molly's skin. It was completely smooth and spotless. "Sorry. I don't see a thing."

"Nothing? Crap! Well, be prepared for screeching and wailing tomorrow morning." Molly stomped her foot. "Shoot! I wish it was morning now. I'm never going to be able to sleep tonight."

Rae could see this was going to be a long night if her

roommate continued to be all Molly-ish about it. As interested as she was about the process, she'd had a really long and draining day and wanted to get some sleep. She had to think fast. "Maybe the ink process acts like the tooth fairy. It won't come unless you're asleep. If you stay awake, then maybe it'll wait until you're not paying attention to mark you."

"What? Heck, then what're we waiting for? Hurry. Let's get to bed. We need to have the lights out, curtains shut and both of us asleep so I can hurry up and get inked. This is going to take forever if I'm awake all night." Rae gave herself a mental high-five. *Mission accomplished.*

"Sounds good to me. I'm exhausted again." Rae headed to the bathroom. When she returned, she saw that Molly had already closed the curtains. She lay curled up in her bed, covers pulled up tight. She popped her head up just as Rae reached for the light switch.

"Oh, I forgot to tell you. Dean Carter stopped by. He wants you to meet him in his office after breakfast tomorrow."

Rae's brain registered the name, realizing that this was also someone she wanted to talk to, but she felt too tired to get excited. "Thanks." Rae yawned and snuggled down in her covers. "Now get some sleep so we can find out what hidden talent's going to wake up inside of you."

Chapter 7

Tatù

"RAE...RAE...RAE!!!" The annoying whispers wouldn't stop.

Rae rolled over, trying to force her eyes open. In the darkness, her watch's bright light kept her from seeing the time. She threw the pillow over her head to muffle out the hoarse voice coming from the bed near her. Hadn't she just gotten into bed? It couldn't be morning already.

"Four hours," Rae mumbled. "Then I'll do anything you want."

"Come on. Wake up and tell me if you see anything on my back."

Maybe having my own room would be nice. "Do you know what time it is?"

"About two a.m., but I swear I felt something and want to see if anything's there. Come on. I'll do it for you..."

Rae sighed. *Way too early.* She groaned when she heard Molly flip on the light and felt the thump of Molly's pillow on top of her own.

"All right. I'm up, I'm up." She rolled out of bed, rubbing her eyes at the brightness. She stumbled over to Molly's bed and with one eye open, lifted the back of Molly's nightshirt to peek at her lower back.

"What do you see? What is it? Ohhh...I can't look myself. I'm so excited! It's there, isn't it? What is it?"

"Nope. Nothing there but your pale white skin. No tatù, no ink, nothing. It's too early. Too early for the tatù and too early for me." Rae yawned and flipped the lights back off. Dropping onto bed she pulled the duvet over her head. "Go back to sleep and don't call me until it's at least seven. I like my sleep, or the little I can get."

"Fine. I'll try to keep quiet, but I'm positive I felt something. I'm just having a hard time sleeping. My dad told me if I get something really cool, he'll buy me a car. They don't allow them until our senior year, but maybe the headmaster or the dean would let me have one here this year. What kind of car do you think I should get? Hey, are you awake? Rae? Oh man, you're asleep again! Damn English-American!"

Rae rolled over and drilled Molly's pillow back at her. The thud muffled Molly's voice, but only for a few seconds. Exhaling a long, silent breath, she blocked out the noise and went back to sleep.

At half past seven, Rae drifted back to consciousness. Sleep tempted her, but as she cracked her eyes open, she noticed Molly dead to the world, facing the wall, her pj top slightly lifted. Curiosity made her crawl out of her bed to get a closer look.

There, right along Molly's spine, rested a unique tatù. No swelling or redness around the ink that hadn't been there hours before. It seemed like it had always been there, like a birthmark. Fascinated, she got closer and could see a bolt of lightning, along with something else. She couldn't make out the circle ink and didn't want to touch Molly's shirt to see it better. Straightening, she debated waking Molly but had a feeling her roomie probably hadn't been sleeping very long.

Crawling out of bed, she slipped out the door and headed down the stairs. At least marble didn't creak like the wooden stairs back home. *Speaking of home...* She checked her watch. It was pretty early in New York. She picked up the pay phone and then hung up. Her hand hung midair, debating if she should call Uncle Argyle.

Screw it. He owed her an explanation. Swiping the phone card with more force than was needed, she grabbed the head piece and punched the numbers into the phone. She tucked the phone under her chin and leaned against the wall. Out of habit, she tapped her bare toe against the heel of her other foot.

Nine...Ten...Eleven...Twelve...No one picked up. *Middle of the night and no answer?* Either they were out at some bed and breakfast or they had turned the ringer off at for the night. She'd try again later. She trudged back up the stairs and quietly slipped back into her room.

Now what? She stood in the center of the room, not quite sure what to do. Seeing her desk, she went and sat down at it. Gingerly, she opened the drawer, trying to avoid the squeak. She pulled out a sheet of stationary and a pen. At least if she wrote a letter, she could get some of her thoughts organized. There was no sense in e-mailing Uncle Argyle. He wasn't computer literate. Rae toyed with the pen before putting it to paper.

> *Dear Uncle Argyle,*
>
> *Why didn't you tell me? About you, or Mom? Or any of this? I had a right to know before coming back to England. It's pretty crappy of you not to tell me.*
>
> *I want to know more about my parents, my mom **and** my dad. Everyone here seems to know about my past -- everyone but me.*

Call me when you get this.
PS. Please tell Aunt Linda I'm settling in
fine and am enjoying myself.
Love, Rae

She reread the letter, noticing how deeply the writing was embedded into the paper. She'd been pressing down hard with the pen. Shoving the letter into an envelope, she quickly licked it shut and addressed it, too scared she'd chicken out. She stuck it in her bag. Later, she'd ask one of the students where to post it.

Rae heard Molly stir and swung around in her chair around to watch. Molly sat straight up, a huge goofy grin on her face.

"Happy Birthday." Rae smiled, literally feeling the excited buzz in the room.

"Thanks. It's there, isn't it? I know it is. I can *feel* something's different inside of me -- like there's something new running through my veins. I bet this is better than sex." She hopped off her bed and jumped to the mirror.

Rae waited quietly on her chair as Molly examined her tatù.

"What is that?" She turned left and right, trying to get a full view. "I see the zigzag. Oh...it's a bolt of lightning. Cool." She inched closer to the mirror, squinting. "What's the thing beside it? A ball? I wonder if it's supposed to be a balloon. It's shaped kinda weird. Crap. I got a boring ink. There's nothing sexy about this." She dropped her shirt, only to lift it back up again. "The one mark's detail's so small compared to the bolt of lightning. Is it a cloud? Does this mean I'm going to have to wait until it storms to figure out what my gift is?" Molly ran to the window and looked out. "I heard it isn't supposed to rain for, like, two weeks."

Rae grinned. "I don't know much about these tatùs, but I'm pretty sure you're not gonna have to wait until it storms to figure out how to use your gift."

"Can you take a closer look?"

Rae nodded and pushed her chair back. Squinting, she leaned in and rested a hand on Molly's hip to steady her. "Sorry. My hands are cold," she murmured when Molly twitched.

"It's fine. I'm just wondering if anyone else has a lightning bolt."

"Hmm...not sure. If it helps, my mother had a tatù of the sun."

"I heard she was marked inked but couldn't remember what it was. I wish she was here so she could explain mine."

"Me, too." *More than you could ever know.* She stood up to look more closely at the ink. The detail was ten times better than any real tattoo Rae'd ever seen. She stared at the circle-thing beside the bolt. She slapped her forehead with the palm of her hand.

"I know what the circle-thing is!"

"What?" Molly twirled. "If you can tell me, that'll be the best birthday present I've ever had -- besides this tatù, of course."

"I think it's supposed to be a kite. You know, like Benjamin Franklin when he flew his kite in a thunderstorm?"

Molly scrunched her face into a puzzled look, then suddenly she brightened. "Holy crap! You're right. I'm going to be able to create electricity or something super cool like that. Oh my goodness, this is going to be so awesome." She swung around and grabbed Rae's hands as she jumped up and down.

Rae went flying across the room. She slammed into the wall and slid down onto the bed. She rubbed her head, just above her ponytail. Shocked, she stared at Molly who stood with her mouth open, surprise written across her face.

They both started laughing.

Molly offered Rae her hand. "I'm so sorry. I didn't

think...I had no idea..."

Rae crawled around the outstretched arm, shaking her own hand. "Thanks for the offer, but I think I'll avoid the hand contact for a bit." She stood. "I'm fine. Just wasn't expecting that."

"Neither was I." She spread her arms wide, bumping the wall. The lights dulled and then began flickering above them. "What the -- ?"

"Hand." Rae pointed. "On the wall." Shouts sounded outside the hall.

"Oops. Guess I'd better figure out how to control this." She stuffed her hands into her pockets. The lights stopped flickering and the shouts outside stopped.

A knock at the door made Rae turn around. When she opened it, Haley came barging through, Maria trailing behind. Haley pulled Molly's shirt up to see the tatù.

"I *knew* it was you." Haley crossed her arms. "I knew if the walls starting shaking, or torrential rain storms started today, or anything weird happened, it'd be you not being able to control your gift.

"Ohhhh yeah, it's me," Molly squealed and jumped up and down, hands still firmly stuffed in her pockets. "This is gonna be sooo awesome!"

"Let's go eat. I'm starving." Haley pulled Molly and Maria out the door, ignoring Rae.

"Don't worry 'bout me," Rae mumbled. "I'll catch up." She thought about Molly and her new skill. Hopefully, Molly didn't end up frying somebody. This seemed a lot like giving a kid a gun, but not giving them any lessons in proper handling or safety.

She headed over to the Dining Hall.

The birthday cake was perfect – almost perfect. Julian walked in, carrying the cake with all the candles lit, and Nicholas, Andy and Riley began singing "Happy Birthday." Molly raised her arms.

"Wait," she said. "Something's not right." She spread

her arms and knocked all the lights out in the dining hall. "Now sing."

Rae giggled as Julian came by, his long hair standing straight on end from the static in the air.

Molly slapped Nicholas' hand as he reached for a slice of cake and sent him flying about three feet backwards. "Wait your turn!"

Rae died laughing when Molly tried something on Haley, a crackling and popping noise whizzed by her ears. When Haley pulled her hand away, the air around them smelled crispy. Her hair looked like the picture from an old Bon Jovi album cover Rae's aunt had from the 1980s. Rae couldn't stop giggling every time she shot a glance at Haley's frayed ends, or Molly's constant apologizing.

"Does anyone want to head over to Aumbry House an' hang out?" Molly blew her bangs out of her eyes, exasperation written across her face as Haley stomped away to drop her tray off.

The boys didn't need convincing. The four of them stood simultaneously and rushed to clear the table.

"Let's get everyone and we'll have a games challenge," Nicolas said. "Like a games competition of juniors versus seniors. That is, if you older boys are up for it?" He laughed, directing the last sentence toward Riley.

"Dude, you're *so* going down. We'll even let you have Devon to make the teams more even."

"You can keep him. Just don't give future-boy," Craig nodded his head at Julian, "a pen and paper to show the outcome or you guys won't even play." He ducked as Julian threw an empty plastic cup in his direction.

"We'll meet you there shortly. Pick some events, but make sure the rest of the girls actually want to play before you set up to destroy their game room," Andy said.

Julian turned to Rae. "You interested in participating in this crazy challenge?"

"Heck yeah! But I'm supposed to meet Dean Carter

after breakfast, and I don't exactly know where his office is, or who he freakin' is."

Devon leaned his elbows on the table. "Dean Carter's in charge of the school. Where Headmaster Lanford's in charge of the students, Dean Carter takes care of the buildings, the alumni and the financial end of the school."

Andy and Julian both cut into Devon's academic explanation at the same time and blurted out, "I can walk you there." "I'll take you."

Devon rolled his eyes and sat back in his chair, crossing his arms, not saying a word.

Rae glanced back and forth between the two guys wondering who to choose, wishing it had been Devon who had offered. "Julian, if you don't mind...I'd really appreciate it." Seeing Andy's disappointed face, she added, "Don't you have to set up the competition?"

"It can wait. I don't mind walking you." Andy nodded, whether in agreement or defeat; Rae couldn't tell.

Julian pushed back his chair like he had a tatù gift for speed. He grabbed his own and Rae's trays to dispose of them. Andy stood and headed toward the front exit with the girls. Devon stayed in his seat, playing with the egg yolks on his plate. He kept his head down. Rae couldn't see his eyes.

"You gonna play, too?" Rae asked quietly.

Devon looked up and grinned, showing Rae his dimple. "Wouldn't miss it. Should be interesting to see how the young lads fair against us big boys."

His attempt at smack-talk made her grin. "Hey, there're girls competing, too! I'll be in the young lads group and plan on kicking your butt!"

Devon's smile turned sly. "Ohhh yeah. That's why I think the younguns are going to struggle -- all this fresh, feminine DNA is going to confuse them."

"And, of course, you big boys don't have that problem?" Rae taunted.

Devon didn't miss a beat. "Maybe just Andy and Julian."

Rae saw the glint in his eye. "You're going down for that."

"Just don't come sobbing to me afterwards when you lose." Devon laughed back.

Julian returned, and Rae stood up to leave. She gave Devon a dirty look as she walked by, and, in return, he stuck his tongue out at her.

They left the Refectory, heading toward the main building of the school. Ten minutes later, Rae stood looking upwards. She marveled at the structural design of the main building. It reminded her of Hampton Court Palace her parents had taken her to when she was about five or six. The main entrance included a large, round tower on each side with beautiful, probably original, leaded oriel windows in between on the second floor above the archway.

"The architecture of the building's amazing, isn't it?" Julian watched Rae.

"Totally awesome. Is the dean's office inside?"

"It's in the right tower of the main building. Enter these glass doors and go up the flight of stairs. There's a main lobby where the dean's secretary is, and you can wait there. It's the room above us, with the big leaded windows."

"Thanks." Rae headed toward the door, then turned back. "Oh, one more question. Is there a place I can buy a stamp to mail a letter to America?"

"Lucky guy." He sounded disappointed.

Rae felt her cheeks burn at Julian's assumption. "No boyfriend. Just a letter to my uncle."

Julian grinned, appearing happy and pleased once again. He pointed along the brick building. "The door with the small red flag hanging on the side is the student post office."

Rae headed into the main building as Julian turned back to the dormitories. She ran up the now familiar-looking black and white checker marble steps into the lobby. Rae gave her name to the secretary and watched her disappear behind a door down the hall. She was too antsy to sit, so she walked over to the oriel windows and admired the view; so much so that she completely missed the secretary coming back into the room.

"Dean Carter will see you now, Ms. Kerrigan," the secretary said in an extremely chipper voice.

Rae felt a knot settle between her shoulder blades. She wondered why she felt a vague sense of foreboding.

Chapter 8

Dean Carter

RAE turned to follow the secretary into the dean's office. She stopped short just inside the door. The bright room was round and completely brick, like the outside of the tower. Ancient-looking portraits hung on the walls, alongside *fleur de lis* emblems etched into the red stone. Curved bookcases lined half the room. They must have been custom built a couple of hundred years ago, maybe when the vines outside had started growing. While warm and humid outside, a cool draft circled the room, making it feel like the frigid breeze from her aunt's window air conditioner back home.

A thin gentleman sat in a black leather chair, his long, spidery legs sticking out from under the large oak desk. His expensive grey suit made his dark hair appear black. He wasn't what Rae would call handsome, but his features were striking. He had a straight jaw shaved perfectly clean, a straight nose and dark eyes, which seemed slightly larger than normal.

"Good morning, Ms. Kerrigan." His crisp, business-like voice punctuated his sentence. "I assume you've settled into your dorm and met a number of our students?" He didn't glance up from the paper he was signing until he'd finished. The secretary took the documents and headed out of the office, closing the door behind her.

"Yes, thank you, Dean Carter. I appreciate being given the opportunity to finish my high school education here." She babbled nervously. She continued to look around the room, concentrating on the paintings, probably past deans and headmasters, and not one of them smiling. *I bet he fits right in.*

The dean harrumphed. "Your parents would've wanted you to attend Guilder, so we had to find a way to make this work. It would have been easier, of course, if you had been a boy, but Mother Nature had to have her way."

Rae stood silent, greatly insulted, but not sure how to respond. *Cranky old geezer.*

He rested his elbows on the edge of the desk, interlacing his fingers. "Seems the board thinks the school needs to modernize, allow women in." He harrumphed again. "There was nothing wrong with the system being an all boys' school. You'd have thought, with all our resources, they'd have built a separate one for females."

Excuse me? Ouch. Seemed the dean wasn't too pleased with the new enrollment rules. Rae swallowed, holding back a snide comment about being old-fashioned and chauvinistic. Not a good way to impress the dean and change his mind about girls being allowed on campus. An inner sense told her she didn't want this man to know how he made her feel. It'd be like giving him ammo or something.

"What do you think of my office, the Round Room?" Dean Carter leaned back in his chair.

Rae bit her lip as she glanced around again, trying to

think of something intelligent to say. "It's interesting. Is there a reason it's round or just easier for the builders, back in the day, to keep the inside circular to match the towers?"

"Round rooms were very important to the Catholic church, at least in Wolsey's time." He stared down at her. "Do you know who Wolsey was, Ms. Kerrigan?"

"Sure." Maybe the man also thought females were dense, on top of not good enough for Guilder. "Thomas Wolsey was a Cardinal, and I think he became the Archbishop of York. He's the guy who helped King Henry the VIII -- well, until he couldn't get King Henry's divorce from Catherine of Aragon." *Score one for the GIRL*, Rae inwardly cheered.

He snorted "It seems American schooling has taught you a bit of our British history."

Surprised? Women not equal to men and now he considered America less developed than England? What was this guy smoking? "Actually, my mother and my uncle always had a fascination with the monarchy, especially the Tudor history. I guess the interest got passed down to me."

Dean Carter leaned forward at the mention of Rae's mother. "What else did your mother, or your uncle, teach you?"

*Common courtesy, politeness, respect...*stuff his parents obviously forgot. She shrugged. "Not much. My uncle has the habit of only saying what needs to be said."

Dean Carter looked like he wanted to push the topic more, but apparently changed his mind. "So, do you have an idea as to the reasoning for this Round Room?"

Rae glanced around and out the window. "I'm not sure, to be honest. Is the other tower an office as well?"

He ignored her question. "The room is round because Wolsey felt these were the safest rooms in the college. Not for architectural reasons but religious. In here, the devil, or

73

his demons, can't trap you in a corner."

The last sentence hung in the air. *Is that supposed to mean something to me?* Rae shifted her weight. *What a miserable guy,* and he looked like he was only forty. *What bug crawled up his ass?* It was just a stupid old tower room, not some sacred religious sanctuary. He hadn't even hung up a cross or crucifix.

"Ms Kerrigan, is everything all right?" His concern didn't sound sincere.

Oops. She must've been making some kind of face, probably a scowl. "Fine...sir. I think I'm just a bit jet lagged from my flight." Rae knew it was a lame excuse, but she wasn't about to tell him he made her, and probably the entire human race, feel uncomfortable.

"Be sure and rest up. Classes begin Monday. I'd hate for you to get behind even more since you already have quite a bit of catching up to do." He looked at his watch and stood up. "I have a meeting with a trustee alumnus who likes to give a lot of support to this school." He began walking toward the door. He turned just before reaching it. "You're not inked yet, right?" He didn't wait for her to answer. "Well, you will be by Christmas. That's the reason I asked you to come by. There's a festive dinner with the alumni before the holidays. I guess we'll have to invite a few female students to it as well. Consider yourself on the list."

Mortified at the thought of being the freak in a room full of tatùed adults, Rae tried to think of an excuse not to attend. Maybe she could go back to the U.S. a few days early and see her aunt and uncle.

"Relax. Don't look so terrified." He shook his head and muttered something that sounded like "women" under his breath. "We invite several of our students each year to attend the dinner. There's food. You eat and talk to the trustees for an hour. Let them know their money is continuing to be well spent." He buttoned up his jacket.

"Please feel free to stop by any time if you have any questions. Have a good day."

Like I'm ever going to come back here to see you. I'd rather eat dirt. He pointed with his hand toward the door. Rae noticed his sleeve slide slightly up. She caught a glimpse of his tatù -- a hand with an eye inside. She guessed he had the ability to strike fear into the heart of everyone he met. *Miserable old git.*

"You, too...sir. Have a *great* day." She strode to the door. It almost hit her behind on the way out. She quickly smiled at the secretary and headed straight for the stairs, determined to get outside. Rae walked the first few steps and then remembered the competition starting at Aumbry House. She ran down the rest of the way.

Once outside, she took deep breaths to clear her lungs and then continued jogging back to the dorm. She stopped by the little post office for a stamp and dropped the letter from her bag into the red post box inside. *Hello Uncle, send answers,* she thought as she jogged the rest of the way back to Aumbry House.

Chapter 9

Competition

LOUD laughter and chatter greeted Rae as she slipped into the games room. Somebody had drawn a scoreboard on one of the chalk slates, naming the teams junior vs. senior. A snooker game between a pair of seniors against a pair of juniors had just started. Molly, standing beside Brady, threw darts, competing against Andy and twin girls Rae hadn't met yet. Haley seemed deeply involved in a game of cards against Julian.

"Is there space for one more player in this challenge?" Rae asked to no one in particular.

Everyone paused in their competition to turn and stare. The silence in the room gave Rae an overwhelming sense that she didn't belong here and made her shift and edge back toward the door. *Maybe I'll give Uncle Argyle a call instead.* Just as she was about to cut and run, Andy grinned and waved. *Shoot. Saved by a grinning wolf. That can't be good. Now what?*

"I'm, uh, I just need to use the phone. I'll be right back." She slipped back out the door as fast as she could. Her heart felt like it had plummeted into her intestines. She'd never fit in here.

The foyer was empty and the pay phone unoccupied. She punched in her uncle's number, now desperate to hear his voice. She'd have even settled for an answering machine but Aunt Linda refused to use one. Rae tried once more and slowly put the phone back on the receiver. *Ah, come on Uncle...I need you. Why won't you answer? Are you hiding from me or something worse?*

Glancing up the stairway, she debated just heading to her room and skipping the competition. Loud laughter and muffled cheers erupted from the games room. Someone hollered, "Nice point, Nic."

Rae paused, her hand on the banister. She'd never fit in if she didn't try. With a renewed sense of determination, she changed direction and headed back to the competition. Stepping through the door, she walked straight over to Andy and the twin girls, a smile pasted on her face. They'd moved to the other side of the room, where a game of cards was going on. She ignored a loud harrumph coming from the dart area.

"Hiya, I'm Rae." The girls wore shirts like the old *Lavern and Shirley* TV show Aunt Linda liked to watch: one was marked with an "N," the other an "A."

"Hi," the twins said at the same time.

"This is Nadia and Aidan," Andy said.

"Cool," Rae said. "Your names are the same but spelled backward."

Both girls' eyebrows shot up. Nadia spoke, "Most people don't figure that out unless they see our names written down, and even then, hardly anyone notices."

Rae shrugged and smiled. "I've got an uncle who loves to play with words. He's kinda brushed off on me." She glanced at the door, wondering if she should try calling him once again. "Are you both here, waiting to see which one of you gets tatùed?"

"We're already inked, both of us," Nadia said.

"No way!"

"Totally." Aidan grinned. "We've got the stamp of Morpheus to prove it."

"Morpheus? I know he's a god, but which one?"

"According to Greek Mythology, he's the god of dreams," Nadia said.

"We can make people dream in their sleep," Aidan added.

"You both have the same power?" At least Rae wasn't the only special case in the female department.

"Yeah, except Aidan can make some seriously scary dreams, and I'm much better at the happier ones."

Andy put his arm around Nadia. "Looks like you're the gal I need to stick with." He glanced over at Aidan, slipping his other arm around her shoulder. "Maybe I'd better be nice to you…payback would be a nightmare."

"Rae *Kerrigan!*" Haley shouted over by the dart boards. Everyone turned to stare at Rae. "We need a junior to compete." It seemed like she was trying to keep a straight face, but the corners of her mouth kept twitching.

Determined not to be wimpy or shy, Rae strolled over. "I'll help, but I've never played before."

Riley, leaning against the wall, straightened. "Never played darts? Sounds like you've been Americanized."

Haley snorted.

Rae pushed her shoulders back. If Haley had PMS, that was her problem. "You've got topless darts in Britain. If those bimbos can play, so can I."

"Impressive," Riley said. "Seems like Kerrigan's got some guts after all." He grabbed some darts. "Here. Have a few practice tries, and then you and Haley can square off."

Rae shrugged. "I'll try my best."

The darts were smooth with a grooved end near the tip. They were heavier than Rae thought they'd be. She figured they'd weigh as much as a pen and tried to hold it the same way. Walking to the line, she turned and faced the board.

"Just aim for the red dot in the middle, or the green ring around it," Riley said.

Haley wrote their names on the little chalkboard beside the board. "We're playing around the world. You need to hit every number on the board once, plus the bull's eye." Haley wrote one to twenty and two bull's eyes down the board lengthwise. "I'll keep your score and you do mine."

"Fine."

"That way you can't cheat," she added loud enough for to make people to look their way.

Rae dropped her arm to her side. "I don't cheat."

"Like father, like daughter." Haley shrugged.

What a bitch. "You never even met my dad." Her uncle's words pounded inside her head. Rae shook it to clear her thoughts and defend her family. "You're such an as-- "

"Cool it." Riley stepped forward. "Put your claws away, girls. Just shoot the darts. We don't want to be here forever."

"Fine, let's play." Rae threw a shot and cringed when the dart made a solid thud into the wall above the board. The next one barely hit the black rim, outside the point range. Closing one eye, her tongue out to the side, she tossed the next one just above the bull's eye.

"Good shot," Devon cheered from across the room.

Rae's mood lightened and she turned, eyes searching for him only to realize that he had actually been encouraging a teammate playing some game on the Wii. Embarrassed, she stepped toward the scoreboard as Haley erased the twenty on the board. She stepped to the line, shoulder shoving Rae as she passed. *Ugh! Mean-spirited bitch.*

Haley threw two of her darts, each one landing on a number. Rae grabbed the eraser and rubbed the first number off. Double checking the second dart, Rae reached for the two darts and jumped back in surprise when another whizzed by her ear. She ducked low to the ground.

"Oops. My bad," Haley said loudly with false innocence. "That one slipped. You shouldn't grab the darts until I'm finished throwing." She tsked.

If Rae hadn't shifted to check the last dart, she'd have the last one stuck in her head. She was blistering mad, but she said nothing. *I won't let her get to me.* She grabbed her darts and went to the line to take her turn.

The game continued for twenty minutes with Rae falling miserably behind. But when Haley had only the bull's eye left, Rae managed to hit her remaining numbers and bring the game to a tie. The two went back and forth, aiming for the red dot, both unable to hit it.

"This is taking forever. How about we go one last turn?" Riley said. "You each get one dart. Closest to the bull's eye wins. Haley, you go first."

Haley threw, nicking the metal around the center and landing just outside.

Rae set her feet on the line, one slightly in front of the other and closed her left eye, then her right. She moved her arm in practice, following a make-believe arc where the dart would go. Calm, she exhaled and held her breath to stop any movement. Completely focused, she opened her eyes and tossed the dart, knowing, before even releasing, it would stick in the center.

The dart traveled and at the last moment, arced to the left, just outside of Haley's. Rae opened her mouth about to protest but kept quiet when Riley patted her shoulder, then walked over and high-fived Haley. She stared at the trickster, who wiggled her fingers at her in a wave.

"Nice try," Haley said. "You lose."

Riley went over to the team scores and added a point to the seniors.

Rae moved beside Haley, erasing the scores. "You cheated," she hissed quietly. "You used your tatù."

Haley covered her heart with both her hands. "I'd never. " She batted her lashes and grinned wickedly. "Can't even lose fairly, can you?" She clucked and shook her head. "Just like dear ol' daddy."

The pounding in her ears grew deafening. Rae wanted to say something snide back to Haley but knew the girl would love that and it would only feed into the situation. She didn't want to feed anything, she wanted to win, so she knew she had to leave this alone. "Whatever," she muttered and turned to leave.

Suddenly November seemed a long way off. Once she had her hidden talent, she'd show Haley she wasn't her father. She just had to be patient.

For the rest of the Sunday afternoon and evening, Rae read in her room. Molly flitted in and out, her mouth never stopping. Rae nodded and responded when needed, which seemed to suit Molly perfectly. Rae was secretly pleased with herself having found a way to "manage" her roomie without too much effort. After a quiet dinner, Rae headed back to the dorm and into bed for an early night, congratulating herself on a day well-spent.

Monday morning, wet drizzle created puddles everywhere. Rae and Molly veered left and right along the sidewalk trying to avoid them. Cool wind rushed against their faces, making them shrug down in their rain slickers and wrap their arms tightly around themselves. Their schedules were identical -- morning classes were regular educational courses and afternoon classes were scheduled in the Oratory Building.

The first class of the morning began with Professor Stockheed. He stood at the front of the class, short and slight. Rae sat a few rows back, but closer to the front than the back. *No better place than the middle for fitting in.*

"People." His voice stopped all the conversation floating around the room. It sounded like it had a hundred different accents, but Rae couldn't place one of them. "I know you're excited with the new school year, but we've got work to do." He strolled by each desk and handed out a lined sheet of paper.

Rae watched the professor as he walked down the aisle and continued to speak. Her paper slid along the desk and, without looking, she put her elbow down to stop it from slipping off.

"I'd like each of you to think of the most memorable book you've ever read. Tell me the story, without sharing the title or the main character's names. You've got ten minutes to explain it."

The Lion, the Witch and the Wardrobe. Rae turned back in her chair, ideas already forming in her mind on how to start the first paragraph. Grabbing a pen from her bag, she went to write her name on the top right corner.

Her hand froze midair.

On the paper in neatly capped black letters lay a note. Rae's head pounded a delirious rhythm. This couldn't be good. She glanced around the room, but no one sat watching her. They were all busy writing, heads bent over their work.

Exhaling slowly and deliberately she cringed, not wanting to look down.

"Is something the matter, Ms. Kerrigan?" Professor Stockheed's voice floated from the back of the room.

"No, sir." Rae bent down, resting her left arm on the table, elbow bent to cover the paper. Forced to look, she read the note.

KERRIGAN
NOBODY WANTS YOU HERE. NOT AT
GUILDER, NOT IN ENGLAND. GO
BEFORE SOMETHING HAPPENS TO
MORE THAN JUST YOU.

Rae's stomach dropped into her sneakers. Another Rae-hater. The professor? What did he mean by "more than just you"? Was this the reason she couldn't reach her uncle? *No, I won't do this, I won't freak out...*

"Five minutes, class." Stockheed stood by his desk.

Rae spread her hand over the note, her sweaty palms sticking to the paper. With a will of their own, her fingers curled into a fist as anger coursed through her veins. The crinkling noise of the sheet as it crumpled into a ball made the students nearby stare at her. She didn't care. She hadn't done anything wrong and these people were still judging her.

"Ms. Kerrigan?" A fresh, blank sheet slid onto her desk from an arm entirely covered in tattooed flags. It reminded Rae of a quilt her aunt once made, like a mosaic. "Shall we try again?" The professor smiled. He looked spooky with his crooked teeth. He strolled up the aisle without saying another word.

By lunchtime, Rae's stomach was eating itself. Molly and she headed to the Refectory for lunch. Rae piled her plate high. Depression made her hungry. She wished she could bury her face inside of her pile of food when she heard Devon's voice.

"Rae, you up for some tutoring tonight? Or do you prefer to eat the entire cafeteria out of all its food?" He laughed. "Headmaster Lanford suggested we meet two nights a week. Whatever works best for you..." He let the sentence trail off.

"Tonight'd be great. Thanks again. I really appreciate

your help." Silly girl for stacking her lunch plate with enough food to feed a small country.

"Tutoring?" Nicholas interrupted her thoughts. "From the sounds of your answers in our classes this morning, I don't think you need any tutoring."

"It's just to help get her up to speed on the tatù and gift classes she hasn't taken," Devon explained. "Shall we meet in Aumbry's library? Say, around eight then?"

"Whatever time works for you is great for me." Rae wondered if she should mention the note to him from class. Maybe see if the professor had a grudge against other students.

"See you tonight." He turned and walked away, Rae's heart hammering away in her chest. *He's got a cute butt.* Her cheeks grew hot. Between her nervous heart and fire-burning cheeks, she hoped she didn't have a heart attack.

"Shall we get going to our first 'magic' class?" Nicholas said.

"Magic? I thought -- "

"Not real magic. There's no such thing. It just seems like it when we use our tatùs." He smiled, excitement flashing in his eyes. "I've been waiting for this moment for three years!"

Chapter 10

Magic Class

RAE walked into the grand room of the Oratory and felt like she'd stepped back in time. It appeared to still be in the sixteenth century.

The same black and white marble that appeared in every other building decorated the floor. Dark stained oak with hundreds of intricately, detailed carvings covered the walls. The grand room stood at least three stories high with long windows set near the pinnacle of the room. Rae wondered who set the windows so close to the ornately carved wooden ceiling almost five hundred years ago. They must've used one heck of a tall ladder.

Antique chairs were stacked along one wall, but there were no desks or tables. The room was as big as a football field.

Eyes wide, she ended up in the center of the room, doing a 360 degree turn to take in the entire view. She wondered if time did actually stand still inside this amazing place. *It sure looks like it.*

"We have class *in here*?" Rae whispered to Nicholas.

The atmosphere felt too reverent to speak louder.

"Some classes are down the hall." Nicholas gestured to the far side of the room. "It's where the younger kids study skills until they turn fifteen. Then you graduate to here. I think Lanford's office is somewhere down the hall, as well."

"Where do seniors have class?"

"It's switched. Seniors in the morning, then we have the place after lunch." Rae had been too pre-occupied to notice the other students coming in so it was a shock when she looked around and saw the room now filled with people.

Headmaster Lanford glided into the room, tapping his walking stick to get the students' attention.

"All of you here are inked. Well, almost everyone." Lanford nodded at Rae, but not in a discouraging way. "I'd like you to form groups of four and explain -- "

He paused in his talking and glanced toward the back of the room. Rae turned to see Dean Carter come in and stand at the back of the room. He appeared ticked off, his arms crossed tight against his chest, and a scowl etched deep on his face.

"...Please introduce yourselves to each other."

Rae blinked, trying to refocus on Lanford.

Nicholas motioned to the boy beside him. "Charlie just had his birthday this summer. Show us the new ink."

Charlie walked over and rolled up his sleeve to show a tatù of a hand-drawn man.

"Cool tat." Nicholas let out a low whistle. "What's it do?"

"It's the Vitruvian Man. Let's me heal quickly from, like, everything."

"How?" Rae was curious. Out of the corner of her eye, she saw the dean head over to Lanford.

"You know the Vitruvian man, right? Leonardo da Vinci drew him and used him to relate proportions of the body. The tatù shows I'm able keep all things proportioned."

"Skip the da Vinci crap." Nicholas let out a deep, hearty laugh. "Isn't the Vit- man the same symbol for the medical profession?"

Charlie glared at Nicholas, then the corners by his eyes began to crinkle and he smiled. "Yeah, you're right. Just thought the da Vinci shit sounded way better." He slapped Nicholas on the back in a friendly gesture. "What about you?" He turned to Rae.

"Nothing...yet. I won't be sixteen 'til November." Rae sighed, wishing her birthday had already passed.

"Students. Your attention, please." Headmaster Lanford tapped his cane on the marble. "Dean Carter would like to have a few words." He leaned back, as if sitting, but with nothing behind him, not a chair or stool.

"The annual interaction with the Roe Hampton students isn't far off. I'd like to remind you all: there's to be no tatù use during the evening. I expect you all to be on your best behavior."

Rae could've sworn he was staring directly at the female students. She averted her gaze when his eyes rested on her.

Molly's hand skyrocketed into the air, and she waved it furiously.

"Yes, Ms. Skye?" Lanford said.

"Will there be normal boys coming as well? Maybe we could invite the students from Oxford."

"No." Carter spoke sharp and swift. "We've enough trouble with you lot." He harrumphed and turned to leave.

Molly, sitting by Haley, whispered loudly. "It's not fair. We should get a dance of our own then."

Carter paused in his walk, pulled the end of his jacket down crisply and puffed out an exasperated breath. "Yes, let's do that. Let's spend thousands of pounds on a special evening just so the female students of Guilder can be happy. Let's address the alumni board that two dances a year are not enough. Our female students need to have an evening every weekend so they can find a suitable spouse since they cannot do it on their own time." He scanned the room, his gaze resting directly on Rae. "Heaven forbid we have a catastrophe of one of you falling for one of our Guilder boys."

Every pair of eyes shot over to her. She didn't know where to look or what to think. Part of her wanted to disappear and another part wanted to throttle the dean for singling her out. He had no right. She hadn't asked the question. She hadn't made her parents fall in love. She didn't want more dances, or to cost the school tons of money. Feeling persecuted and madder than hell, she refused to drop her gaze and stared at each student until they glanced away.

"All right," Lanford spoke. "Let's get back to work, shall we?"

Dean Carter made his way to the door, but not before Rae saw the grin on his face.

What a chauvinist. He had purposely embarrassed the girls and got a kick out of it. Rae turned her shoulders, deliberately showing her back to the dean. She focused on Lanford, already missing part of what he'd said.

"...each ink is different, like a snowflake in a way."

Rae watched Lanford as he spoke. She cocked her head to the side and tried to see what he sat on. "What's your tatù?" she interrupted. "...sir."

"Levitation." He pushed up his sleeve to show his tatù. A man sitting in a yoga position, floating above the ground, rested neatly on his large forearm. He motioned for Rae to come forward.

She walked up to the front and stood to his right. Lanford stayed in his seated position, and raised up both of his arms slowly.

"What the -- ?" She felt weightless and lightheaded.

Looking down, her breath caught. She hung suspended in the air, her feet dangling three feet off the ground..

Lanford wiggled his index finger, bringing Rae up so her feet dangled slightly above his head.

It turned out to be the weirdest sensation, not so much feeling suspended, but more like gravity had left her body. Lanford floated her across the room. She was almost disappointed when the feeling of gravity returned as he set her back down gently. Like jumping on a trampoline for an hour and then trying to walk on the hard, flat ground.

"Next time, Ms. Kerrigan, please raise your hand to ask your question." Lanford smiled and pointed to where Nicholas stood. "You can return to your spot."

Not long after Rae jumped, surprised to hear the buzzer sound to signal the end of class. She reluctantly grabbed her bag and walked out into the rain.

What if she woke up on her birthday with no mark ink on her back? A claw of worry tightened her stomach as she realized that it might always remain blank. No one seemed to know what would happen. What if she really was just a normal, boring teen? She couldn't go back to the way things had been before.

She stopped in the middle of the sidewalk. Her uncle must've felt awful when he learned her mother had been given the mark tatù instead of him. What gut-wrenching disappointment he must have felt. *Wow, that must have really sucked, to be taken away from all his friends, from my dad, and to realize he wasn't the special one.* Rae pondered this new side of her uncle's life story as she wandered along the sidewalk.

Using her bag as an umbrella, Rae slipped into the dining hall and grabbed a few buns off of a table. She stuffed them in her pockets, along with a few mini butters. The idea of just hanging out in her dorm room doing homework until her meeting with Devon seemed like the perfect idea. With her pockets stuffed with snack supplies, she set off to do just that.

With her notebook and pen, Rae headed down to the library ten minutes before eight. She tried her uncle on the phone one more time. No answer. But Aunt Linda had called earlier and left a message with Molly, so Rae was no longer worried. She hadn't been sure if Rae had been trying to get a hold of them. They had no machine and had been away and planned another short holiday for a few nights. Rae figured her aunt was enjoying some time with just the two of them. Her uncle probably said yes to the trips just so he wouldn't have to talk to her. *Coward*. She shrugged off her disappointment with her Uncle and focused instead of the tutoring session to come.

Her heart skipped at the thought of seeing Devon. She tried telling herself it was because she wanted to learn more about her past, but knew that wasn't the only reason.

Rae slipped into the library, picking a table toward the back. The last thing she needed was anyone, especially Haley, within hearing distance.

She sat down on the antique oak chair, rubbing her palms against the smooth top of the table. After a few minutes, she began tapping her pen against her binder. Eyes glued to the entrance of the library, her heart rate doubled when Devon walked through the oak doors.

He'd just showered. His dark hair still damp, and he'd changed into jeans and a white t-shirt. He moved with an easy confidence. She liked that. He raised a hand when he noticed her, arriving at the table in seconds, the speed of his gift carrying him. He moved so fast, his image had appeared blurry from the speed.

"Sorry I'm late." He plopped down across from her. "The guys had a football rematch after tea and I lost track of time. Then I had to shower, 'cause I stunk." He grinned and wrinkled his nose.

Rae relaxed at his easy-going tone. "No prob."

Leaning forward to rest his elbows on the table, Devon dropped his chin into his hands. "How'd your first day of classes go?"

The scent of Devon's musky cologne wafted over her. Rae sat back to concentrate better, but the lure of his cologne tempted her to lean forward again and smell his delicious scent.

"Cl-classes were all right. Professor Stockheed seems... uh, interesting." Rae inhaled a deep breath through her nose, trying to not appear obvious. If Devon said anything bad about the teacher, she'd tell him about the note.

"He's fine. A bit strange, but he's harmless. What'd you think of the Oratory?"

Nope. She wasn't going to mention the note. She focused on his question. "When you walk in the place, I swear, time freezes."

"Yeah, the Grand Room does seem to hold some special power or quality. Maybe that's why they called it the Aura-tory." Devon dropped back in his chair, his hands clasped behind his head. He had long, muscular arms. The corners of his mouth twitched, his dimple winking at her.

"That's a *really* bad joke." Rae laughed despite herself.

"There are plenty more where that came from." Devon stretched his legs out under the table. "Did you like Lanford's class?"

"Definitely the most interesting." She felt her cheeks burn. "He's got an awesome tatù."

"Oh no," Devon laughed. "Who was it? Someone not paying attention or fooling around?"

Rae's face got hotter and Devon's laugh got louder.

"You?" He shook his head. "Last year, he lifted Riley up while he was mucking about. Dude didn't catch on and tried to fight it. He looked like a cat thrashing about in the air. Legs and arms going everywhere as he tried to get his feet back on the ground. Took him a while to figure out

Lanford held him there."

"Mine wasn't that bad. Thank goodness." She smiled, relieved. "I love the Oratory."

"Did you know the school dance next month is held there? It's looks pretty surreal once decorated. You'd expect King Henry himself to show up."

"Cool." Rae didn't know what else to say. She pictured them dancing together and then she thought about his girlfriend and wondered if Beth'd be there.

"How about we get started?" Devon reached for a pen. "Tell me what you want to know."

"Me? Shouldn't you have some lesson plan all mapped out?"

"Nope." Devon laughed as he shook his head. "These sessions are to help you with any questions you've got."

"Okayyy..." Rae drummed her fingernails against the oak desk, her eyes traveling along a grain in the desk's wood. "All rightie, let's start with something obvious. My parents. What do you know about their ink?"

"Skip the small talk and get right into the deep stuff, don't you?" Devon began doodling on a sheet of paper inside her binder. He rested his chin in his free hand. "I don't know a lot about your mom. Story is she fell in love with the wrong kinda guy." He shrugged.

"Then tell me what you know about my father."

Devon paused in his doodling and exhaled. "You say you don't remember much about your dad. Maybe he acted different with your mom. To the rest of this secret society of tatùs, he chose the dark side of his ink. I don't know the hows or whys." Devon glanced at Rae, quickly dropping his gaze. "He'd be the poster child for the debate about kids growing up evil. Others joined him. This group of men let greed and power rule the choices they made in their lives, with no care or consideration for who got hurt."

"People who aren't inked live like that now. That's no different than the norm of today's society." Her dad couldn't have been that bad. After all, there were terrorists in other countries blowing people up just to say they did it.

"Yeah, but normal people don't have powerful tatùs to work with. Your dad...he did some pretty bad shi—not so nice things to a lot of innocent people." Devon paused, setting the pen down on the table. "There are still inked people who agree with what your father believed and are determined to continue with his plans..."

"I get what my dad was. I know there were times when my mother seemed terrified of him. As a kid, I thought it was normal. But my uncle... he never spoke the same way to my Aunt Linda or acted angry. And, it seems, he had good reason to be mad." She chewed her lip. "You know, when my father was happy, he was good, but if he was mad or in a dark mood..." Rae shuddered and whispered, "Maybe that's why I forget so much. Maybe I've blocked it out because it was so awful. What I do remember certainly isn't all hearts and roses. I still have nightmares."

Devon played with his pen cap, unable to look Rae directly in the eye. "Your father had big plans for himself and his little coven of followers. It got to the point where something catastrophic was going to happen. The Tatù Privy Council was terrified of what he planned to do, knowing they'd be unable to stop him. The fire at your house changed everything." Sympathy filled his eyes. "Miraculously, you survived. Officials were unable to find the cause or source of the fire."

"It'd be nice to see those reports. Maybe there's something I'm forgetting." Rae couldn't remember anything more significant about that day than losing her mother.

"If you'd like, we can look up the newspaper articles on another night."

Rae rubbed her temples. "I'd like to remember something no one else knows. Try and right the wrong he did." She paused, unable to decide if she should voice the hope nagging inside. "Or maybe my dad really wasn't that bad, and it's all just a big misunderstanding. Maybe..." She knew how silly she sounded. It was childish, wishful thinking, wanting her dad to be a secret super hero instead of the villain of the story.

Devon took one of Rae's hands in both of his. He held it for a moment before slowly releasing it. Rae could still feel the warmth from his touch. She stared down at her fingers.

"Deep down, I think I always knew my father couldn't be a good person. I never knew details, but I always figured..." She blinked rapidly, trying to stop the burning in her eyes. Unable to talk, she half whispered, "I'm terrified I'll end up like him when I get my tatù. What if his ink changed him? It could happen to me, too." No wonder the school wanted her here and why the other kids acted weird around her. She glanced up at Devon, forcing a tiny half smile. A long, sad breath slipped out. "Would you mind if we maybe called it a night?" She didn't think she could hold the flood works back much longer.

"Sure." The pity in Devon's eyes made Rae look away.

Devon's chair scraped as he stood. "Go get some sleep and don't worry. Tonight was just a lesson in history. It doesn't mean anything, and it changes nothing of who you are." He waited until Rae gathered her things. He didn't push or question her request. Together, they walked down the center aisle of the library and went their separate ways in the foyer.

It means everything to me. How can Devon think it doesn't change who I am? It's like an ink stamp on my forehead. Like I'm already labeled by everyone here. Rae trudged up the stairs and into her dorm room, feeling relieved when she saw that Molly wasn't already there, with her constant chatter and questions. She just wanted to crawl into bed, cry and disappear into the darkness..

Chapter 11

American Cheeseburger in London

SCHOOL life settled into a steady rhythm in sync with the English rain. Unlike the rain, school was never tiresome: Predictable, yes, but not tiresome. She became friends with a few of the students, said "hi!" to them on the way to and from classes, and even spent time with them after hours. In short, she began to fit in and enjoyed the feeling.

Rae loved afternoon classes best. Studying tatùs and learning how each student grew with their abilities made her more excited each day. September passed by quickly. Rae knew the first weekend of October would be Parent's weekend and she dreaded it. But when it arrived, it turned out to be even worse than she had imagined.

She wasn't naïve enough to think that her uncle would fly over for the weekend. Deep down, she didn't want him there. She wished her mom, or even her dad, were alive to help her through this. When Rae had finally gotten through on the phone to the U.S., Aunt Linda had answered. Each time she called, Uncle Argyle managed to be out or unavailable. The previous week, she'd finally spoken with him, but he'd been evasive since Aunt Linda had been in the room. He hadn't answered any of the questions she asked.

Over the weekend, other students' parents avoided her. Most of the students did as well. She felt, once again, like she didn't belong at the school, and it hurt. Thank goodness Devon's father turned out to be polite. Otherwise she'd have disappeared and hung out in her dorm.

Just like his son, he didn't seem to judge her just because of who her parents had been. He talked about Devon the entire conversion, which she didn't mind at all. Headmaster Lanford interrupted their pleasant conversation to say how ecstatic he was to see Mr. Wardell. He quickly dragged Devon's father off to speak with Dean Carter. While being pulled away, Mr. Wardell smiled apologetically. She noticed he had the same dimple as Devon and decided she both liked and trusted him, just as she did his son. He seemed the kind of guy who wanted the moon and stars for his kid.

Meeting Mr. Wardell turned out to be the easiest part of the weekend. The rest was like having her fingernails ripped out -- she actually thought that might be less painful. Any conversation she tried to have with a parent, Dean Carter stood within earshot to tell them who she was and what she'd been doing since her arrival. He seemed nervous with all of the female students, yet stuck to her specifically, like glue. Almost as if he thought she'd blurt out to the parents without tatùs how special her ink was going to be or how she wanted to take over the world with it. She thought she'd never been so happy to go back to class Monday morning.

Sitting at her desk listening to Professor Stockheed drone on about the importance of punctuation and how grammatically correct sentences allowed people to understand you better, she assured herself that the isolation of the past weekend would dissipate.

As the days progressed, the weather turned cooler and Rae noticed the trees began to glow with hues of red, orange and yellow. The school dance became the focus of everyone's attention. Molly, determined to ask someone to the dance, was disappointed to learn no one actually took a date.

"I'm gonna ask a boy, anyways," she told Rae later that evening.

"Ask Craig. His ink is water, and you know it's an excellent conductor of electricity." Rae waited for Molly to start laughing, but Molly didn't get the - obviously very bad - joke.

Molly just continued to pace the room and talk like she'd never heard Rae. "I'm dying to have my first kiss. Here I am, the sad age of sixteen and I've never been kissed. Well, I've been kissed, but not *that first kiss*." She ran out of the room, shouting Haley's name and hollering if she'd ever French-kissed anyone. Rae idly wondered why Molly hadn't asked her that question rather than Haley, but dismissed the thought just as quickly as it came into her head. It was blatantly obvious Rae had little experience in the world of kissing. *More important things to do anyways.*

She grabbed her backpack and headed downstairs to meet Devon. He was already there, waiting for her at their usual table at the back of the library. He sat chatting on his cell phone as she walked down the aisle. Noticing her, he waved.

Not wanting to eavesdrop Rae slowed her pace, but

still caught the end of the conversation.

"...Sounds great, Beth. I can't wait to see you on Saturday, too. Yup, me too...I, uh, gotta go. I'm tutoring tonight."

The tone of his voice made Rae feel like an obligation, a job, and that hurt. She'd come to consider him a friend and thought he felt the same. It certainly hadn't sounded that way.

"Who's Beth?" She tried to make her voice sound normal.

It took a long time before he answered. Rae watched him concentrate on putting his phone into his backpack. He exhaled, in what sounded like frustration.

"My girlfriend."

"Oh. How long...have you guys been toget--dating?" Rae blushed, hating that she couldn't keep her curiosity contained.

"Since the summer after I turned fifteen."

Rae did the math. His birthday was in March, so they'd been dating almost two years. They might as well be engaged, in to her mind.

"Yeah, we kinda grew up together. Her parents are friends with mine, so it was kinda...She goes to RH." His words were rushed and jumbled together. "Anyway, I'll introduce you at the dance."

Yeah, Rae'd like to meet this Beth and throw rotten bananas at her, along with a few moldy tomatoes. *Might as well make sure she's wearing something white and very expensive so it ruins everything.* Rae smiled sweetly, hoping her thoughts weren't transparent. "Does she know about your tatù?

"No. I haven't told her anything about Guilder or the ink-stamps. She thinks I got the tatù when I turned sixteen to copy my dad's snarling fox. She laughed and thought it was adorable I got a little fox with big ears as a tattoo instead of a skull or something more masculine." He shrugged indifferently.

What a jerk! Can't you see that, Dev? Come on, I'd be SO much better for you than her. Rae shifted, surprised at her own thoughts. "Funny. I never thought of your tatù as cute." She cleared her throat and tentatively reached out to touch his ink. She traced it lightly and quickly pulled her hand away when she pressed against his warm skin. "It's got a lot of hidden depth: speed, agility, awesome hearing. Fennecs have strong vision and aren't they supposed to have an easy-going nature? Definitely a useful tatù, especially if want to be a secret agent or spy." She'd checked out fennec foxes on the Internet the day after she'd met Devon.

Devon grinned and straightened in his seat. "I like your definition of my ink. Makes me sound a lot tougher than some tiny, cute, little desert animal." He laughed.

She glowed with pleasure, but quickly dropped her head down, determined not to show how much his words affected her. *Get your game face on Rae,* she coached herself. "Don't you hate that you can't say anything to Beth about your, uh…gift?" She played with the zipper on her bag. "I'd want to be able to tell the person I lov-cared about. Who wants a relationship built on lies?"

"No way." Devon shook his head. "It's hard enough to figure out how to deal with the skill, let alone tell other people. Our society would never allow us to do it anyway. It goes against the code."

Keep your tatù a secret to the outside world. Use it to the best of your ability. Don't try to create or evolve what has naturally been given to you. That includes scientific experiments, crossing DNA with each other or creating life. Blah, blah, bull-crap, blah, blah, and so on, and so forth. Rae stopped the mental reciting of the code and rested her hands on the table and leaned forward, curious to know why Devon walked the straight and narrow. He sounded scared to go against the grain or disappoint anyone. He definitely played by the rules. She scrunched her nose, annoyed that Uncle Argyle's little proverb itched in her memory. Compared to someone like her father, it was no wonder people here considered her a freak and were afraid of her.

She straightened in surprise when Devon stopped doodling and went stock still. His head cocked to the side as his eyes shot to the computer area near the library doors.

"Did you hear something?"

Rae looked around and held her breath, listening. The only sounds she heard were the hum of the lights and the fans from the computers. "Nothing unusual," she whispered.

"It's probably nothing." Devon shrugged, glancing behind him. "I thought I heard something click shut."

"Might've been one of the computers going into hibernation mode."

"Yeah, probably nothing." Devon lifted a large volume book. "This covers the entire history of tatùed people in Great Britain. One section even lists the people who attended Guilder." He opened the book to a random page. "To the unknowing eye, the book represents tattoos students from Guilder have gotten over the years since King Henry's time." He tapped his forehead with a finger and gave a knowing smile.

Devon picked up a scroll leaning against the desk. He and Rae unrolled it on the table to study the chart's tatù markings. The chart divided tatùs into four sections: common, distinct, rare and unknown.

"I've seen some of these here." Rae pointed to Andy's ink and a few others.

Devon tapped a drawing with his finger in the rare section. "That's your mother's ink stamp." He then pointed to another one. It was one of only three ink in the unknown section. "And your dad's."

Rae studied the sun marking with the rays coming out

of it. She traced it lightly with her finger, swearing to herself it felt warm. Ironic that it looked exactly as she'd pictured it. She hesitantly brought her hand over to her father's. "What's this supposed to be?" She leaned in closer, squinting at the detail. "Some little wizard in a robe?"

Devon coughed. "Kinda. I think it's supposed to be a warlock."

"A male witch?" Rae grinned. "You scared?" She covered the ink with her hand. "You think it might rub off on me if I touch it?"

"No." Devon's mouth said no, but his action of sliding her hand away spoke volumes about how he really felt. His reaction, and the meaning behind it, bothered her. But she wasn't willing to explore it at that moment.

She pointed to the title. "Why're there only three here?"

"There's no written code for the unknown section. I always thought of it as more of a black-gifted section. Though no one can say for sure, everyone says that unknown ink is dark. These three shown here were dark throughout our history -- the last one being your father's. The other two are from over hundreds of years back, one being from King Henry the VIII's time.

"I wonder which category mine will fall under.'" Her gut clenched as she stared at the unknown section. Would she be dark-gifted like her father? Surely not. Between her mother's and father's gifts, there had to be a happy medium...right?

"It's just a chart, a theory." Devon touched her hand lightly with his fingers. "It doesn't mean anything. It just gives us something to look at, like the periodic table." He pointed to his heart. "What matters is who you are on the inside. How you let the gift grow inside of you."

"Smarty pants." Rae grinned, all the fear she had felt a moment ago gone.

"Headmaster Lanford taught me that."

"Okay, he's the brilliant professor. Is he the brilliant-mad professor?" Rae winked. "Seriously though, he cares a lot for the school, doesn't he?"

"Everything he does is for the good of this school. Anyone who's attended Guilder pays homage to it. Famous, rich or whatever, they all give back to the school and, in turn, send their kids here. My father's a huge supporter and a big fan of Lanford's and he's been bragging about Guilder ever since I can remember."

"I've a feeling my father wasn't as big of a fan." Rae's watch chimed and she doubled checked it in disbelief. "Shoot, it's ten already, and I've got a lab I need to write up." She stood and started shoving her stuff back into her backpack.

"I promised Julian I'd help him with a vision-drawing he had yesterday. He can't figure it out so I said I'd take a look." Devon pushed his chair back and placed the chart back into its tube-holder.

They headed out of the library and went their separate ways. Rae spent the rest of the evening trying to do her report, but constantly thought about the chart. She went to bed still wondering how the inking worked and what kind she might get. Restless throughout the night, she couldn't relax and drop into a deep sleep. Around three she woke from a nightmare, her heart racing, fearful her entire body had been inked, even her face. She dropped back onto her sweat soaked pillow with relief when she realized she'd been dreaming.

The next afternoon Andy stopped by Rae's dorm room.

"You wanna go for lunch before the dance Saturday? There's this great little pub in town that serves American food. It's called 'American Cheeseburger in London.' It's awesome." Andy let out a growl. "I'll bring the werewolf."

She couldn't stop the explosion of laughter that

escaped. "S-sounds like fun. Why don't I meet you at your dorm around noon?"

Thumping and banging erupted from Rae's closest. Andy growled and jumped into the room, ready to protect her from the unidentified danger.

"That's it! I'm taking you shopping." Molly stepped out of Rae's closet and slammed the door. "You have absolutely nothing to wear to the dance."

"I was just--"

"No, you aren't." Molly grabbed her purse. "We're going now. I'll call a cab from downstairs."

Andy relaxed, laughed and stepped out of Molly's way. "I'll let you two get going. I'll even offer to drop you off at the shops if you'd like."

"Perfect." Molly snatched Rae's hand and dragged her to the door.

Rae dreaded shopping. She didn't have a knack for finding things that actually went together. However, the afternoon turned out to be fun. With Molly's help, Rae found a simple dress, fitted on top but when the material reached her hips, it relaxed and the chiffon ruffled down to her knees. The dress was simple but elegant, in a beautiful turquoise blue-green with tiny sparkles sewn into the chiffon. Molly even talked her into buying loads of little winged clips with rhinestones on them.

"Your hair is super long, and with your curls they'll look fantastic. I'll clip them in and do you hair." Molly pulled a tendril of Rae's hair from her ponytail. "It'll look like it's been pinned up by a million little butterflies."

"It sounds pretty." Rae's aunt had always gone on about how pretty she was and how she looked like her mom. Rae had never given it much thought. Of course, her aunt would say she was pretty. She was family, that's what family did. But no one else had ever really said it so Rae didn't really believe it.

"As long as we show those Roe Hampton girls up, the

evening'll be a success." Molly raised her hand, which Rae promptly slapped, returning the high five.

The following day, Rae ran up the stairs to the second floor of Joist House. Andy had told her his room was the last one at the end of the hall. Reaching the end of the hall, she glanced left and right. There were two doors at the end and she wasn't sure which one belonged to Andy. After a quick eeny-meeny-miny-moe, she knocked on the one on the right. Her jaw dropped when Devon opened the door.

"Hey, what're you doing here?" He grinned, his eyes bright.

Rae swallowed. He looked awesome in just a pair of jeans and white t-shirt. "Hi! I, um, I didn't know this was your room. I, uh...actually I'm trying to find Andy's room." Rae felt the heat creep into her face. Why'd she always have to blush? It was so annoying.

His face registered surprise, which quickly disappeared and his features became unreadable. "Andy's room is across the way." He pointed behind her.

"Thanks." Rae turned, hoping he'd shut his door. She wasn't that lucky. Devon leaned against the door frame, crossing his arms and watching with a smirk on his face. Andy opened his door before Rae finished knocking.

"Ready to go? I'm starving." He noticed Devon. "Hey, Dev. You want us to bring anything back for you? I'm taking Rae to lunch." Andy put his arm around her shoulders in a possessive gesture. "We're going to the American Cheeseburger in London."

"I'm good. Thanks for the offer." Devon's smile disappeared, his face unreadable again. "I gotta give Beth a shout. I'll catch you guys at the dance." He headed back into his dorm room, firmly shutting the door. Rae couldn't keep from glancing back at it as they walked down the hallway.

Andy drove to the pub in his little Volkswagen. Rae

giggled when he ran around the car to open the door for her.

"Very chivalrous of you." She stepped out. "Guilder should be proud."

Andy grabbed her hand and gave it a squeeze. "Ignore those old professors. They're so behind on the times."

Rae nodded, wondering what he meant. She smiled, happy to have her hand back when Andy opened the wooden door to the pub. The smell of fried onions, vinegar and beer filled her nostrils. The old pine floor showed years of foot treading, spilt drinks and polish. The tables and chairs were all Jacobean with twirly-carved legs. A few guys sat at the bar, watching TV as they munched on french fries and chicken wings. Other than that, the place seemed empty. Andy and Rae settled in at a table near the fireplace with actual logs burning inside – not a gas one like you'd find in an American restaurant. The place looked English, but the menu was completely American. Rae loved the casual, cozy atmosphere and couldn't wait to eat food from back home.

After ordering drinks and burgers, Andy leaned back, resting an arm on the back of the chair beside him. "So," he drawled, "are you starting to feel settled in?"

"A bit." Rae played with her utensils and scrunched up her nose. "Everyone still seems put-off by my family history."

"Ignore them. Loads of the guys think you're hot." He winked at her and bent forward. "You know, not everyone is scared of the old myths about tatùs dating each other. I'm definitely not chicken. I'm up for the challenge...if you are."

Rae blushed. It started at the base of her neck and burned all the way to her hair follicles. She got his implication loud and clear. Boy oh boy, she was *not* interested. "Um...thanks." She licked her lips. "That's uh...really nice of you to say."

"Don't worry." Andy grinned. "I don't bite. Just save me a dance tonight. I can bide my time." The look on his face turned to an "oh-crap" expression as his focus caught on someone over her shoulder. He straightened in his chair, suddenly intent with his menu.

Rae turned in her seat to see the dean enter the pub. He frowned when he noticed the two of them, his eyes narrowing when he stared at Rae.

Thank goodness the waitress brought their food. Rae stuffed a chip in her mouth right away, avoiding further conversation and not looking at anyone else in the pub. Andy chatted between bites about Guilder, classmates and the English weather.

Rae responded when she needed to. She tried using her peripheral vision to spot where Dean Carter sat. Andy seemed oblivious, constantly hinting the two of them should go out to a movie, to dinner or a club. Shortly after one, she used the excuse of having to get ready to cut their afternoon short. She stood, relieved to see the dean no longer there.

They drove back to Guilder, Andy talking most of the way.

"All rightie, you get going." Andy parked in the school parking lot and unclipped his belt. "I've two younger sisters. I know how it goes."

He leaned toward her, and Rae wedged herself against the door, terrified he might try to kiss her. She reached for the door handle, about ready to make her escape. Andy's eyes traveled down her arm. In one motion, he was out of the car and racing to the passenger side. He opened her door and helped her out. As he led her to Aumbry House, he said, "Remember to save me a dance, princess. You promised."

Rae watched him saunter over to Joist House, whistling as he walked. He turned and yelled, "Now you've had lunch with a werewolf at the American

Cheeseburger in London! Not a lot of people can say that."

Rae grinned, despite herself. She could still hear his laughter as she dashed up the stairs. Grabbing her toiletries, she rushed to the showers, avoiding telling Molly about her lunch date. *Crap, that's what it was. A date.* She had only meant to go as friends, but obviously Andy's intentions were completely different. He seemed like the brother she had always wanted. Obviously he considered her...*ew! I can't even finish the thought! It can't possibly be a worse mess.* Then the dean had to be there. With her luck, he'd probably taken notes and planned on sending a letter to Andy's parents and mentioning the entire thing at the Alumni Dinner at Christmas. She scrubbed her scalp harder, trying to clear her thoughts. She wanted to have fun tonight and, no matter what, she was determined to do so.

While putting the butterfly clips in Rae's hair, Molly grilled her on lunch. Not getting any answers, Molly finally fell silent and focused on Rae's hair. Rae felt a twinge of discomfort not talking to her roomy, but the whole thing had been uncomfortable for her and she really didn't want Molly to go blabbing to everyone about it, possibly hurting Andy's feelings. The one thing Rae was absolutely certain of when it came to her roommate was that she couldn't keep a secret if her life depended on it. *Better not even ask her to try. I'm already a freak. I don't want to be the freak who broke Andy's heart. What would Devon think then?* That brought Rae out of her thoughts with a start. She mentally lectured herself not to think about Devon since he had a girlfriend, whom he'd be dancing with tonight. *And I'm going to have fun, too.*

The tray of clips empty, Molly offered to put on Rae's makeup. Thirty minutes later, she rolled Rae's chair in front of the mirror. Rae suddenly felt nervous and stared down at her hands.

"Quit avoiding. Your hair's fantastic. And the make up

isn't over done, I promise. You're really going to turn some heads! Who knew?"

Fluttering in her stomach, Rae peeked. Her eyes widened in surprise. Molly had put clips around each tendril of curl. Every direction Rae turned, sparkles shown through her curls and bounced of the blond and dark parts. It looked like movie-star hair. She swore she could hear the other girls down the hall laughing. She glanced at Molly and grinned sheepishly.

"Don't be so shocked. It's about time we got to see what you really look like. You've been so busy trying to keep up with classes and learning about tatùs, you never bother to put any effort into your physical appearance. I don't think I've ever seen you put more than mascara lip gloss on, or had your hair out of a bun or ponytail."

Rae could only smile.

"We'll show the boys of Guilder there are girls here worth a second glance!" Molly put her hands on her hips. "And we'll let everyone here know you're not just a stupid name."

Rae wanted to hug Molly. That was the nicest thing anyone had ever said to her. *I have the best roomie in the world.*

Chapter 12

The Dance

HEADING off to the dance half an hour late, Rae noticed the empty Roe Hampton bus in the parking lot. Rae, Molly, Haley, Maria and the twins all headed up the path to the Oratory. They all jumped simultaneously when a deep voice spoke front a bench in the shadows.

"Good evening, ladies. You're all splendidly charming." Dean Carter stepped from the shadows. "Might I have a quick word with Ms. Kerrigan?"

Pounding echoed in Rae's ears. She reminded herself that she planned to have fun tonight, no matter what. *Creepy old goat.* "Go on in. I'll meet you inside." Rae turned her attention to the dean, abruptly feeling less confident than her voice had sounded. She tried to ignore Haley's snicker.

The dean waited until the others went in. "I wanted to take a moment to ask how things are going." He didn't wait for Rae's reply. "I also wanted to mention you'll be sleeping in the Infirmary on the fourteenth of November." He frowned. "So we ca--may see you on the morning of the fifteenth. This is one of the conditions we set with your uncle on your being allowed into our school. That's all. Have a pleasant evening." He stood and walked away, leaving Rae frozen in her spot.

What? That had been totally abrupt. Why'd he have to tell her right now? The guy was off his rocker. She slowly made her way inside, shaking her head, thankful again no one knew her birthday was actually the thirteenth. It would give her a couple of days to prepare for the English Inquisition she'd have on the fifteenth.

The dance seemed to be in full swing as Rae entered through the double doors. She felt like she'd stepped back in time. The Oratory had been transformed into a ballroom during King Henry's time. The stage on the far side resembled a castle. There were long tables with flowing linen cloth covering them and old wooden benches where students sat talking and eating grapes and other fruits. Fire-lit torches lined the walls, casting wonderful dancing shadows over the wood carvings. Between the feeling the Oratory emitted and the decorations, Rae couldn't tell if it was the fifteen hundreds or the twenty-first century.

She spotted Molly with the girls on the other side of the hall. She sensed everyone's eyes catch and stare as she walked across the marble floor.

What's wrong? Crap, did my hair mess up when we walked from the dormitory? Is my dress split? She glanced down at her shoes, gave her dress a tug, and then gently patted her hair. *Nothing has fallen out of place, and I don't see any obvious problems. Did Dean Carter do some voodoo thing to me?*

She'd become accustomed to the stares, but this gawking felt ten times worse – like she'd turned into some exotic fish inside a tank instead of just the freak with a bad family history. Suddenly walking became her single focus; too afraid she'd trip in her heels and end up on her face in front of everyone.

Andy stepped in her path and came to her rescue.

"Stunning." He let out a low whistle.

Nicholas came up behind him, smiling excitedly. "Rae! My lab partner, how are you this evening?" He let out a whoah-hoah.

Rae stood rooted. Thankful for the low lights, she was glad no one could see her face. "I'm good. Thanks." Glancing behind the boys, she pretended to see Molly waving at her. "Oh, Molls needs me." It was tempting to break into a run, but still terrified she'd trip in her heels, she forced herself to walk. Simply focusing on breathing in and out seemed about all she could handle at the moment. This attention felt so foreign.

"*Everyone's staring at you.*" She could hear Maria's soft voice inside her head. She sounded sweet and sincere. "*It's totally different than when you first arrived. It's like they're seeing* you *for the first time. You know, not the name Kerrigan, but the girl, Rae.*" Maria giggled. "*You should see the faces of the girls from Roe Hampton. Totally jealous! Molly's mission is accomplished -- you know she'll never shut up about it now!*"

Rae glanced up toward Maria and started laughing. Maria's last sentence was totally true and exactly what she needed to hear to drum her out of her nerves.

"Rae," whispered Molly when she reached them. "If you could feel the electricity in the air like I can, man-oh-man. It's priceless. All that time I spent on your hair...totally worth it."

"I think I'd feel like a princess tonight, if I wasn't so nervous. These heels you made me wear are killer high." Rae giggled. The heels were only about an inch, but having never worn anything but sandals or tennis shoes her whole life, she was not good at teetering on heels of any height. "I have a feeling the Roe Hampton girls aren't too happy with the fact they have to share the boys now. Come on, let's go get some punch.

A live band began setting up on the makeshift stage. Rae felt a flutter of excitement when she noticed Devon. He stood on stage chatting with some of the band members.

A pretty, blonde-haired, girl walked up on stage and put her hand in Devon's. Rae tried to squelch the jealousy that rose in her chest. She squinted to get a better look at the girl she assumed was Beth. She had gorgeous, naturally blonde hair, with those natural highlights that made it look like it almost sparkled in the lights, and it sat poker straight across her shoulders. The kind of hair celebrities had in magazines that you never believed actually existed. Could hair really by *that* shiny?

Her eyes traveled down Beth's body. She had olive-colored skin that probably stayed tanned all winter long. Miss Perfect Body wore a strapless, designer dress. If Rae ever tried to wear something similar, it would fall down as she had nothing on top to hold it up. Beth, on the other hand, had plenty to keep the dress, and seemingly Devon, in place.

Rae sighed in defeat. She couldn't compete with someone like that. How could she?

Andy appeared at her side, offering a glass of punch. "I have to tell you again how great you look. It's, uh...you're pretty hot." He nodded toward her dress.

"Molly picked it out." She purposely turned her back on the stage and Devon. She reminded herself that he wasn't the only guy in the room and even though Andy was more big brother than big romance to her, it felt nice to be noticed.

"There's a new James Bond movie coming out next week. D'you want to go see it?"

"That'd be fun. We could see if Molly and Nicholas want to come with us as well." She pointed to the punch table. "They seem to be having a laugh at the moment."

A look of frustration crossed Andy's face. Then he

smiled, like he'd just thought of something. "Except, I'm the only one of us who has a car and it's pretty tiny."

"Maybe we should ask Julian or Riley to come along then, too."

"Where we going?" Riley sauntered by. He stopped directly in front of Rae, blatantly checking her out. "Wow, Kerrigan, you clean up nice. I heard some of the Roe Hampton girls bitchin' but didn't realize they were referring to you. It seems like we might have a bit of a competition heatin' up here." He elbowed Andy. "If we're really lucky, a good catfight!"

"I'd prefer a mud fight," Andy said. The two guys roared with laughter.

"*Sooo funny.*" Rae rolled her eyes. "Andy wondered if you wanted to go to a movie this weekend. We need another car."

"Movie? As long as Andy's not asking me out." He smirked at the scowl on Andy's face. "Then sure. I can drive as long as you promise to ride shotgun in my car." Riley grabbed her hand and gave it a gently gentle squeeze but didn't let it go. "Come on. Let's get this party started."

Before she could reply, Riley pulled her to the dance floor and began twirling her around to an upbeat tune the band played. Others joined them on the floor as the music continued. Molly wiggled in beside her and wouldn't let her leave.

When a quiet song finally slowed things down, Rae expertly dodged the reaching hands of several boys and made her way toward the punch bowl. Pouring herself a glass, she stepped back toward the shadows near the wall. She planned on staying there until her breathing slowed. She leaned against the cool wood and looked around the dance floor. Devon and Beth moved in sync near the stage. Determined to make every effort to ignore them, she physically turned her attention to whoever had just come up beside her. It was Riley. *Crud.*

"Are you going to hide here all night when the slow numbers come on? You do realize ninety percent of Guilder is planning on asking you to dance."

"I'm not hiding. I just needed a little breather." Rae took another sip of her punch and realized she'd already finished her cup. She snuck one more glance toward Devon and Beth.

"It's none of my business, but they seem very happy together."

"Pardon? Not really sure who you're talking about." Rae kept her eyes roaming around the dance floor, pretending to look through the crowd. Her heart seemed to have jumped into her throat. She tried to swallow it back down.

"Devon and Beth. They belong together. Plus, they've been dating for, like, ever." Riley pushed his sleeves up, his tatù reflecting from the glittery lights. "You know, of course, Devon's father approves of Beth. She isn't in *our* circle." Riley took Rae's hand and pulled her toward the dance floor again. His cheetah tatù seemed like it was moving from the swaying reflection of the torch flames. "Some people frown upon inked people being together. Heck, almost everyone at the school follows the unwritten rule. There are a few of us who disagree…Why shouldn't inked people like us stick together and make stronger talents? How can that be wrong? Shoot, royalty does it all the time."

Rae stared at Riley in disbelief. She'd been thinking it in the back of her mind but wouldn't admit it, even to herself. It had always felt wrong somehow. But now…What was so bad about being with someone you liked? If Devon was so determined to follow the rules and please everyone around him, then let him. Her parents had married, bore her and she felt completely fine. When she received her tatù, she'd show everyone how good and strong she could be. A new-found sense of confidence started to grow inside her.

She tucked a hair behind her ear, enjoying the soft feel of hair curling against her skin. "You've got a good point. What harm would it there be to in going out with someone from Guilder? Dating doesn't mean you're getting married. Guilder's thinking's as old as their buildings sometimes."

"Exactly!" Riley spun her away and back to him, dipping her. "So, when're you and I gonna go out?"

Rae froze in his arms, relieved when he pulled her back up to a standing position. She hadn't been expecting that. She figured Riley'd been talking about Devon's lack of courage to go against the grain, not angling the conversation around to hooking up with her himself. She'd gotten the impression he didn't really like her. *Surprise, surprise.* But she didn't feel the same. *I have to be careful how I handle this though.* Going out for lunch would be less embarrassing than telling Riley the truth, and possibly better than turning him down. "M-Maybe next weekend or something."

"Perfect! Let's plan on Saturday afternoon."

She blinked. "O-Okay."

When the song ended, Rae dashed off to grab another glass of punch, terrified Riley'd follow. She glanced back, relieved to see him dancing with a pretty blonde from Roe Hampton. She took a deep breath and considered the first part of the conversation she'd had with Riley. Rae suddenly realized that he had neatly backed her into a corner, leaving her no alternative but to say yes to his invitation. *Sly move, Cheetah boy..* She made a mental note to be better prepared the next time she talked to him.

"Excuse me, do you mind?" A silky soft voice interrupted her thoughts.

Realizing she still held the punch ladle, she turned to apologize. The act of contrition stuck in her throat. The airy voice that had asked her to move was none other than

Beth's, *Devon's Beth.*

"Sorry." Rae handed her the ladle, almost dropping it before quickly moving to the other side of the punch bowl. "Beth, right?"

"How do *you* know my name?" Beth's eyes narrowed.

"I, um..." Rae paused, her heart hammering. "I noticed you on stage with Devon and just assumed. Everyone knows he has a girlfriend at Roe Hampton."

"An' who are you?" Beth didn't seem as sweet as Devon had said. In fact her attitude screamed Queen Bee. Rae knew all about that type. They were always the ones who tried to make her life hell back home, if they didn't ignore her. But things were different now. She wasn't invisible anymore and suddenly, that didn't seem like such a bad thing.

"I'm Rae, Rae Kerrigan."

"Ohhhh..." Beth smirked. *"You're* the kid who needs tutoring. Devon told me about you. Don't you think it's strange you made it into a school like Guilder, and you need help with your classes? Your father must be loaded or have some excellent connections to get you in." She crossed her arms. "Maybe your mom slept with the dean?"

Rae blinked in surprise. Then Beth's last comment about her mother sunk in. It made her livid. Wishing she had a tatù to shrink Beth into a bug she could squash with her shoe, she stiffened. "I got in on my own merit, thank you. My dad's dead and my mother passed away as well. No loads of cash or connections. Guilder actually sought me out. I live in New York."

Beth had the decency to appear slightly embarrassed, but only for a moment. She glared at Rae before storming past her.

"It was nice meeting you," Rae said cheerfully, wiggling her fingers at Beth's back. A small driftwood of guilt floated by. She'd been brought up better, but the satisfaction the look on Beth's face had brought made it

116

worth it.

A warm breath against her neck sent shudders down her spine. She jumped.

"Were you teasing Beth?" Devon whispered.

"Crap! You scared me." She slapped him lightly on the shoulder. "No sneaking up on people tonight. It's against the rules."

"Rules? I didn't know there were rules. Any more I should know about?" He laughed.

Rae rolled her eyes at him. "For the record, I didn't bug Beth. She asked me if my parents had money. I told her my parents had passed." She shrugged. "I guess she felt embarrassed for mentioning it."

Devon's dimple appeared. "After seeing you walk in tonight, I guess Beth's got some issues with me tutoring you." He grinned. After pausing a moment, he pointed to her head and quietly added, "I like it. It's different than your usual ponytail."

Rae touched her hair, twirling a lock around her fingers.

Devon coughed. "Well, I should probably get back over to Beth, or I won't hear the end of it." He sighed, his eyes traveling back and forth from Beth to Rae. His gaze lingered on her.

"Are you banned from talking to other girls tonight, or is it just girls from Guilder?" She tried putting on her most innocent face. *Seems I'm not the only one with rules.*

"Originally, it was just the Guilder girls, and then you walked into the Oratory looking all beautiful. When Beth found out you're the girl I tutor, I was mainly banned from talking to you." Devon grinned mischievously. "Personally, it's worth the risk. However, I'd better head over before she has a coronary."

Rae didn't want him to walk away but didn't know what to say to make him stay. She clenched her hands, feeling her nails dig into her palms. *Beautiful...he thinks I'm* *beautiful...*Rae was full of competing emotions.

Devon took a few steps toward Beth. A slower country song started playing and he paused. "Ahh, screw it." He turned around, his dimple appearing on his cheek.

"Pardon?" Rae raised her eyebrows at him, wondering what he meant.

He reached for her hand and pulled her to the dance floor. "If she can't understand I'm only trying to help a friend fit in, then she can brew."

Like a witch. Rae's heart stuttered faster than her feet as she stumbled to keep up with him. She suddenly felt lightheaded, his warm, rough-skinned hand against hers her the only anchor she knew. She wondered if he worked out. It felt like even the tendons in his hand were super strong. If Beth stood scowling at her, Rae had no idea. She couldn't focus on anything past Devon's back, then his face when he turned around. He released her hand and slipped his arms around her waist, pulling her tight.

His body felt firm and muscular as she tentatively brought her hands around his neck. They fit together in all the right places. Perfect. Not too tall and her forearms rested comfortably along his chest and shoulders. She felt his upper body shake and brought her eyes up to meet his. She was shaking deep inside, as well.

Then she saw the crinkle by his eyes and realized he was laughing. Not mocking, but a guy's way of giggling. "Wha -- "

"The song."

She cocked an ear and tried to make out what the band was playing. When the chorus started, she recognized it and smiled, whispering the words to the song. "...Things will change...People will see...The walls...la la na de da...will fall."

"Don't know the words? Just seems to be your song. Things changing, you knocking down some walls, you against the world."

"Hey, you're the one who taught me about my past. This is your fault." She squeezed his neck lightly, loving the feel of his soft hair against her fingers.

He pulled her tight against his hips, trapping her arms against his lean chest. His eyes grew wide, but he didn't release her. Neither said another word and too soon, the song finished.

Devon's hands slid across her back as the last chord rang out. She took a small step back, only to bump into someone very warm and tall.

"Hey," Andy said. "I planned to ask you to dance. You didn't have to jump right into my arms." He winked at Devon as he spun Rae around in a circle. "Your girlfriend seems pretty pissed."

It seemed like it took a conscious effort for Devon to pull his eyes away from Rae's. "Who...What? Oh shoot, Beth. I gotta go." He slipped away before Rae had a chance to say anything.

"So," Andy said as an upbeat slow song came from the band on the stage. "You've had your American cheeseburger, what about the British werewolf?"

Rae stared at him blankly. Her thoughts were still on Devon, wondering what he was doing behind her.

"The movie. You know, *American Werewolf in London*. It's from, like, eons ago. Probably the seventies." Andy's large, sweaty, hot hands pressed against her mid back as he stepped on her toe. She couldn't help but compare his clumsy presence to Devon's effortless performance.

"Oh yeah. I watched that with my uncle years ago." Rae began concentrating on keeping her tender toes from turning into mashed potatoes. She didn't get Andy's joke or what he hinted at.

"My bad. I'm a bit into all the werewolf movies at the moment." Andy swung her around and Rae banged into a couple dancing beside them, earning a pair of dirty looks.

Thankfully, the song ended in time to save her toes and

eardrums from Andy. He was really nice, but she just wasn't interested. *I thought he'd never stop talking!*

The rest of the evening sped by. As Molly and Rae waited for Maria and Haley to come outside, they watched the Roe Hampton girls step into their bus. Unable to turn away, Rae watched Devon walk a now happy Beth to her bus, then kiss her in front of everyone. The taste of jealousy lingered in Rae's mouth and no amount of swallowing helped.

Chapter 13

Mail

OCTOBER drifted, like the leaves, into November. Her magical dance with Devon and the subsequent disappointment of seeing him kiss Beth didn't fade so much as it became lower on her list of important things. Midterm exams kept everyone busy. Rae excelled in all her classes, pleased to send a good midterm report back home.

The week of her birthday she received a thick letter in the mail from her uncle. She dashed up the marble stairs, hoping Molly wouldn't be in their room. Instinct told her she needed to be alone when she read it.

Rae opened the door and stopped dead in her tracks. Molly sat at her desk working on her laptop. Rae glanced around the room for an escape. She spotted her wool sweater on the back of her chair. She ran in, grabbed the sweater and turned back for the door.

"Hey, you just got in. Where're you going now?" Molly didn't bother to look up from her computer.

"Hi." Rae quickly hid the letter under her sweater. Not

that it mattered, Molly paid her no attention. "I'm just going to head out for a walk before dinner. For once, it's not raining."

"Cool. I'm still trying to fix my computer." She hit the top of her desk with a vengeance. "I buggered it up the other day when I tried to use my tatù in the room. Stupid electricity!"

"Good luck." Rae pulled the door shut behind her.

She trotted down the stairs and outside into the brisk air. She thought about the past week as she headed down the concrete steps. Dean Carter had come to talk to her over the weekend to remind her again he expected her to sleep in the Infirmary the night of her birthday. He said the school felt it would be in her best interest if she was there when she woke up with her tatù -- a better way to help explain her ink and learn to control it. She couldn't be sure if the dean felt it was for her benefit or for the school's. She didn't argue, only because it hadn't really been a choice or a question and it didn't really matter in the end. So, whether she liked it or not, Rae would be spending the night of the fourteenth of November at the stupid Infirmary.

She'd kept silent about the mix-up on her birth certificate. *It's the one thing I can do on my own. I've every right to experience this the way I want, like everyone else.*

Striding past the buildings, she decided to take the path that led through the forest. She'd been on it a number of times in the past month, on walks with Andy, Riley and Nicholas. She felt like a broken record, always maintaining she just wanted to be friends with each of them. Each said they understood but continued to vie for her attention. Even reminding them of the unwritten code didn't seem to deter them. It soon got tiring trying not to hurt anyone's feelings.

As she headed toward the forest, she contemplated telling Devon the truth about her birthday. After all, it would be nice to have one person she could completely confide in. Checking her watch, she stumbled, realizing her birthday fell on Friday -- the thirteenth. No way would she tell Devon. Plus if he got caught knowing, Dean Carter would probably have his head on a platter and she didn't want to leave him in that situation.

Rae entered into the quiet forest, continuing on the path until she came to the first park bench and plopped down. The cool wind turned into a light breeze inside the forest. The temperature actually felt a few degrees warmer. Relieved no one was around, she pulled out Uncle Argyle's letter.

Inside the large envelope were two cards. One a faded pink with creased corners and rather thick, and the other had Uncle Argyle's quirky handwriting with a note for her to open first. She tore the backing, pulling the card out. A single sheet of paper lay inside, again in the quirky writing.

> *Dear Rae,*
> *I thought to write or phone you many times. I simply did not have the courage to answer your questions. I'm sorry for that. I promised your mother a long time ago I wouldn't tell you about your ink until the right time. It never seemed to be the right time. When Guilder offered me the chance to have them explain, I believed that was in your best interest. The school knows how to tell you, and the students are whom you'd need to be around. I'm sure you've learned about your mother and me. Please do not think ill of me. I never once felt jealous of your mom, and I tried to help her as much as I could. Your mother was very special, and it broke me when she fell in love with your father. I was frustrated with her and kept telling her she'd be making the biggest mistake of her*

life. I should have done more but, as always, I lacked the courage. When you were born, you became her lesson of love. You were worth everything she had sacrificed and endured.

I hope you're able to remember her and recall how much she loved you. Your father had other plans and grew furious when she refused to give him another child -- the son he so desired. She knew something was going to come to pass. She sent me a letter to ask me to take care of you should anything happen. She also sent an envelope I should give you on your sixteenth birthday. I've enclosed it with this letter.

Your aunt and I wish you a wonderful birthday. Aunt Linda knows nothing about the ink-stamp, as I have never told her.

I fear for you and what your ink might be. You are a smart girl and I see so much of your mother in you. However, I repeat the words I told you before you left:

You can't undo the past. The sins of the father are the sins of the son. I wish you all the best as you figure out your talents and find out who you are.

Sincerely,
Your uncle Argyle

Rae sat staring at the letter for a long time. It took all her courage to turn to the decade-old envelope beside her. Inside were the last words her mother had wanted to tell her, the last piece of advice she would ever give Rae. Tears welled up in her eyes for the mother she'd lost. It felt like she was losing her mom all over again. However, this time she knew what she'd be missing and how much it hurt.

Wishing desperately her mother could be here with her now, she tried to swallow the lump in her throat. Her uncle's letter brought little comfort. *No surprise, it's typical of him.*

What if she turned into something bad, something evil? Maybe it would be better if she weren't on her own. *What if I hurt Molly?* Even by mistake it could be serious.

She understood from her lessons the ink's powers would grow with her. It would be weak when it was born and would take time to strengthen within her. So she had assumed all this time that she wouldn't be a danger to anybody. What if she were wrong?

Rae shook her head, confused and unsure what to think or do. She debated about waiting to open her mother's card until Friday. She stood and paced around the bench. Blowing her bangs away from her forehead, she swore. Walking in circles didn't help.

Angry at herself for being so indecisive, she plunked down onto the bench. She ripped open the envelope, pulling the card out quickly, making it impossible to change her mind.

The cover of the card froze Rae in her tracks. It was very pretty, something a young child would like -- something *she* had loved as a kid. Instantly the tears fell and no amount of blinking could stop them. Loads of sparkles in different shades of pink covered the card, with a beautiful princess in the middle.

When she was five and six she loved to color and do crafts with sparkles, glitter glue and markers. She always used pinks. Her mom would hang everything up in the conservatory. The memory brought on a fresh flood of tears. After the fire she never used the color pink and seldom did crafts or coloring, unless she had to at school. She swallowed, wiping her eyes and exhaling a long breath. With shaking hands, she reverently opened the card. Inside sat a letter in her mother's neat cursive. She remembered that writing. When she was little, she had thought it the most beautiful writing in the world. Taking another deep breath, Rae slowly read the page, trying to absorb everything straight into her heart, to a secret place where she could keep it all safe forever.

> *My Dearest Rae,*
> *Happy 16th Birthday, love!*
> *It seems surreal I'm writing this letter to you now, as you sit here beside me drawing a picture, and only six years old. I don't want to write this, but when something happens, I want to be able to explain to my daughter the choices I've made in my life. I also want you to know I am very proud of you.*
> *I'm sorry I'm not there to be with you when you receive your ink. I've wondered so often what your gift will be. You're such a beautiful, talented little girl right now. I'm assured you will have that same inner beauty and talent go into your ink. I pray you will have the splendor and goodness from my gift and the capability of your father's.*
> *I have asked Argyle to tell you nothing, unless he has to, or until you are close to sixteen. I'm sorry I never told you about the tatù, but your unknowing will have saved your life more times than you will ever understand.*
> *You will, by now, know what kind of man your father was. I'm sorry I didn't see his true self at first, and sorry again that I couldn't change him. I loved him once, despite his faults. That love gave me you and for that, I have no regrets. I may not have been able to help him, but I am able to save you.*
> *FLAMES TO DUST. That is what my father taught me of my ink. That was my destiny -- **my destiny**, Rae, so that you will live. Others will see this differently, but never lose sight of the bare truth -- you would live and become*

what you are meant to be -- that is YOUR destiny. One day, I hope Argyle will tell you about your grandfather.

*Always stand tall and walk proud, Rae. You have such wonderful promise and I know, difficult as it may be, you'll find your way. Your father's demons will try to tempt you, but don't listen. You're going to be more powerful than your father ever was and that is why he **fears** you. The wrong temptations will challenge you, but every time you don't give in to them, you'll strengthen your gift. You have a tough road ahead of you, but I know you'll create your own path and make your own stamps in life. Don't ever lose sight of that, and know that you are special.*

Through you, I will always shine. My tatù is a sun and that is why I named you Rae. You are my Rae of Sun, my Rae of Hope.

I love you more than life itself,

Yours truly,

Forever,

Mother

XOXOXO

Rae read the letter again and again. Her throat felt so painful and tight, she could barely breathe. No amount of swallowing made the throbbing lump disappear. She could hear her mother saying the words as if she were right beside her, whispering in her ear.

When she tried reading it again, she tenderly put the letter away, fearing her salty tears might ruin the ink on the sacred paper. Her mother had sacrificed everything. She'd planned everything to make sure Rae reached her sixteenth birthday.

Rae slipped the letters inside her coat and slid off the bench to walk.

You can't undo the past, Rae. Her uncle's words jeered at her as she plodded further down the path. She wished her uncle was standing right in front of her so she could scream at him. She'd curse just about anyone right now.

Glaring up to the encroaching darkness, Rae checked her watch and realized dinnertime had already started. She felt like skipping the evening meal, heading back to her room and locking the door to have a good cry. The idea of trying to hold a conversation with anyone filled her with dread.

Swearing, she turned around to head back to the dorms. With her birthday only days away, now was definitely not the time to show the professors anything might be amiss. The last thing she needed was more of them breathing down her neck, constantly monitoring her every move. She pounded the ground with each step, getting angrier and more frustrated by the moment.

Exiting the forest, she made a conscience effort to take some deep breaths. She focused on putting that anger deep inside, to use at another time. She needed to act like everything was perfectly fine by the time she got to the Refectory. Counting to five with each inhalation and exhalation, she willed herself to relax. She ran her fingers under her eyes and checked to make sure no mascara had run down or smudged.

By the time she reached the Refectory, she appeared physically calm. She nipped inside, quickly hanging her coat up before checking the seating chart. Relieved to be sitting at Andy and Devon's table tonight, it would save trying to make conversation with Molly or trying to avoid Maria's worried gaze.

She tried to walk inconspicuously into the hall but could feel eyes of the professors and students turn toward her. She smiled at Headmaster Lanford, determined to hide her true emotions. He nodded back, and then returned to his meal. Rae slid into the empty seat between

Andy and Devon and reached for a bun. She put all her concentration into lathering it with butter.

"You're a bit late tonight," Andy commented.

"I went for a walk and lost track of time." She could feel Andy stiffen as he glanced up toward the door. She followed his gaze and watched Riley enter the dining hall.

"Did you walk alone?"

"Andy! Give her a break. It's none of your business." Devon leaned behind Rae, punching Andy in the shoulder. Andy gave him a dirty look but grinned sheepishly at Rae.

"Sorry," he said.

"No biggie." Rae shrugged. "I got a letter from my uncle."

"Everything okay?"

Rae grimaced at the concern in Devon's voice. "Yeah," she lied. "He sent a card to wish me a happy birthday and hoped everything'll go all right on the day."

"It'll be the best day of your life." Andy hugged her shoulders, seeming reluctant to remove his arm to eat. Rae sighed, wishing he meant it as a comforting gesture, but knowing that it was a possessive move meant more for everyone who was looking than for her. She felt like a pawn in this little game the boys played with her. But as of yet she couldn't find a way out of it that didn't include breaking their hearts and making her position at Guilder worse than it was.

Toward the end of dinner, Devon asked if she still wanted to get together for a tutoring session. He seemed preoccupied, so she offered him an out, saying they could resume again on Thursday. She certainly wasn't in any state to be alone with him anyway.

Devon got up to leave as soon as the meal concluded. Rae wasn't far behind. She slipped her coat back on, instantly feeling for the letters inside her right pocket. She panicked when she couldn't find them. Grappling into her other coat pocket, she sighed with relief when she felt the soft paper material.

She scratched her head as she walked outside, sure she'd stuffed them into her right pocket, not the left. A large gust of wind shook her thoughts. Pulling her coat tightly around her to avoid the cool wind, she rushed to get inside the warmth of her dormitory.

It felt like forever before her wristwatch finally read nine and she could fake a yawn and big stretch as a show to Molly. "I'm exhausted. It feels like it's been a really long day." Which did hold some truth to it. "Molls, do you mind if we cut the lights out early?"

Molly sat at her desk, with two textbooks open and a spiral pad full of writing. "Really? I've got a report do tomorrow and I just started."

Rae's spirits dropped. She didn't have the brain power tonight to try and argue.

Molly must have seen the look on Rae's face. She dog eared the textbooks and began tossing stuff into her backpack. "I can go down to the library and finish this. I'll use the computers there since mine's still broke." She moved to the door. "'Night."

Rae made a trip to the bathroom to brush her teeth and shower, all the while thinking of her mother, her sorrow, her situation and her roommate, who was turning out to be entirely more considerate than she had ever imagined. Guilt mixed with her pain, swirled her emotions into turmoil. She crawled into bed and, thankfully, drifted into oblivion before her tears flooded her pillow.

The next few days passed at a snail's pace. The boys, as she had persisted in thinking of them, were miraculously leaving her alone, for once. She spent some quality time with Molly, making her guilt over hiding things from her roomy lessen just a bit. Even the depression over her mother's letter began to disappear as her birthday drew closer. Happy when Thursday evening finally rolled around, Rae began to get excited to meet up with Devon. It would make the night pass quicker. Then she could head off to bed to wake up for her "secret" birthday.

Opening the library door, she noticed him already waiting in their usual spot. "Hey, how you doin'?" she whispered when she got to the table.

"I'm all right. How 'bout you?" He grinned. "Only a few more sleeps 'til your birthday. Anxious?"

"Anxious isn't the word." Rae rolled her eyes as she plopped into her seat across from him. "I've no idea how anybody survives this. I've only known about this since September. You guys've known basically all your lives. How is it none of you ended up in the loony bin?"

Devon threw his head back and laughed. Madame Elpis peeked in the door from the foyer outside Aumbry's library to shoot them a dower look and shushed them, which only made Devon's shoulders shake harder.

He finally calmed down enough to answer her. "Your comment had me picturing a large group of tatùed people in some psych ward. Could you imagine what the *other* patients would say?" He grinned. "They'd be telling tales of wolves and bears, or seeing people walk through walls. The psych doctors would keep them under lock and key." He started chuckling again. "Then Madame Elpis shushed me. Could you imagine her in a psych ward?"

Rae had to hold her belly to try to keep from laughing aloud. It felt awesome since she hadn't done it in a while. Once the moment was over, they sat quiet, smiling at each other. She gathered her courage to ask Devon something that had been bothering her since she'd read her mother's letter.

"Devon? What d'you know about the fire?"

He looked at Rae, surprised at her sudden seriousness. He stared down at his fingers, drawing imaginary circles on the desk. After a few moments, he slowly lifted his head. "The house fire killed your parents, and really should've taken you as well, but it didn't. There's no record of what actually happened -- just that you were saved and the two other people inside the house died. Somehow you managed to escape. I'd guess it probably had something to do with your mom." Devon shrugged his shoulders.

"I think so, too. In fact, I'm positive my mom had something to do with the fire."

Devon's face registered shock.

Rae gushed on, before losing her courage. "My mom made me go outside before it happened. She told me to go play in the tree house and she'd come get me. *She* sent me outside.

"Maybe you're right. I only know fleeting stories and bits of adult conversation from the week it happened. I've read the newspaper articles but that was a long time ago. Why the sudden interest? Is it because your birthday's around the corner?"

She debated making something up but decided the truth would be much easier than lying. "I got a letter from my uncle and inside was a letter my mom wrote ten years ago. She asked my uncle to give it to me on my sixteenth birthday."

"Oh...Umm...Do you want to tell me about it?" Rae watched him run his hands along the table, his knuckles pure white. He seemed more nervous than she felt. *How odd, and sweet.*

"Yes...No...I don't know. There's nothing secretive inside, or some hidden message." She shrugged, not sure what to say. "It's just weird she'd know to write a letter...like she knew something might happen." Rae stared at her hands. "It just makes sense – her ink was a sun, and the sun's made of fire..." The conclusion seemed so obvious now. But she just couldn't finish the sentence.

Devon paused, biting his lower lip. "It's possible. Everyone assumes your father started it and your mother was the casualty. Is it really important to you now?" He stared intently into Rae's eyes. "What's bothering you, if the letter isn't so bad?"

Rae sighed and picked imaginary bits out of her clean nails. It seemed he knew how to read her without even trying. Glancing up, she quietly said, "I want to know my father's gift. Or curse, if you want to look at it that way."

"You've seen a picture of his ink, the male version of a witch -- like a warlock or sorcerer. He was unique." Devon ran his fingers through his hair. "Has no one explained this to you?"

Seeing her shake her head, he continued, "He could mimic other people's gifts."

"Mimic?" Rae's eyebrows shot up.

"He had the ability to copy the ink of other people, do what they could do. You know, use their tatù." Devon stared intently at her, as if waiting for her reaction to the news.

"You mean he could copy your ink or if he wanted to, he could turn around and copy Andy's?"

"He had to come in contact with a tatùed person in order to imitate their gift."

"So he could do anything then?"

"Kind of. He could copy their ink, but if he touched someone else, he'd then take over the power of that tatù. He wasn't able to retain a gift to use again. Great power, but it still had its limits." Devon's eyes met her gaze and didn't waver. "Does that make sense? Maybe Headmaster Lanford can explain it better."

"I get what you're saying." *Holy crap. I DO get it.* "If my father wanted more power or to use his ink to his advantage, he'd need a lot of people around him so he could use their tatùs." Rae's mind swirled as memories pushed forward. "I remember he never seemed to be on his own. He told me the people with him were his bodyguards."

Devon shrugged and stared at his hands. "I only know what I learned here, so I don't know much about him. My father was assigned to watch him once so he knows a lot more than me. Sorry I'm not much help."

"Dev, you're a huge help! You've been a great friend and I'm lucky to have you mentoring me. You have no idea how much you've taught me already." Gushing on as she was, Rae almost let it slip that her birthday was tomorrow. She bit her tongue just as Madame Elpis opened the library door and in a voice worthy of a drill sergeant, suggested it was time for them to finish for the evening.

Without saying a word, Devon and Rae gathered their books and walked toward the library doors, trying to hide their amused smiles. She paused halfway there and turned to him once more.

"Hey, is everything all right with you? You haven't seemed yourself the past few days. We spend so much time talking about my past and ink-history I sometimes don't even ask how you're doing." She put her hand on his arm as she spoke. Her palm tingled where their skin met, and she felt the energy of it running all the way up her arm.

He gave her his signature dimpled smile. "I'm all right. There's some stuff I'm dealing with, but everything's going to be fine. Just concentrate on yourself for the next few days and hurry up and get that tatù so we can start seeing the crazy things you get to do." He patted her shoulder. "I'm not sure anymore who's more curious to find out, you or me!"

"You'll be one of the first to know, aside from Dean, who has me staying in the Infirmary the night before. After I'm tested and prodded like some lab rat, I'll let you know."

"It won't be that bad. The school wants to help you."

"Yeah, so I can ask any questions I might have. Right.

It's only so they can monitor my ink. I think they're worried I'm going to morph into my father the minute I'm inked." Rae smiled halfheartedly, trying to make a feeble joke of the situation.

"Guilder tends to know what's best for us, so it must be a good idea, then. Not the turning into your father part but helping you out with your ink."

"Probably." It irked her the way he always agreed with, and followed, what Guilder thought was right.

"Madame Elpis is about to open the door again. Let's get outta here."

"G'night, Devon."

He paused. "Good night, Rae."

It would be a good night, life-changing in her opinion. *It just sucks I've got no one to share it with.*

Chapter 14

Gifting

TRYING to fall asleep knowing what would happen seemed next to impossible. Rae had empathy for what Molly had gone through back in September. She wished she could talk to her now. But Molly lay snoring on her bed, and Rae had no intentions of waking her. Instead, she lay buried in her sheets, thinking about Devon's knowledge of her father. As she grew drowsy, her thoughts stayed on Devon and she fell asleep dreaming about him. It turned out to be a night full of vibrant and pleasant dreams.

Rae felt herself waking and tried to will sleep to pull her back down. She liked her current dream. It was vague but nice. The feeling of Devon being beside her, his hand warm on her lower back, keeping her safe. She wanted to enjoy the feeling a few moments longer. However, sleep didn't return, and the dream slipped out of her grasp. Lifting her head to check the time, she suddenly remembered what day it was.

Tempted to jump off the bed and rush to the mirror, she had to fight to control herself. Rae settled for trying to tell if anything felt different inside her. She started cataloguing every twinge, twitch and pulse searching for something that might stand out.

Molly's alarm stopped her train of thought. She watched Molly, still lying prone on the bed with her eyes closed, hit the nightstand and then the wall with the back of her hand.

The light went on without the switch even being touched. Impressed, Rae realized Molly was getting better with using her ink. The last time she'd tried that trick she'd blown out all the fuses in the building. Madame Elpis went around with crazy hair that day because she couldn't use her hair dryer to tame it. Since all the other residents of Aumbry house had been in the same predicament, no one had laughed. Molly had gone on about her business as if nothing were wrong. The memory made Rae smile.

Molly groaned and slowly sat up, rubbing her face. Rae quickly shut her eyes and pretended to still be asleep. She heard Molly stumble to the closet and grab her toiletries. Something heavy and soft landed on Rae's bed, followed by an "oops." She must've dropped her towel and brushed against Rae's arm as she picked it up. Molly flipped the light switch off and shut the door.

In a flash, Rae hopped out of bed, grabbing the wall to steady herself. She flinched when she got a shock and blinked at the sudden brightness. *Dummy! I hit the light switch.* She rubbed her eyes. *No worries. The better to see my new ink with.*

Dashing to the closet, she swung the door open to the full-length mirror. She lifted her pajamas as she turned. She stared in stunned silence.

The tatù was there all right, and quite large -- bigger than the other girls' inks she'd seen. It spread across most of her lower back. On her pale, white skin lay a beautiful, unique figure with…Rae squinted to see an outline behind the ink…wings. A fairy etched in hues of pink, purple and green with glittery sparkles on the dress and wings. How in the world did it sparkle? She'd never seen anyone's tatù glitter before?

Rae craned her neck to see it again. Below the inked girl lay an ornate design with Celtic detail and small circles with wiggly lines. Excitement flowed through her veins. They were miniature suns, part of her mom's ink!

The tatù looked totally awesome. Not scary at all. It wasn't some witch or warlock or sorcerer. Hers was delicate…tender. Like a fairy.

She spun around and spoke to her image in the mirror. "The sins of the father are not the sins of this daughter. I might not be able to undo the past, but I'm not being punished for something my father did!" She did a happy dance, wiggling her butt and moving her arms alternately in a pumping motion.

Today was the best day of her life. Nothing could ruin it -- no proverb of truth, no Friday the thirteenth, nothing. *Finally, my birthday, my tatù!*

Now, she just needed to figure out how to use it. She had less than forty-eight hours before she'd have to pretend it was her birthday all over again.

Rae stopped dancing and stood perfectly still in the middle of the room. Closing her eyes, she lifted her arms and focused on every feeling inside of her, trying to determine if something felt different. She sensed a quiet buzz but wasn't sure if it was coming from the room or inside her. "Probably just the hum in my ears from the excitement."

A light tingling in the tips of her fingers caught her attention. Different than when your hand falls asleep, but she couldn't figure out just how. Going back to the mirror, she took another look at the tatù.

Definitely a fairy, wings and all. *Hmm…wings…* Maybe

she could fly or levitate. Shutting her eyes tight, she focused her thoughts on flying and slowly opened one eye to see if she'd floated off the ground.

Nothing. Not even a hint of fluttering or flying. She sighed, running her fingers through her hair. She had no idea what she could do or how to do it. If only she'd told Devon about today. At least someone could help her figure it out.

It wasn't hard to see she had a unique ink, but were any other tatùs similar? "I gotta check at that bloody chart again." Too bad you couldn't look it up online...or maybe? Her laptop only needed to be opened and she'd have full access to searching.

Rae glanced at her watch and realized Molly could be back any moment. Deciding to give the ink probing a break for now, she grabbed a random pair of jeans and top from her closet.

One look in the mirror had her ripping everything off. The jeans dropped too low and the shirt would lift if she bent or leaned over. *Too easy for someone to catch a glimpse of my Celtic pixie.* Scrambling through her closet, she pulled out a charcoal black dress, the only dress she'd brought from New York. It was short sleeved, so she'd need a jacket, but at least no one would be able to see her tatù. She huffed and puffed doing the fastest change job of her life, trying to make sure she fully covered her ink before Molly returned. Finally the last thing she needed to do was fix her hair. *Hmm...up or down?*

Hair down, she held two barrettes in her mouth and pulled the sides up to clip it out of her face. Laughing to herself, she added a few of the butterfly wing clips she'd worn at the dance.

Molly returned just as Rae leaned close to the mirror, blinking mascara on the way Molly had shown her.

A whistle erupted from the doorway. Molly looked Rae up and down. "Wow, girl, you're all fancy for classes this morning. 'Bout time you started listening to my style suggestions."

Rae almost poked her eye with the mascara brush. "I-I figured I'd dress up...since we don't have classes on Sunday. You know, for my birthday."

"Great idea!" Molly came and stood behind her. She touched Rae's back, making Rae step forward and bash herself into the mirror. "Careful, you've got a few lose hairs stuck to the back of your dress. I like that you're wearing you hair down. It flatters the outfit. I keep telling you that you need to dress up more often. However, it's too cold for short sleeves." Molly disappeared into her closet, clothes flying out and landing on Rae's bed across the room. Molly stepped out with a short-length, beige leather jacket with a simple plaid pattern inside. "It's Burberry. You can keep it if you want. I never wear it."

Rae slipped it on. It went perfect with the dress.

"Thanks. I love it!"

"Consider it a birthday present." Molly laughed.

Rae's smile faltered. Did Molly know? Then she realized her roomie didn't have a clue, and instead of being nervous, she felt guilty. *Sheesh, if it's not one thing it's another.* "Th-Thanks, again."

"Don't mention it. Now, can we head down and get some breakfast? I'm starving."

Rae leaned over and hugged Molly. "I'm glad you're my roomie."

The two made their way to the Refectory. Filling their trays, Rae bumped into Maria in line, her hand banging into Maria's as her tray slid along the aisle. "Oops, sorry. I wasn't paying attention."

"It's fine. I think you shocked me," Maria rubbed her hand.

They sat down at their usual table. Haley sat babbling to the twins something about her family planning on going skiing in Switzerland over the Christmas holidays. She glanced at Rae, her mouth open but no words coming out. She narrowed her eyes. "My goodness, who're you trying to impress?"

Rae could feel her cheeks heat up.

"No one." Molly plopped down beside Haley. "It's for her birthday this weekend. She's wearing my Burberry coat."

Haley rolled her eyes. "About time you get that sacred tatù the entire school has so anxiously been waiting for. Finally, it'll be over so we can all move on."

Rae wondered if hot tea would do permanent damage to Haley's face if she threw her cup at the bitch. The girl knew how to take the wind out of someone's sails, didn't she?

"*Ignore Haley*," came Maria's quiet voice. "*She's just green with envy. She's jealous of your looks, your personality and the way every guy in this school stares at you. You have a history to talk about. She can't compete.*"

Rae nodded at Maria, the voice invasion no longer as daunting as at the beginning of the school year. *Thanks Maria, I know you can't hear me, but I appreciate it.*

Maria's smile faltered and her eyes went huge. A glass of juice slipped from her hand. Girls sitting beside her quickly jumped up to avoid the spill. Everyone reached for napkins to absorb the orange liquid.

Maria stared at the table, extremely focused on cleaning. Without looking at Rae, she inner spoke again. "*How the heck did you just do that? I have NEVER had anyone reply to my thoughts before. Your birthday's Sunday, but you can talk to me now? Are you having some pre-power?*"

Rae froze with a spoonful of oatmeal halfway to her mouth. Had she thought-spoken to Maria? She could feel the inner buzz inside of her again. Staring directly at Maria, she tried again. Panic set her heart racing, but curiosity won over.

You can hear me?

Maria nodded, still staring down.

This is crazy. Rae shifted in her chair, trying to appear like she was just eating, not going out of her mind with anticipation. *I can't believe it. Sorry I scared the crap out of you. I had no idea I could do this.* She paused, debating if she should tell Maria and decided to go with her gut. *Can you keep a secret? My actual birth date's today, but everyone here thinks it's the fifteenth. I just wanted to see what my ink was before the school started treating me like a lab rat, so I didn't tell anyone about the mistake.*

Maria smiled at her bowl of cereal. No one at the table even noticed the two of them. *"It's all right, you don't need to apologize. You just surprised me by answering back. If I were in your shoes, I'd probably keep it a secret as well. What's your tatù? Is it the same as mine?"*

Rae found it easy to converse this way. She noticed Maria picked up her pace as well -- like they were just thoughts, not words in a conversation. *My ink's different. I'm going to check the chart later.* She paused, unsure if she should share the ink's image. She liked Maria and needed to tell someone. *It looks like a fairy, with wings and everything! There's also a neat Celtic design along the bottom.* She shrugged. *I guess my gift's some kind of telepathy. I thought it meant I could fly. I was really hoping, but I tried getting airborne this morning. Unfortunately, gravity wouldn't le me go.*

Maria covered her mouth to hide a laugh. *"I'm glad you didn't try jumping out your window to see if you could fly. Remember, your gift's pretty raw at the moment. It'll take some time to strengthen and sort itself out. You have to learn to work with it and train it. Or have it train you as some of the professors say. I'm excited for you and, to be honest, I'm a little excited for me. This'll help improve my skill, as well."*

Rae nodded as Molly leaned over, tapping Rae's temple.

"You listening in there? I just asked if on Sunday, after you get back from the Infirmary, of course, you want to sneak out? You know, celebrate your birthday properly?"

"Ummm..." Rae didn't know what to say. She glanced around the table.

"Come on, be devious," Molly said with a mischievous smile. "You're the last of the gals to get inked. We'll head out to the sporting fields. I'm sure we can get some of the guys to come as well."

"That'd be a riot," Haley said. "Except we'll get caught on the fields. Too obvious from the buildings."

Rae saw the disappointment on Molly's face and just couldn't let it stand. "There's a clearing behind the forest. I walk there all the time."

Molly jumped around, all excited. "Wouldn't it be a riot?"

Haley tapped her long, manicured fingernails against the tabletop. "I'm sure Riley, or one of the older guys, could get us some festive drinks."

Molly's voice dropped to a whisper. "You mean, *alcohol*?"

Rae nodded absentmindedly. She'd been listening but also trying to talk to Maria since Molly'd poked her. Had she lost the telepathy? Or, since her gift was still new had it somehow powered down? She could still feel the electrical buzz running through her body but couldn't figure it out.

"Rae! Yes or no to the party?" Molly poked her in the ribs, creating a shock. It actually made Rae and Molly jump apart. "Sorry! That was a strong one."

"I'm okay." Rae laughed, rubbing her side. "The party sounds like fun. However, aren't we a little young to be drinking?"

Haley snorted and tried mimicking an American accent. "Well, in big ol' America, yous peoples huv to wait 'til yer super old, like twenty-five to drink."

"It's twenty-one." No way would Rae let Haley ruin her birthday.

"Whatever. We'll get the guys to bring the booze and

those of us looking for a good time can enjoy ourselves," Haley said.

Molly clapped her hands. "I'll spread the word. Let's plan on meeting at ten, once Madame Elpis shuts her door for the night."

It wasn't long before the entire girls' table whispered excitedly about the prospect of the party and being sneaky. Something none of them had dared to try since arriving. They continued whispering plans as they put their trays away and started to head off to morning classes.

Maria touched her arm and began walking beside her. *"Let's make sure we're close by each other in the Oratory today. Then we can work on your gift without anybody else knowing."*

Relief flowed through Rae when she heard Maria's voice back in her head. She only had a few hours to do this and she didn't want to waste any of them.

They stepped out into the crisp morning air, heading to the Scriptorium for English.

Julian caught up to them. "Hello, lovely ladies." His eyes traveled over Rae. "Hot bod in the dress. You had our entire table in shambles. Looks like several guy's made bets on who's going to take you out to lunch tomorrow. Lucky you!" He laughed, giving her a warm hug.

"Thanks. I appreciate you sharing that with me." Rae pursed her lips and let out a groan. "Now I can spend the rest of the day avoiding any males except you."

"Who said I wasn't in on it?" The look on his face said he was teasing her.

Haley called out to Maria. Julian and Rae continued walking while Maria waited for Haley.

As soon as they were out of earshot, Julian leaned in toward Rae. "This morning I had a drawing vision of you. I'm not trying to scare you, but I just wanted to show you. See if it makes any sense." He pulled a piece of paper from inside his jacket and opened it up. Hand drawn, with intricate detail, a picture of Rae as a fairy lay on the sheet.

The depiction of her face appeared almost like a photograph instead of a drawing.

"You drew that just this morning?" Rae stopped walking.

"No, I drew it last night, just before midnight. I'm sorry I don't know what it means, but I wanted to show you. Can you make anything out of it?" Julian pushed a lock of hair away that had fallen across his face.

Rae shrugged, hoping her eyes didn't give anything away as she thought about the tatù on her lower back.

"Maybe it has something to do with your birthday." Julian folded the paper and handed it to her. "Take it." He chuckled. "I don't plan on hanging it up in my room. I can just imagine what the guys on my floor would say and who'd try to buy it from me."

"Do your drawings make you money?"

Julian squeezed her shoulders in a friendly, comforting way. "You're the sweetest, most naive girl in the entire world. How can you not see every junior and senior boy is in lust with you? The way you looked at the dance only drove them deeper. Now today, again..."

Rae started laughing. Julian was pulling her leg, trying to get her to blush. She playfully punched him in the arm. "Nice try, Juls. I'm not gonna fall for that. You can dream on if you think you're going to embarrass me. I'll keep your drawing, though. It's the prettiest picture I've ever seen, even if it is of me."

Julian shook his head and chuckled. "I've got to get to class, but I'll see you around this weekend." He winked before darting off to the Oratory.

She watched him go, and as she continued walking, she noticed the humming sensation again. Then the strangest thing happened. She could see where she was going but at the same time, she saw a vision of Julian. He was lying down and suddenly got up to his art easel and began to sketch. She watched him draw the same picture he'd just given her. Weird. It was like she watched him have his vision -- like she'd been in the room, staring down at him. As quickly as the vision had come, it disappeared.

What the heck was that?

The rest of the morning continued with little moments where Rae could feel a bit of her gift growing, but then fizzled out. It took more work than usual to concentrate in her classes. There were times when she felt she was on the verge of grasping her ability, and then it would flutter away and leave her feeling empty. She was relieved when lunch was over and it was time to go to class in the Oratory.

Maria met her inside the hall and grabbed her hand. She immediately began talking to her by thought. *How's it going?*

I keep having all these weird sensations. I tried to talk to you again this morning but couldn't.

Maria nodded in sympathy. *It's normal. It took me over a week before I could even communicate. My father has the same ink so I knew what I was going to be able to do. I'd try and the wrong thoughts would go out or I'd scream in frustration and he'd get my scream. It's a pretty complicated process. Don't worry. Rome wasn't built in a day, you know."*

Rae sighed in frustration. She only had one more day before she'd be in the Infirmary, under the watchful eye of Dean Carter and whoever else. She wanted to get this sorted out before then -- before they had a chance to judge her or say she was just like her father and lock her away forever.

Headmaster Lanford entered the hall, handing out a copy of the inking chart. "Students, please gather 'round. I'd like to discuss everyone's sixteenth birthday." He stared directly at Rae as he spoke, and she thought she saw him wink. "Let's discuss the process. Who wants to go first?"

While he spoke, Rae folded her sheet of paper,

knowing she wasn't going to be able to answer anything without admitting the truth. She folded the paper one more time and ran her fingers over it to make the crease tight. As she did so, she felt the paper slice deep into her skin, between her thumb and index finger.

"Ow!" She dropped the sheet of paper and turned to look at her palm.

Charlie stood beside her. He grabbed her hand to see what had happened. He touched the inch-long cut lightly with his finger. "Just a flesh wound." He grinned. "I'd heal you if I could, but my ability only works on me."

Rae noticed blood running down her finger. "I'll grab some tissues from the bathroom."

Walking toward the bathroom, the familiar inner buzz ran through her body. She kept her left hand over her right, pinching the cut so it wouldn't bleed all over. The pinching also seemed to relieve the sting of the cut. Pushing the door open with her hip, she slipped into the bathroom and turned the faucet on to run her hand under the cool water.

She stared down at her palm in surprise. No cut. At all.

She brought her hand closer to her face, unable to even find a small lift of skin. It was like the wound had disappeared. It was like...Rae gasped and stared at her stupefied reflection in the mirror.

The cut had healed by itself.

Charlie had touched her hand, and then she'd held the cut and healed it. Her head started to spin with images and thoughts throughout the day. She'd talked to Maria this morning because...And Julian. The vision. The powerful shock from Molly had been because Molly had touched her first. She hadn't even realized, even considered. Chemistry was easy because Nicholas had touched her hand to correct the way she held a wire.

Rae leaned against the cool limestone wall and slid slowly to the floor. She covered her face with her hands, not sure if she should cry or scream.

She'd been inked with her father's gift. She could mimic other people's tatùs. Her uncle had been right all along -- *the sins of the father are the sins of the son, or daughter.* She was being punished for what her father had done. The school would go crazy with the news of her gift. They'd lock her up or send her back to New York.

Her mother had wanted so much more and now Rae was going to make her turn in her grave.

Rae sat up as she thought of her mother. Her mother's letter had forewarned her. She knew she'd have a powerful gift. She'd also said Rae had goodness inside of her. She was her mother's Rae of Hope.

She needed to use her gift for good. No one had ever had a inking like hers before. That was pretty obvious. No one would know what to expect, and she could hide some of her abilities. She had two days. Two mornings, two nights.

Staring up at the ceiling, she spotted a box of bandages on a shelf by the soap dispenser on the wall. Grabbing the box and ripping it open, she stuck one over the spot where her cut had been, then ran back to class. She needed to listen to everyone today and remember all of their abilities.

She snuck back to her spot beside Charlie. Rob stood telling the other students about when he realized he could shape-shift, and immediately knowing he was an eagle. He said it took him weeks to get the courage to try to fly. When he finally did, it turned out to be the best feeling in the world. Plus, the view was amazing.

Charlie began giving his spiel of DaVinci versus the medical marking of the Vetruvian Man.

Rae listened closely to everyone, captivated by each story. She was amazed to learn she wasn't alone. It had taken days, even weeks, for each person to figure out how to use their gift -- even if their parent had had the same marking. Rae had already accomplished that in a few hours. She nodded as each person spoke, as if now hearing and understanding for the first time.

"That's it for today," Lanford said.

Rae looked up, shocked class was over.

"We'll continue our discussion on Monday." He smiled at her. "With a new ink-stamp able to share and ask questions."

Rae began collecting her things and, as she turned to leave, had a sudden thought. She raced over to Rob and touched him on the arm.

"Hey." Fluttering her eyelashes, she hoped she appeared coy, not stupid as she felt, "Has Molly or anyone mentioned we're having an outdoor party on Sunday night?"

He gave her a huge smile. "Yes, she told me about it. I'll see you there, I assume?"

"I wouldn't miss it for the world." Making sure she didn't touch or bump into anyone, she dashed out of the Oratory.

Running to the dorm, she quickly changed clothes and grabbed her backpack, throwing in a pair of jogging pants and a sweatshirt. She tore down the marble stairs of Aumbry House, rushing out the back door toward the path that led to the forest. She didn't stop running until she reached the other side of the forest, where the open area for Sunday's party would be. No one was around; it was completely vacant, just as she'd hoped it would be.

Dropping her backpack against a tree, she concentrated on her marking as she ran. Instinct took over. She closed her eyes and spread her arms out wide, dipping down before taking a small leap.

Everything changed in an instant. It was like she'd dropped her body...and tumbled into the soft earth, rolling. However, when she straightened, claws and feathered wings were her balance. If a bird could smile, she was grinning ear to ear. She fluttered about, managing to get up to a branch in a surrounding tree. A memory of the drive into school came flashing back. She remembered seeing a bird flying by the bus. It must've been Rob. Closing her eyes, she jumped, letting herself fall and arched upwards toward the sky.

Wind whipped by and ruffled her feathers. She opened her eyes, flapping her arms in excitement when she realized she was actually flying. Arching her new body toward the clouds, she glanced down and enjoyed the view high above the treetops.

She tried to let out a whoop. It sounded like a caw. She'd copied Rob's gift and was now an eagle. How cool was that?

After half an hour of flying, Rae checked out the school from the view she had, constantly keeping an eye on the area where she'd left her backpack. No one ventured onto the path or into the small forest. Deciding it was time to head back, she flew back over the grounds one last time. She saw Julian and Devon get into Julian's car and drive away. She noticed the twins come out of the post office and Riley head over to Dean Carter's office. She spread her arms (wings) wide and enjoyed one last view from that height before heading back.

Focusing on landing, and then trying to shift back into human form took a few tries. She was laughing by the time she'd it figured out. Glancing down, she was relieved she'd changed clothes from her dress and had brought some spare ones along, and also that she'd managed to change all of herself back. She'd been a little worried about getting stuck with tail feathers.

Rae stood naked, her old clothes lying in tatters in the grass. She grabbed the pieces as she quickly ran back to her pack to throw the spare sweater and jogging pants on. Heart hammering furiously, she was terrified someone would see her in her birthday suit. *Can't afford to try to explain this.* Then she pictured actually trying to come up with an excuse for being naked in a field, and laughed. *What a scene that would be!*

Heading back to Aumbry House, Rae recalled the conversation she'd had with Andy during the first week of school regarding shape-shifters. Andy had been right -- Rob was the lucky bugger who could fly. The exhilaration and sense of freedom she'd experienced was by far the best thing she'd ever felt. *Rob maybe the lucky bugger who gets to fly, but I am, by far, the luckiest kid in the world!*

Giddy with excitement, she skipped along the pavement. She had a fleeting thought to run over to Devon's dorm and tell him about it but remembered she'd seen him leave with Julian.

She grinned foolishly to herself as she came up with a plan. She'd touch Devon and figure out how his ink worked before she told him. Imagine the look on his face if she surprised him with that kind of knowledge! Maybe she could teach him a lesson or two.

Chapter 15

November 13 + 14

ECSTATIC over figuring out her tatù, Rae couldn't wait to tell Devon. The rest of the afternoon she touched anyone within reach, wanting to experience everything. During dinner, she looked around for Devon. Slightly disappointed she didn't find him, she figured it didn't matter, she'd catch up with him the next day.

Thinking about the next day and what would happen dropped her back down to earth with a resounding thud. Hopefully, Lanford would be there. She trusted the headmaster, and if they had a moment alone, she'd like to ask what he remembered about her mom. She'd gotten the impression from previous conversations that Lanford had barely known her mom. But, any information would be more than she had now.

"Have you been able to figure anything else out?"

Rae heard Maria's voice and searched across the room for her. She sat by the wall. Maria gave a small wave before turning back to the boy sitting beside her. Amazed at how clear Maria's voice came through from across the room, Rae wondered if Maria could communicate even further away.

How far away can you talk to someone? Same room or house or further?

"I can reach about a mile away. My father has the same gift. My family's in Cork, so we can't reach each other."

Before Rae could respond, Craig, who sat beside her, touched her arm. Rae lost the ability to communicate with Maria. Her attention shifted, immediately focusing on what Craig's ability so she could mimic it. She knew it had to do with water, but that's all she remembered. She stared down at her plate and, using her peripheral vision, glanced at the tatù on his arm -- ink art of a lake, an igloo and a cloud. A light bulb went on in her head as the buzz flew through her veins, she realized he could change the state of water from frozen to liquid or gas and vice versa.

"Sorry, what were you saying?"

"Just wondering where you were? Your body seems to be here, but I think you left your brain outside. Nervous for Sunday?" Rae felt a pang of guilt. He sounded genuinely concerned and here she was hiding her tatù from everyone.

"A little. I'm constantly thinking about what it's going to be like."

"It's really cool, and kinda disappointing at the same time. You wait so long to be marked and then when the full marking is there, in plain sight, you have to figure out what it means. It's a process -- a fascinating, hair-pulling one. A process you love to hate and hate to love."

Rae leaned back in her chair and dropped her shoulders. A dull, tight ache disappeared between her blades. She exhaled a slow breath, enjoying the feeling of letting the tension out. Obviously Craig had thought a lot about this. *Might as well learn from him.*

"So, Mr. Philosopher, how were you able to figure out

what you can do?"

"By accident, actually. I was in the shower." He raised an eyebrow, his eyes teasing her. "The water was freezing, so I turned it to hot. I turned it too far. Trying to avoid scalding my back, I flung the tap back the other way, accidentally using my ability in the process. I actually froze the pipes in our house."

"No way!"

"And it was the middle of summer! My father thought it was hilarious. My mother kept calling the utility company. She thought they'd done something to the water pipes."

Rae burst out laughing, choking on her glass of milk. She managed to swallow it back before spitting it everywhere.

Craig patted her back. "It took me a few days to get the hang of controlling the state of H two oh, but I did try some really cool and crazy experiments. Great way to make a quick cup of tea." He held his cup in front of Rae so she could see the steam rise from the water in a matter of seconds.

Rae's mouth hung open. "What's the largest amount of water you've ever changed?"

"Coolest thing I've ever done on a large scale?" Craig smiled, rubbing his chin as he pretended to consider. "One time we wanted to have a scrimmage football match on a Saturday morning. It'd rained the night before, so the pitch was soaking wet. It took about five minutes, but I dried the entire pitch so we could play on fresh, dry grass."

"You're jokin?" She wished it'd rain right now so she could test this tatù out.

"The best part was the look on the professors' faces when we came in for lunch a couple hours later -- none of us were wet or muddy."

"I can't wait to try – I mean, I hope I get something like your tatù." *Whew! That was almost a major slip.*

"My father can decontaminate water and works for the country's treatment center. He's the only one in the country who can ever save us if we run out of fresh water. He already has plans for me to work with him. *His* talent is handy. Mine's boring compared to his."

"You don't really believe that, do you?" Rae was appalled. *How can anyone think they had boring ink? That's horrible!* Rae felt a strong need to convince him that his ink was special.

"Think about it. If there's ever a drought or serious flooding, it's going to be you who can aide the country, not your father."

Craig grinned and rubbed the top of her head. "You're pretty cool. We were taught about your dad. You know, what he tried to accomplish, and how you were going to finish what he started. You're nothing like what they said. You're a good person...pretty cute, too."

Her face burned and along with the embarrassment came a twinge of guilt. She'd intentionally started the conversation because she wanted to figure out how to use his gift, but she couldn't wait to show everyone she wasn't her father.

"I hope I can be half as gifted as the students here." She played with her empty tray. "I think I'm gonna call it a night. I have a feeling I won't be getting much sleep in the Infirmary tomorrow."

Rae stood and cleared away her tray before Craig could reply. She wove her way through the sea of tables to the front lobby to grab her coat, keeping her head down to avoid eye contact with anyone and headed out of the Refectory.

Rushing, she bumped into Julian and fell backward, landing on her butt.

"I'm so sorry. You all right?" Julian bent down to offer his hand. "I was lost in thought and didn't even notice you."

"I'm fine. The fault's mine. I wasn't watching where I was going." Rae let him help her to her feet. She looked behind him. "Where's Devon?" She stepped back, realizing Julian had no idea she'd seen the two of them leave together. He had no clue she'd been an eagle. And no way did she plan on telling him either.

"I dropped him off at the train station about an hour ago. There was a family emergency."

Her heart stopped. "Everything all right?"

"Yeah, I think so. His mom slipped on some ice by their house. It looks like she mighta broke her leg. He's planning on coming back on Sunday's train."

Her heart resumed its regular beating. Devon was safe. Strange how he created such inner turmoil inside of her. *I'm just a caring friend. He has a girlfriend so...I'm just a concerned friend...right?*

"Rae?"

"Yeah?" She chewed on the inside of her cheek, nervous he might know she'd already been inked. He did see the future after all, so it wasn't outside the realm of possibility.

"Be careful, ok?" It looked like he wanted to say more, but just stood staring intently at her, his eyes full of concern. He gave her shoulder a squeeze before walking off, not saying another word.

Rae shook her head, brows furrowed. "O-Okay." *Does he know? Did he see it in a dream and draw it? Wouldn't he have said something? Did he say something already? To the Dean?* With doubts and unanswered questions assailing her mind, she slowly walked back to Aumbry House.

She caught sight of a familiar silhouette at the main entrance to the dorms. "Molls!"

Molly turned and waved. "Hey! Where've you been all afternoon? I haven't seen you since the end of Lanford's class."

"I fluttered around and lost track of time." Rae grinned

at her own private joke. "You heading up?"

"Uh-huh. I want to try to fix my laptop one more time. I had a paper due today, and the only copy I have is on the bloody laptop."

They quietly walked up the stairs. Rae pulled her key out and reached for the lock.

"It's not locked. I --" Molly started, bumping hands with Rae as she opened the door.

Once in their room, Rae headed to the bathroom with her toiletries. Molly settled in front of her computer. When she returned from her shower, Rae plopped onto her bed and watched Molly continue trying to jump start her computer.

Molly slapped the keyboard with both hands. "Damn it! This is so stupid." She shoved her chair away from her desk and grabbed her bathrobe. "I need a break and a shower. I'll try it once more after. Otherwise, I'm gonna have to stay up all night and rewrite the paper."

Molly stomped from the room, muttering about curses and how it was all bullshit. Rae stared at the closed door and rubbed her fingers over the pad of her thumb. She'd picked up Molly's tatù when they had bumped hands and the hum of electricity felt prickly against her skin.

Needing a book, she leaned over the bed to grab her backpack. She spied Molly's computer and stole a glance at the door. *I could give it a try...but what if it doesn't work?* "I'll just have a peak."

Sneaking over to the blank-screen laptop, she lightly touched the keyboard. She could feel the electricity inside of it humming against her fingers, begging to be ignited. On a whim, she lightly ran her hand overtop of the keys. The hum's rhythm changed cadence over one spot. It seemed...out of tune or sync somehow. Rae tried rubbing her fingers together over the spot, like she was trying to smooth out the hum's cadence. A second later, the hum became similar to the rest of the computer. The unwinding rhythm became steady. The screen lit up and Rae watched the main page start up. Surprised, she quickly stepped back from the computer. *Holy guacamole! It worked!* She did a quick happy dance, careful to keep quiet. Hearing a noise in the hall, she grabbed a random textbook and hopped onto her bed, afraid she might get caught.

Molly came in a few moments later, her head wrapped tightly in a towel with some fancy name-brand robe draped over her shoulders, but not tied, flopping open with each step. Rae thought she looked like a rich housewife, only missing the blue face cream to complete the effect. Rae had to stifle her giggle.

Molly sighed loudly and strode over to her computer.

"What the -- ?" She let out a holler and jumped in excitement. "I should've just hit the stupid thing a week ago!" She dropped down on the chair, clicking on the wireless mouse. "Had I known that would've fixed it, I'd have thrown it against the wall!"

Rae smiled and nodded, not daring to look for fear she'd burst out laughing.

The printer began whirling and spewing sheets. Molly shuffled her report and stapled it. She swung around in her chair. "It's a shame you can't be here tomorrow night. I'd love to be the first to see your ink. You know, before everyone else, like you did with me." She stuffed the report into her backpack.

Rae sighed inwardly, guilt wiggling its way into the area by her heart. *Good ol' Molly.* "I'd rather be here, too."

Molly undid the towel on top of her head and started picking through her hair with her fingers. "Not to sound teacher-ish, but it's probably a good thing you're in the squeaky-clean infirmary. The professors will be able to help you better than anybody." She scrunched her face and grinned. "It's only one night. Then we're having that outdoor midnight party."

"Hmm..." Rae yawned, shut her book and crawled

into bed. She didn't feel like talking about it tonight. She had mixed feelings about the party, about hiding her tatù from Molly and huge stress worrying about being in the infirmary the next night, waking up to Dean Cardell poking and prodding her. *Ugh! It's too much!* Thankfully Molly distracted her from the worry circling her mind like vultures.

"Hey, watch this." Molly twiddled her fingers and switched off the light. The bed across from Rae's creaked and the sheets snapped about. "I'm getting better with practice. G'night."

Rae lay there in the dark, her hands clasped behind her head. She felt like she was sitting on a seesaw, constantly weighing the pros and cons of everything. Sleep eluded her but shortly after two, her brain finally gave in and let her slip into darkness.

Morning rolled in with heavy rain and dark, dreary grey clouds that looked oppressive from the dorm window. The weather matched Rae's mood. She wasn't looking forward to the evening. Wishing every minute would take an hour, the day rolled by much too fast. Rae tried to act like she was invisible when she sat down for dinner, not really wanting to talk to anyone.

"What's the dean doing here? He's never around for meals." Nicholas pointed to Dean Carter. He stood by the fireplace, frowning.

"It's 'cause Rae gets inked tonight," Haley whispered loudly.

Rae wished she could sink lower in her chair. If she tried, she'd be sitting under the table. *Not an entirely bad idea. I wonder if anyone would notice?*

Riley walked over during dessert and sat across from Rae. He completely ignored Andy who sat beside her talking her ear off as usual.

"I thought we had a lunch date? I came by your dorm,

but Molly said you were out."

Oh no! Rae slapped her hand to her forehead. "Did we make plans?" She tried to remember what they'd talked about at the dance, which felt like eons ago, and only came up with a big blank. The one thing she really remembered from that night was the way she had felt in Devon's arms when they'd danced.

"Riley," Andy sounded annoyed. "Get a life. It's her birthday tomorrow. She's got enough on her plate." He put his arm around her and rubbed her shoulder.

"Watch it, wolf-boy. I wasn't talking to you. I had a date with Rae and wanted to make sure everything was all right." Rae could hear the fury in Riley's voice. It made her squirm uncomfortably. *When will they stop this?*

"Guys, please. I can speak for myself." Rae tried to keep her voice low; heads were already turning their way. "Everything's fine. I just forgot. Maybe we can go next Saturday?" The last thing she needed was to attract the dean's attention. He'd love any excuse to have the girls eat at a separate time from the boys. *And wouldn't that just be fabulous? I'd be ostracized forever.* So she sighed in relief when Riley accepted her compromise.

"Sure. It's a *date.*" He emphasized the last word and shot a smug look at Andy. "Do you want me to pop by and see you at the Infirmary tonight?"

"I'm not sure if you're allowed." Rae leaned forward, trying to escape Andy's over-warm arm.

"I asked Dean Carter yesterday if it'd be all right."

Rae just barely managed not to roll her eyes. *Of course he did. Backed into a corner once again by cheetah-boy, while being smothered by the hairy beast.* Andy gripped the table, his knuckles white and the veins in his arms bulging. With her luck, he'd probably shift into a wolf and fight Riley right here. Rae grinned, despite her wariness. It'd be an interesting fight. Riley, with his cheetah tatù, was quick. She pressed her shoulders back. She might like the idea, but had no intention of letting it start.

"It may be kind of boring. I doubt I'll get much sleep." Rae hoped she sounded like she was excited. She tried to think back to how she had felt Thursday evening and all she could picture was hanging out with Devon in the library. She wished he was here.

"I'll come by around nine. Keep ya company." Riley winked, then stood without a second glance at Andy. He headed to the front where he disappeared into the evening dusk.

"I don't understand how you can stand that guy." Andy's ears seemed to puff with steam like an angry cartoon character. "He's such a...a...Richard Cranium."

"A what?" She blinked, wondering if he'd gone off his rocker.

"You know, a Richard Cranium." He smiled, then made a face that looked like he'd been eating raw onions. "I'm trying to make up for being an idiot and make you laugh. I don't think it's working."

"I don't get it." The name "Riley" didn't sound like "Richard" to her.

Andy pinched his nose, closing his eyes. He mumbled, "Consider the short forms for the two words."

"Richard, Rich, Rick, Dick...Cranium, brain, skull...Ohhhh...I get it, a Dickhead!" Rae started laughing.

"Oh, brother, I don't even know why I open my mouth sometimes." Andy rolled his eyes but grinned. He straightened, now happy and bright.

"I'm the slow one today. My uncle talks in riddles all the time. I should've jumped on that one." She winked. "I'll have to save that for the summer when I go home."

"Just don't call him one and say it was me who taught you." He put his hands up to fend off her fists.

Rae threw a playful punch when he dropped his arms.

"Are you going tomorrow night...to the COP?"

"COP?"

"Covert Operation Part -- " He paused, glancing behind her.

She froze, scared a professor had just heard and would ruin everything.

"Ms. Kerrigan, are you prepared for the change?" Dean Carter leaned forward as he drummed his fingers against the table. *Oh...of course it's him. A teacher would be good luck and that's not what I have.* Rae made a conscious effort to avoid touching him, afraid his miserable attitude or gift, whatever it was, would rub off on her.

Professor Stockheed came up behind Carter. The dean straightened and pulled on the pockets of his suit jacket. "If you have a moment, Dean Carter, I'd like to have a word."

The dean sighed. "Of course, Professor Stockheed." He stared at Andy and frowned before walking away with the professor.

"Creep," Rae muttered.

"Richard Cranium," Andy said. They both laughed.

Madame Elpis met Rae at Aumbry's main entrance and walked her to the Infirmary.

"Have a pleasant sleep." She patted Rae's shoulder. "Enjoy the roller coaster ride."

"I'll try." Rae instantly mimicked Madame Elpis' tatù, watching her leave the room without turning. The headmistress' gift was pretty handy. No wonder the woman never missed anything that went on at Aumbry House. *Talk about eyes in the back of your head. Freaky!*

She glanced around. It was a simple white room, like any typical hospital room, with four single beds and a crappy view from the window. The sharp scent reminded her of bleach and some sort of cheap scented cleaner. The buzz from the fluorescent lights sounded like the cicadas back in New York. She wished her uncle were there with her. Even though she was still kind of ticked at him, he was family and he cared.

Trudging to the far bed, closest to the window, Rae dumped her backpack on it and plopped into the ugly orange vinyl chair beside it. She let her head fall back to rest against the chair and put her feet, sneakers still on, onto the white bed sheets.

Dean Carter walked into the room. A lady in scrubs covered with dancing clowns followed behind him. She could sense their movements thanks to Madame Elpis' gift.

Carter stopped at the foot of the bed and crossed his arms over his chest. A glimmer of a smile made his lips twitch. It looked like it took a great deal of effort for him. *I wonder if a full on smile would make his face crack?*

"Excited?" Dean Carter seemed to be attempting to have a relaxed conversation with her, but his body language seemed all wrong. Rae couldn't figure him out.

"Sort of." Like she was going to tell him she already knew what happens. Or that she dreaded the thought of staying here tonight. The more she thought about it, the angrier she got. "Why all the bullsh—crap? Why do I have to stay here? It's just an ink stamp. No one else has to do it this way! It's not fair!"

"No one ever said life was fair, only eventful, Ms. Kerrigan."

The dean closed his mouth when Professor Stockheed and the science professor strolled in.

Rae's eyes grew big. "You've got to be kidding me." Now she felt like the monkey doing tricks at the circus. The lady with the dancing clown shirt was obviously the school's nurse. She probably treated everyone here like they were five years old.

The dean strolled over to the newcomers, and the three men conferred quietly.

"Let's check her back now. We'll photograph and check every hour to see if the ink art appears instantaneously or in parts." Stockheed reached inside his coat pocket and pulled out a digital camera. "She might be different."

Rae froze, terrified they'd see the ink already there. She wondered if the bathroom had a window she could escape out of. She was so screwed.

Carter waved his hand. "No need. There's no documented proof." He coughed. "We don't have approval." He nodded his head at Rae.

"I'd really like to do some blood work," the science teacher said. "I'll call her uncle to get his permission. I'd like to see if there's a change in her DNA from tonight to tomorrow. Let's see if the markers on the genes differ, or if hers are unique to the others."

"No needles," Rae said. The men all turned and stared at her surprised, like they'd forgotten she was in the room.

"I'm just cur-- " science-guy started.

"No! I'm not a lab rat. I have a say in this. If I want my genes or DNA or whatever looked at, I'll ask." She huffed. "It's my ink-stamp." *Not my father's.* It took serious effort of press her lips together and not say the last part out loud.

She slid off her chair, grabbed her bag and went into the bathroom. Like any typical hospital, there was no lock on the door...*and no flippin' window.* She spied the hospital gown on the back of the door, hanging on a hook. Rae snorted. No way would she wear that. If they saw her tatù before morning, they'd probably slice it right off her back to examine it. She pulled her pajamas out of her bag and changed quickly, not trusting she'd have any privacy if she didn't hurry.

Rae planted her ear on the wooden door, trying to hear what the dean and professor were talking about. Through the wood, the deep muffled voices were impossible to decipher. She didn't want Stockheed here. He was creepy and weird in class. Plus, she'd never figured out who left the note at the beginning of the year. She kind of thought he'd written it but wasn't sure.

The room on the other side of the door became quiet. Rae straightened, her eyes shooting around the room. What if they were listening to her? Watching her? She quickly threw her pj's on, ran over to the toilet, flushed it and then ran the tap to wash her hands. Taking a deep breath, she opened the door and stepped out.

Except for the beds and chairs, the room was empty. Bare feet silent on the cool concrete floor, Rae tiptoed and peered out the door down the hall. Heart thumping erratically, she went back to the bed and organized her backpack. She'd packed a book and some magazines to read and set them on the nightstand. No one came in.

She sat down on the bed, swinging her legs back and forth. Checking her watch, she slid off the cot and went to check the hall again. Empty.

"Weird." Her voice sounded hollow against the bare walls. They caged her here like a lab rat, but backed off their "tests" at the first sign of opposition from her? She didn't trust it. But what else could she do?

The bed frame looked as old as the buildings. It was one of those old metal ones with a crank to bring the head part up instead of by remote. She wondered why something so lacking in technological advancement would be in a school that prided itself on providing students with the best of everything? It didn't fit. She leaned over and flipped the handle open and began turning. The groan of protest from the hinge made her jump. She gave it a few more turns, hopped on the bed and organized her pillows. Twiddling her thumbs, she watched the door and cocked an ear for the sound of shoes tapping against the floor. Nothing.

It was mildly disappointing really. She'd been expecting something a bit more...sinister for tonight. *Well...maybe they plan on doing all their nefarious deeds tomorrow?* Rae sighed and tried to relax. She knew her imagination was running rampant.

Alternately curling and uncurling her toes on each foot, she sat on the bed and waited. Before long, her breathing became steady and her lids grew heavy.

I'll just close my eyes for a moment. Focus on my hearing. A large yawn slipped out, and Rae rubbed her eyes. She could feel her head begin to bob so she rested her chin against her hand. Tired of trying to listen for the dean's return, she grew weary and let herself slip into the darkness.

She bolted awake, the hair on the back of her neck on end. She blinked rapidly, trying to force the edges of sleep away.

"Who's there?" She coughed and cleared her throat. She sat up on the bed and glanced toward the door. No one came in.

Kicking the sheet off her legs, she hopped out of bed. She turned her head and glanced out the window, seeing something out of the corner of her eye.

"Crap!" she screamed and jumped away from the window. She laughed when she realized the person she'd thought she'd seen was her own reflection. Grabbing her chest, she tried to stop the crazy stuttering of her heart.

"Everything all right?" A cheery voice called from the door, making Rae leap onto the bed.

The nurse stood by the door, a bottle of water in her hand. She looked as startled as Rae felt. "Sorry, dear. You'd had a visitor but he said you'd fallen asleep."

"What? Who?" Rae sat on the bed, trying to think who'd been in. She closed her eyes for a moment, trying to feel if the hum inside her had changed. There was something new tingling through her veins but she couldn't tell what.

"One of your classmates." The nurse set the bottle on the nightstand.

"Devon?" Rae tapped her fingers rapidly against the

bed. The hum didn't feel right. It felt like she'd had too much caffeine, like she couldn't possibly sit still.

"No, not him." The nurse smiled. "He's such a sweet boy. Riley popped in."

Cheetah-boy. That's why she wanted to run and felt twitchy. She wished Devon was back.

"Anyways, you try and get some sleep. It can be a long night of waiting."

"Yeah, I know." She froze, afraid the nurse would realize her mistake. "I mean, I went through this with Molly. Molly Skye. She's my roommate. We, uh, she turned sixteen at the beginning of the school year." *Ugh!* She sounded like Molly now.

The nurse raised her eyebrows. "I'm in the next room if you need me. Just push the button." She pointed at the wall behind Rae. "Sleep tight."

Rae watched her leave and then leaned back into the pillows. It seemed to take forever, but finally she felt herself drifting off. She slept but couldn't relax. Awful visions and dreams kept her jolting awake. Awaking from the fifth or sixth horrible dream, she vowed to never set foot in the Infirmary again after this night. Turning her back to the window, she closed her eyes tight and focused on abilities she'd like to try out.

Chapter 16

November 15

RAE winced as she slowly came awake. A sharp pain in her neck let her know she'd slept on it wrong. She closed her eyes tighter, the morning sun too bright for her still-tired eyes.

She rolled over to her side and slowly let her eyes open and focus. The room was bright, but outside still looked dark. She'd never closed the curtain and forgotten to switch the lights off. Groaning, she checked her watch to see it read only a bit after five a.m. *Ugh! Why am I awake?*

Suddenly remembering where she lay, she shot straight up.

Dean Carter sat, elbows resting on his knees, in the orange vinyl chair. He grinned, wide awake and waiting for her. He stood and the overhead lights caught a flash against something silver he held in his hand.

Rae held her hands up and edged toward the hospital bed, Terrified and thinking that he held a gun, she wondered if she could outrun a bullet, or maybe at least get out of the way.

Slowly dropping her gaze to his hands, she realized he was holding a camera. Not wanting him to know how he made her nervous, she yawned and stretched trying to hide her fear from a moment ago.

"Stand," Carter said. He raised the digital camera, focusing on the lens at the back.

She stared at him, letting the word sink in. She'd finally slept so heavily, her head still felt groggy, even after the scare a moment ago. The bed creaked as her weight came off. "Do you want me to smile and say cheese?" She woke fully when she realized she'd said the sarcastic words aloud.

"Not funny. Not funny at all," The dean snapped. "Turn."

She huffed, spun around, and lifted the back of her shirt up slightly.

"Oh blimey! What the heck kind of tatù is this? It's huge." The camera flashed a number of times. "This isn't the ink of your mother or father."

"May I see it, sir?" Rae smiled mischievously. She got a kick out of having the upper hand knowing that the dean had no idea she already knew.

"What? Yes, here, have a look." He grit his teeth as he tossed the camera in her direction. He disappeared out of the room, his shoes clicking rapidly down the hallway.

Rae turned back to the pillows and stared at the picture on the little screen. The photo showed the tatù in full detail. What Rae hadn't been able to notice the past two days was now seen in full view. The ink design made any real tattoo look like a child's artwork. The fairy seemed to be grinning and watching her as she moved the camera, staring at it from different angles. She was drawn so deeply into admiring the ink art that she jumped when Dean Carter hovered over her shoulder. She hadn't heard him return.

"What can you do? What's your power?" He sounded

frustrated.

"I-I've n-no idea, sir." She stepped out of his reach, paranoid he planned to grab and shake her.

"Neither do we at the moment. Your ink's original, like Simon's."

Rae froze at the mention of her father's name.

"You're up now so let's get started. I want to run you through a series of tests, so we can figure the ink out." It was not a request. It was a demand.

Rae exhaled the breath she'd been holding. Dean Carter didn't know her tatù was like her father's...yet. And she'd just assume it stay that way for as long as possible.

Two hours later, what had started out as a bit of fun by not showing the dean what she could do, had long since become tiring. He'd drilled questions, asked her to try things and only become more and more annoyed with her lack of favorable results. Rae figured Riley must've touched her in the night as she'd been able to react to certain exercises extremely fast and continued to have the overly-caffeinated feeling running through her veins. Interesting, she felt she could control it at times and then make it feel less charged inside her. *My body's still probably trying to figure out how to use this tatù.*

Dean Carter picked up a chair and dropped it heavily back down. It clattered and vibrated against the floor.

Rae jumped, surprised at his frustration.

"This is impossible!" he shouted.

A response flew out of Rae's mouth before she could stop herself. "No one ever said life was fair, only eventful." She couldn't resist using the dean's words against him. "If we can't seem to figure out much about my ability now, maybe it's going to take some time to grow." She wanted to get out of this stupid room.

"Don't mock me, *woman*." Daggers shot from Dean

Carter's eyes. "You've NO idea of my power." He enunciated each venomous word as he spat them at her.

Rae dropped back down on the bed, suddenly terrified. He was right. She didn't know what his ink allowed him to do. The only thing she really knew about him was that he hated women, especially her.

"Do you know what my tatù is?"

Rae slowly shook her head, afraid to speak.

Dean Carter pulled up his sleeve and showed his tatù. On his skin lay a triangle with an eye in the center.

"I've a very unique ability." He stared down his nose at her. "By touching someone, I'm able to see their past. Flashes of it, and usually it's the secrets people prefer to keep hidden. My father had the same ink and did wonders with the police in interrogation rooms, and later in the military with captured enemies. He taught me firsthand how the ink worked."

As he spoke, Headmaster Lanford walked into the room, whistling. "Good morning! How's our birthday student doing?"

Dean Carter stepped away from Rae and turned, a fake smile plastered on his face and his entire demeanor changed from raging to polite.

"She's fine. Her tatù is some new, original ink." Dean Carter tried to put the camera away, but Lanford stopped him, taking the camera from his hands to look at the picture. Dean Carter stayed very still, eyes focused intently on Lanford. "Not like her father's or her mother's ink."

"Interesting...very different." Lanford continued to study the picture as a large, toothy smile split his face. Headmaster Lanford walked over to Rae, ignoring Carter, and sat down beside her on the bed, patting her knee in a friendly, fatherly manner. "Able to try anything?"

"Dean Carter tried about a hundred different tests on me, but I'm afraid I haven't been able to do much so far." She wanted to hug him. She was so happy he'd come. "I figured since my ink has wings, I might be able to fly. However, no go. Something feels different. I just don't know exactly what."

"Hmm...well it's good to see you're trying." He slapped his leg and stood. "When I learned to raise myself up, I had to focus on something outside of what I was actually trying to do. I'd stand in the center of the room and focus on a lift or elevator, something that could rise up but needed assistance." He offered her his hand. "Would you like to try?"

"Sure, why not?" Rae got off the bed. She glanced over toward the dean. He stood with his arms crossed in front of his chest in the corner of the room by the broken chair. He had a scowl on his face, but he didn't say anything.

Rae faced Headmaster Lanford. He held his arms out to her, palms up, so she stretched out her arms with her palms down. She closed her eyes and focused on his steady voice. She knew it'd work. She'd felt the power of his ink run through her veins when he offered her his hand. Within seconds, the two of them were three feet above the floor. When Rae opened her eyes to glance down, she felt herself begin to fall.

"Focus, Rae! Be the cable that keeps you suspended."

She regained control of her balance and gingerly brought her body back up to his level.

"Well done." His steady voice helped make the rest of the room disappear. "Focus on the feeling of letting go of gravity. Think back to the day in the Oratory when I lifted you. This is the same feeling, but now you're the one controlling your own movement." He made large circles with his arms. "Concentrate on the air. See how it appears thicker than you think? It's thick enough to stand on and step up higher. Focus, stay focused."

This is SO FRIGGIN' COOL! Having walked on air for ten minutes, the headmaster decided it was time to "come back to earth". Slowly, they sank back to the ground, with

Lanford's combover now a mess. They landed in front of Dean Carter. The dean's scowl erased Rae's high-spirited mood from a second ago.

"Finally." Dean Carter threw his hands up in the air. "Women! They don't understand anything." He shook his head and turned to the headmaster. "I wish you'd come by at seven this morning. Would have saved us all that time of useless experimenting." He tapped his finger against his lips. "I think this ink has more. If it was just a gravity-thing, the stamp would be similar to yours. Neither of her folks had that ability."

"Andrew, the ink is unique," Lanford said. "We, Rae included, won't figure it out in the course of a day. Give her time. Everything'll be fine."

"Possibly." Carter glared down his nose at Rae. "However, I think we should continue to closely monitor – sorry, *teach* Ms. Kerrigan how she can best use her ability *or abilities*, for the good of the school and her future well-being, of course."

"I've already seen to it." Lanford waved a hand. "Rae's in my afternoon class, and there's a very bright student mentoring her two evenings a week." He turned his attention back to her. "Rae, it's your birthday. Go. Enjoy your day before it's over."

"Thanks, sir." She was so grateful for his presence and his pronouncement she wanted to reach over and fix his messy hair. Instead, she turned, grabbed her backpack and rushed to the bathroom to change her clothes before the dean could change Lanford's mind.

Taking the quickest shower of her life, she dried off in record time with a crappy, stiff hospital towel. She threw on jeans and a sweatshirt, running out of the Infirmary without glancing back.

The fresh air hit her like feathers from heaven. Rae inhaled deeply, enjoying the breeze and slowed to a walk. A lovely warm wind blew and the sun shone from a cloudless sky. She headed toward the dorms, pausing when a familiar voice called out to her.

"Happy birthday!" Andy caught up to her. "I was just going to come see what was taking you so long."

"I didn't think I'd ever escape. The dean's a royal pain in the arse."

He laughed. "How'd everything go?" He grabbed her hand and squeezed it.

"All right." Rae tried to free her hand from the sweaty one holding it. "Carter's a pain in the rear. My tatù's some kind of fairy. Lanford came by and was totally cool. He figured my ink has something to do with gravity." She grinned, wiggling her hand loose. "Looks like I might be able to do some flying."

"Trying to make me jealous?" Andy laughed, reaching for her hand again and missing. "You should tell Rob. I'm sure he'd love to fly without having to turn into a bird."

"It's an eagle. His gift's super cool. I wouldn't change that ability at all." Rae thought back to Friday afternoon and then realized what she'd said. "I-I mean, it s-seems pretty cool. Shape-shifting. You guys are so lucky." She forced a laugh. "I definitely won't be turning into some fairy and sprouting wings." *Maybe...I wonder if that's a possibility.*

Andy winked and grinned. "You'd make one helluva hot fairy." He looked her up and down. "When do I get to see this ink-art?"

Rae blushed and pulled the back of her shirt down, paranoid he might lean back and try to check it out. "Uh... I'm not much for being flashy."

Andy grinned. "I like that about you. Anyways, you're still coming tonight, right?"

"I wouldn't miss it. Sort of like a pretend birthday party for all of us sixteen year olds." She started toward Aumbry House and then turned around to ask Andy another question. "Is Devon back? I, um, was wondering how his mom's doing."

"He got back about half an hour ago. He said everything's all right. She broke both bones in her lower leg, just above her ankle." His face puckered up like it hurt him to think of it.

"Ouch! Glad to hear she's going to be all right." *Awesome! I get to see Devon today!* She started up the concrete steps of Aumbry House. "See you later."

Rae headed inside and met Molly on the marble staircase. Molly screamed with excitement when she saw Rae. She grabbed her hand and dragged Rae up to their room.

As soon as she shut the door, Molly lifted Rae's top. "Oh my goodness, you're tatù's *totally* awesome! By far the best ink art I've ever seen." She lightly touched Rae's back. "It almost like you painted glitter sparkles on the wings. That Celtic design's going to look awesome when you wear jeans. You have to make sure your tatù shows off just above them." She headed for Rae's closet. "Wear low riders so guys can catch a good glimpse."

Rae couldn't stop laughing. Molly was completely and utterly nuts. Molly tossed a pair of Rae's dark blue jeans on her bed, along with a bunch of Rae's tops. "Start trying these on. I'll help you find something hot to wear tonight." She ran to her closet and threw a handful of clothes on Rae's bed. Then she ran into the hall, calling the other girls into the room to see Rae's tatù.

Rae had her head stuffed inside one of Molly's long sleeve shirts when she heard her roommate in the hallway, talking to Maria and Haley.

"It's about time a GIRL has unique ink instead of a guy. And she's *my* roommate."

The girls filed into the room.

One of the twins dropped onto Rae's bed. She turned to Molly. "Awesome clothes. I love designer brands. How do you keep your side of the room so neat."

Rae didn't bother to mention it was actually her side.

"Riley and another senior boy are bringing alcohol." Molly looked like she'd been dying to tell the secret for days.

"There's no drinking on school property." Aiden was the twin on Rae's bed.

"Riley said where the forest ends, and the open field begins, is the end of Guilder's property. So even if we get caught, we technically can't get into too much trouble."

I'm not touching the stuff, either way. Rae grinned. After dealing with Dean Carter, she'd take Molly's verbal diarrhea any day.

"Rae Kerrigan," Molly shouted. "I know exactly what you are thinking and you're wrong! You are going to have *one* drink." She pointed her finger at Rae. "You don't have to get drunk, but you're going to have a celebratory drink."

Rae chuckled. "Whatever, Molls." However, the idea of alcohol made her nervous. What if she started blabbing about knowing her ability or about her birthday date mix-up? Or worse, she said something about crushing on Devon? *Too risky.*

"Let's order pizza," Haley interrupted. "I'm hungry. I'll call Julian and get him to pick it up. He's a sucker."

"Julian's super nice and you shouldn't use or talk about him that way!" Maria's quiet voice came out strong and irritated.

"Sorry," Haley said softly. It wasn't loud, but it made Rae smile. Maria might be quiet, but she stood up for what she believed in and even Haley didn't tread on her. *Go Maria!*

Chapter 17

C-O-P

"*IT* may be November, but tonight's really warm," Molly told Rae as they headed up to their dorm after dinner in the games room. "Julian told me the guys are going to set torches in the ground...give it a *Survivor* kinda feel." She gave Rae a once over. "I've the perfect top to show off your tatù..." She paused and sighed when she saw Rae's face. "Without making it obvious you're trying! Give me some credit here! Have I ever steered you wrong? Let me go through our stuff one more time and see what'll match."

"Um...Okay." Part of her felt excited Molly wanted to help, the other part, nervous. Rae had never been flashy, but Molly had the perfect magazine look, like she'd just stepped onto the runway. They were so different. And yet, Molly had a point. She'd never steered her wrong before, fashion-wise. She seemed to have a knack for knowing what worked for Rae without making her look like something she wasn't.

Molly rapped her fingers against the closet door as she stared at Rae's wardrobe. "You know, besides those dark jeans I picked before, you don't really have many clothes. Your American style is, like, a season behind ours. I really need to teach you to shop properly. If you want, why don't you come to my place over the holidays? We can hit all the Boxing Day sales, and redo your entire wardrobe."

Rae couldn't believe it. "Are you asking me to spend Christmas with you?" She hadn't planned on flying home until the summer so she was free, but she hadn't yet considered the Christmas break and what she would do during it. And while she and Molly had gotten close since they'd met, she'd always thought maybe Molly would treat her like everyone else did when it came down to it. Yet here she was, inviting Rae-the-evil-freak to her house. Plus, staying at school by herself while everyone else went home to be with family, certainly didn't sound fun.

"Sure, but only if you're willing to get a new wardrobe." Molly smiled. "You know what, I'm really glad we're roommates. Hanging out with you is going to be a very good thing now.

Rae's heart swelled even as she rolled her eyes. "Glad one of us thinks my tatù's a good attention getter." *I am so lucky to have you as a roomy, Molls.*

Molly bent down and disappeared into Rae's closet. "You have those cool Converse Pink sparkly runners. Wear them." She tossed them at Rae and disappeared into her own closet. "I have this awesome white top with a Celtic design on the side which runs over the shoulder then down a bit of the back. It'll look perfect with your ink." Molly chewed on her fingernail while she gave Rae the once-over. "We're going to have to do something with your hair. It's braided right now, but I bet if we let the braid out and add a little mousse, it'll be fine."

Molly dressed in a pair of black dress pants with a very

expensive-looking (and chest-flattering) top. She'd done hers and Rae's makeup perfectly. Nothing was missed. Haley tapped on their door and whispered, "Time to go."

Sixteen girls tiptoed down the stairs, sneaking toward the back door. The twins stood by Madame Elpis' door, giggling as Nadia concentrated on sending Madame Elpis wonderful, happy dreams. Aidan had wanted to send the dreams, but everyone had agreed that'd be a mistake.

Outside, the group relaxed and ran toward the trees.

Gale, the senior with excellent hearing, touched Rae's shoulder. "Can you see anything?" she whispered.

Rae pointed to the dancing dots on the east side of the forest. "I think those are torches." She absorbed Gale's ink, loving the feeling the hum gave as it coursed through her veins. Rae's hearing picked up instantly, as if her other senses were put on a slight dimmer and the volume was turned up so she could hear everything more clearly.

When they were free from the forest, the girls quickly dispersed among the boys who were already hanging out in the field. Rae held back among the shadows, suddenly shy.

Riley walked over and handed her a can of cider, smiling sweetly. "If you're going to drink anything, stick to cider and *take it easy*." He held his beer can up. "Cheers, an' happy birthday!"

Rae touched cans with Riley's and reluctantly took a small sip, surprised the bubbly cider actually didn't taste too bad.

Nicholas sauntered over to wish her a happy birthday. He bugged her until she took a sip of his beer. The grimace on her face made him laugh and spill his tall can.

Rae chatted with him, her eyes roaming the field for Devon. Halfway through her cider, she began to relax. So, it seemed, did the other girls. Before long, they were tying the fronts of their shirts up to show off the ink art on their backs.

Rae slipped back toward the outer circle. *No way I'm doing that.* She heard some of the boys talking about her father and comparing her to him. No one knew her ability and she needed to remember to constantly think before saying or doing something stupid.

"Hiding out in the dark?" A voice drifted quietly toward her.

"Devon!" Rae swung around and hugged him. She pulled back awkwardly, surprised at her exuberance. She took a sip of her cider.

"Happy birthday."

"How's your mom?"

They both spoke at the same time.

"You first," Rae said.

"Happy birthday. I got back late this afternoon and didn't see you at dinner."

"We ordered pizza."

"Yeah, Julian informed us of his dinner with all of you." Rae could hear the smile in his voice.

"How's your mom? Andy told me she broke her leg."

"She's pretty sore, but happy that I came to see her."

"I'm sure." *Who wouldn't love to have a perfect boy like you?*

He coughed. "I, uh, picked you out a little gift. It isn't really anything, but when I saw it, I thought of you." Devon pulled out a small box from his pocket and hesitantly gave it to Rae.

Her heart skipped a beat or two as she tore the sparkly wrapping paper and lifted the lid off the box. Inside was a silver cuff bracelet. She lifted it out of the box to read the line inscribed: "*Follow your dreams...*" She went to put it on her wrist. "Thanks. That's really sweet of you."

Devon reached over and held her wrist. "Wait. Don't put it on yet. You have to read the inscription on the inside."

Rae paused, enjoying the tingling burn his fingers

created against her skin. Devon's ability coursed through her. The night suddenly became brighter, her vision spectacular as she turned the bracelet over to read it. "... *But watch your back.*"

Devon laughed. "With all the crap and cool stuff you're dealing with this year, it just seemed... kinda fitting."

"It's awesome. I really like it." She meant it. What were the chances he'd find something like that for her? It was perfect.

He grinned, giving Rae a quick glimpse of his dimple. "What're friends for if you can't celebrate an important day like today?"

A pang of guilt surged through her and she couldn't take it anymore. She didn't do well with lying to begin with, and having kept her own secret for so long she needed to tell someone. "I have to tell you something." Rae wasn't sure if it was remorse or cider talking. She decided to let the words out before she lost her courage. "My birthday was actually on Friday." She snuck a peek at his face. The surprised look made her babble an explanation. "My birth certificate's wrong. My mom had me at home and when they took me to the hospital to register my birth, the doctor put the wrong date down. My mom never bothered to get it corrected. It's not really a big deal." She shrugged. "With this whole tatù thingie being blown out of proportion for me...I just wanted to tell you." She swirled her empty can of cider, now wishing she had a full one in her hand.

"Your secret, not mine." His face turned sympathetic. "I won't tell a soul. I do think, though, if you wanted the experience on your own, Lanford wouldn't have cared." He motioned with his hands. "How'd it go today?"

"Fine." Rae didn't want to talk about it. She wanted to have fun tonight. She tried stealing a sip from her empty can.

"Can I see it?"

"See what?" Rae was about to hide the cider behind her back, thinking he'd give her crap for drinking it. Then it dawned on her -- he wasn't talking about the cider. "Oh, you mean my tatù."

"Is it like either of your folks'?"

Rae turned and lifted her shirt so Devon could see the full ink art. "It's pretty much one-of-a-kind."

Devon didn't say anything or move. Rae turned her head to look at him, wondering what he was thinking. Big pupils shone against the white of his eyes and his mouth hung slightly open. Rae had a fleeting thought of what it might taste like to press her lips against his. She ran her tongue against her teeth, trying to get the picture out of her head.

Finally Devon broke the silence. "That's really something...it's, uh, awesome."

Rae felt his fingers gently touch her skin where the tatù lay. Chills ran up her spine and down her legs, making her knees feel weak. She liked the feeling.

"Did you know she sparkles? It's almost like her wings glow in the dark. It's, uh, very u-unique." Devon cleared his throat and brought his fingers to his mouth, the same fingers that had touched her.

She blushed. "I didn't know it sparkled in the dark." Rae tried to see her back but just ended up twirling in a circle.

Devon chuckled. "She's definitely special."

Rae blinked. Was he talking about her or her tatù?

"Do you know how to use her?"

Should she lie or tell the truth? *Take a chance...* "You can't tell anyone." She playfully bumped his hip. "Or I'll have to kill you. Just kidding. I haven't figured it all out, but I think I've the main gist of it." She reached for his fingers. "Give me your hand." She'd already picked up his ability, but wanted the excuse to touch him. She held on a moment and then relaxed her hand, but Devon continued to hold hers.

She whispered, barely loud enough for him to hear but knowing the rest of the kids would not, except for maybe the senior girl with supersonic hearing. "I can see you perfectly and I know you can hear me." She watched his face turn. "I know exactly what your abilities are now. There's more inside of you I bet you haven't even realized yet." She swallowed, staring up at the night sky. "My ability is like my father's, but different. I don't know how it's different yet, but I *know* it is."

"Wow. I'm stunned. A little curious, as well." Devon squeezed her hand, making her draw her gaze away from the sky and at him.

"Curious?" Rae repeated.

"Yeah, if you've the same ink as me at the moment, can you see as well or possibly better than me? What about your speed or agility or jumping skills?"

"Hey...are you challenging me?" She giggled.

"Definitely. However, not tonight."

"Why not?" She had the urge to take off running across the field, Devon chasing her.

"Maybe we'll save it for a tutoring session which doesn't include cider."

"Wimp. I'm fine." The corner of her lips dropped and she knew she was frowning. *Hopefully not pouting.*

"Sure, that's what they all say." He laughed, rolling his eyes dramatically. "Come on. Let's head closer to the fire. Molly's searching for you, and I think I need to grab myself one of those beers now."

He kept hold of her hand as they walked toward the fire, only letting go when they got near the others. He grabbed a can from the cooler and popped it open.

"Very impolite of you to not offer me one." Rae teased and then leaned over to grab herself a cider. A gasp came from behind her. Worried, she looked up. Devon stared at her marking, his eyes rooted to the spot even as Rae turned around.

"Is something wrong?" She touched her tatù.

Devon shook his head and then smiled at her. "No, nothing's wrong. Your ink art's very, uh…attractive in the firelight." He took a swig of his beer and pretended to be interested in the action going on around them. "It's seductive."

Rae grinned, silently thanking Molly for dressing her. She popped open her can of cider and took a big gulp, not caring about anything but the fact that the way she felt at that very moment, was even better than flying.

Chapter 18

Alumni Dinner

NOVEMBER, like the snow, drifted into December. End of term exams were around the corner. Talk of Christmas holidays soon filled the halls of the school.

Class in the Oratory became more intense. Lanford tested each individual, pushing them to learn and understand their ability in more detail. Rae made a conscious effort to only perform skills which copied what others thought her tatù could do. She still hid the fact that she could mimic abilities like her father. It amazed her that no one caught on. She swore a red light started flashing over her head each time she touched someone, even though she tried to keep it as subtle as possible.

She continued tutoring with Devon. Nothing had changed between them since the C-O-P party. She never mentioned the evening, and neither did he. The only thing they really talked about was her tatù. Only he knew her true capabilities. He promised to keep silent until the end of the year, but encouraged her to tell the headmaster, especially after reading the letter from her mom. Rae refused, but wouldn't explain why. She wasn't one hundred percent sure why she felt the need to keep it a secret. She told herself it was because she didn't want to be hassled and wanted the freedom to learn her tatù on her own, like anyone else. But deep down, she felt it might be another reason altogether, she just wasn't sure what.

The five days before the Holiday break were crammed with exams. Monday morning, Rae wandered towards the Refectory for breakfast so firmly focused on her study notes that she didn't notice Dean Carter until she almost ran him over. He stood rigid, dressed in a long, black leather jacket, matching gloves and a pair of expensive sunglasses. "Good morning, Ms. Kerrigan."

Like a vampire stepping into the daylight. She stifled a giggle at the thought and took a careful step back to keep distance between them. "Good morning...sir."

She wished she'd touched Molly this morning instead of Maria. The dean would probably feel thought projection would need closer examination. Ironically, he actually needed to get his own head examined, at least in her opinion.

"Don't forget the alumni dinner on Friday evening. You're expected to attend. I've been informed you'll be staying with Ms. Skye's family over the holidays, so I've extended the invitation to her as well. She is, apparently, over the moon with the invite," he said sarcastically. "I trust the two of you will be on your best behavior." Rae knew it was a rhetorical question, but she couldn't resist the urge to poke fun at him a bit.

"I'm honored to have been invited and I'll do my best not to chew with my mouth open." She'd rather rip a fingernail off than go, but she knew she had no choice. "If you'll excuse me, sir, I need to grab some breakfast before my exam."

Rae stepped wide to pass the dean, but with lightning

quick reflexes, he reached out and grabbed her arm.

She froze as a new hum spread through her body. Unable to stop it, Rae felt panic settle into her core.

A vision played before her eyes. It was the morning of Rae's real birthday, when she looked into the mirror and saw her tatù. Then the vision fast forwarded through the day, pausing when she realized her talent in the bathroom and ending on her shape-shifting back from an eagle.

The dean now knew she'd lied about her birth date and the power of her tatù. Terrified, she was afraid to move, not knowing what he would do. She'd never really trusted him and now he knew what she'd been trying so hard to hide. Rae cringed inwardly as she waited for his reaction.

Dean Carter leaned forward and hissed in her ear. "I knew something was amiss! You didn't think I'd believe you *that* incapable with an ink this original?" He huffed as he shoved her arm back. "You should have told me. This may have dire consequences," he finished ominously. Then he walked away without glancing back.

Rae couldn't breathe right away. It took a moment for her to remember how to suck air in and her stomach churned so much she lost her appetite. She stumbled to lean against the wall of the Refectory.

What would happen now? Would he tell everyone she was like her father? She knew she had the ability to be, but had absolutely no intention of letting her father's legacy rule her. Besides, her tatù was different from his anyway. Wouldn't everyone see that? *Not here. They're all too blinded by the past.*

Plus, they were about to find out she'd been lying all this time. She wanted to run and hide, but knew she couldn't. She felt sick to her stomach at the thought of going back to having everyone stare at her, and treat her like an outsider or a leper again.

This whole tatù business is complicating my life on a level normal teens don't have to deal with! It's not fair! Just a few months ago she'd been invisible in New York, living with her cryptic, riddle-loving uncle and her clueless but loving aunt, going to school and not being noticed by anyone at all. She'd been nothing special. Then Uncle Argyle had shipped her off to this place where the walls had eyes and it seemed that everyone waited breathlessly to see if she turned into a monster like her father. Special powers or no, she just wanted it all gone from inside her, to go back to being invisible. That was so much better than the alternative. Her shoulders drooped as she shuffled off to class.

Dropping into a chair at the back of the room, she pulled a book out of her bag and stared blankly at the pages, not knowing what to do next. There was no way she could focus on the test now. She sighed and closed her eyes, taking a deep breath, trying to accept the fact she was basically screwed. After all, now that the dean knew, there was no way he'd keep his mouth shut. She thought him entirely too greedy and cruel to keep her freaky ability a secret. Besides, he'd love to make her the main attraction at the Alumni Dinner and she knew it well. All her hard work to fit in here would go up in smoke at the dinner.

She wondered idly who would turn on her first once they knew. Molly? She hoped not. It would be more than she could bear. At least she knew without a doubt that Devon wouldn't turn on her. *But I can't go through life clinging to him as my only friend in the world.* She opened her eyes and stared blankly at the ceiling.

"Rae!" Nicholas came by and held up his hand. "Good luck. I hear this one's going to be a killer."

She automatically high-fived him, a social knee-jerk reaction she couldn't have stopped herself from doing. She instantly felt better with Nicholas' gift coursing through her body, easing the weight of Dean Carter's mental invasion. *And I'm back!* She managed to focus just in time for the exam.

When she finished the exam, she dashed out the door to find Devon leaning against the wall waiting for her. She skidded to a stop

"Hey! What're you doing here?"

He smiled and pushed off the wall to stand close beside her. "You up to anything right now?"

He flashed his dimple and Rae's breath caught. "N-No. My next exam's in two days."

"Lucky you." Devon began walking toward the exit. "I've got a whopper of one tomorrow night." He held the door open for her. "So, that means you're free for the afternoon?"

"Sure. What do you want to do?" She almost started skipping. *He wants to hang out with me!*

"Can we do our study session now? I've got to study later, and Beth wants to take me out for dinner."

Poof! Her happiness balloon just popped. "U-Umm...sure." She glared at her shoes. "We can skip it if you want. Start up again after the holidays." She refused to look him in the eye as she had no intention of letting him see how much the mention of Beth's name bothered her, but then she remembered the dinner. She brought her head up. "Hey, are you going to the alumni dinner?"

"No way." He laughed. "Good food, but so boring." When she didn't laugh too, he glanced at her. "Oh shoot. You've gotta go?" He nudged her with his shoulder. "Don't look so worried. It's not *that* bad."

"Easy for you to say. You don't have a rare ink." *Or an evil father, or the weight of the world on your shoulders...the list goes on.*

They headed into Aumbry House, going straight to their usual spot in the library.

Devon tossed his backpack on the chair beside him. "What do you want to go over today? I'm all yours..." he checked his watch, "for the next fifty minutes."

All hers? *I wish!* Rae dropped into her seat and tried to come up with something interesting to discuss. She tapped the heel of one sneaker against the toe of the other. "What do you know about the dean?"

Devon's eyebrows came together. "What do you mean?"

"He doesn't like me."

"He doesn't like anybody. He's a miserable git."

"Yeah, but the guy's seriously mental. You weren't in the room on my birthday and...and again this morning." She stared at her fingernails, absently thinking they needed a trim.

"What happened this morning?" Devon tilted his head, his forehead creased.

Rae sighed. "I-I guess nothing. He just has a weird gift...and he t-touched me."

"What?" Devon straightened. "How, or where?"

She glanced up and started laughing. She hadn't intended to, but he looked so worried for her and she suddenly realized how her words had sounded. "I don't mean like *that*. I just meant he grabbed my wrist." She rubbed her temple. "It seems kinda silly now. I guess it's no big deal. He's just weird."

Devon fell back against his chair and gave her a slow smile, showing his relief. "I've never seen his gift in action. I'd probably be freaked if he used it on me."

"You know what he can do?"

"Something about being able to see the past."

"It's like a video. He can fast forward, probably rewind and pause it as well."

Devon glanced at the clock on the wall. "Okay. Now that we've cleared that up. What'd you want to do?"

She knew exactly what she wanted to find out. "I want to see if there's a link between Carter and my dad. There's got to be some history to make him hate me." She watched the corners of Devon's mouth twitch.

"It's not funny. The guy knows I lied about my birthday and he knows the truth about my gift. Maybe he wanted to date my mom and she shot him down? I don't know..."

He leaned forward. "Here's the deal. I think you're being paranoid. You think there's something behind a guy who's just a male chauvinist. If we look stuff up and find nothing, you promise to just try to ignore him?"

Rae twisted her fingers together considering the option. She balked at the idea of leaving the dean alone if they didn't find a link. She was positive there was something that made him focus on her with such intensity. e seemed to despise all women, so maybe, the idea of her having something rare just irked the hell out of him. Plus Devon was someone she trusted completely, and he seemed to think there was nothing to find. Maybe she *was* making too much out of this, but she needed to know and he did offer to help. With her head still tilted down to her hands she looked up at him through the fringes of her lashes. "Fine."

They went through the school's enrollment, searching the Web and anything else they could think of to find a link between Dean Carter and her dad, or mom. They came up empty-handed.

It wasn't a total loss though. Rae learned more about the bullying and other more illegal things her father had done and was shocked no one had tried to take him down. Like a modern day Hitler, his plans went undetected until it was too late to stop him.

He had wanted to rule the world and, according to the documents in the files, had created a large group of followers to help him achieve his goal. He had done everything secretly. Even now, very few of his chosen entourage would admit to what they had conspired to do.

Rae remembered the men her father had always kept around him. He'd referred to them as bodyguards. She looked into that, but again came back with more questions than answers. According to the information, very little was known about his mysterious service men. Most of their names, and even some their inks were unknown. It became clear to Rae her mother had been the only one able to get close enough to her father to stop him.

It put more proof to Rae's theory that her mother had used her tatù to start the fire. It made perfect sense. Why else would her mother have written the letter to her and made campaigns for Rae's future if she hadn't planned something big? Like her father's death?

Did she sacrifice everything to save me? Rae craved answers but had no idea where to find them.

The rest of the week went by faster than Rae would have liked. She felt fairly certain she had done well on her exams, but had no real time to worry about it with the dreaded dinner looming over her head like an executioner's axe. No matter how hard she tried, she couldn't calm her nerves that night as she let Molly dress her and fix her hair.

The six students invited to the alumni dinner were required to greet the guests at the front entrance of the Refectory, as they entered for the meet-and-greet cocktail hour prior to the meal. The mess hall had been converted into an eloquent dining room. Rae, Molly and Riley were positioned at the east entrance, with Charlie and two other boys Rae didn't know at the west entrance.

Shaking hands with each person who came through became a nightmare. She kept flipping through abilities faster than she had a chance to realize what they were. It felt like flipping through TV channels too fast to actually see what was on. The buzz in her veins became almost too intense to handle as her tatù tried desperately to mimic every one she came in contact with. She was on the verge of either having her head explode or running way, when one of the professors got on stage and asked everyone to find their seats. Rae wanted to hug him. She sat at a table with Riley while Molly sat with Charlie on the other side of the hall. She tried to remember the names of the ten adults sitting around her, but couldn't, so she continually had to lean over to ask Riley in a whisper what their names or inks were.

Riley acted the perfect gentleman throughout the evening, even looking hot in his tuxedo. He introduced Rae to many of the alumni, got her punch and constantly had a hand on her arm or back. He never left her side. Rae was grateful for all his help, but annoyed with the over-caffeinated feeling his cheetah tatù kept giving her.

After dinner, Dean Carter rose and moved to the podium,. Headmaster Lanford waited quietly beside him, absently smoothing down his combover with his hand.

Dean Carter cleared his throat, rested both hands on the podium and looked intently at the audience, making sure he had everyone's attention before he started speaking.

"I'd like to thank everyone for attending the dinner this evening. Headmaster Lanford and I are pleased with the turnout and, of course, we are thankful for all of your support. Your financial support has been a wonderful credit to this school. It's amazing how generous each talented individual in this room has been in giving back to the school which helped all of you to reach the incomes you've attained. It's like every one of you have a secret power." He finished the sentence with a lascivious grin.

Rae didn't really think it was funny, but most of the adults got a kick out of the comment and laughter floated across the room. She leaned back and relaxed, expecting more stupid comments, but she froze when she heard his next line.

"It's a credit to have the Kerrigan name back at Guilder. Many of us thought all had ended with the terrible fire. How fortunate for us, and for Rae, that Headmaster Lanford was able to locate her and invite her into the school. It's a new experience for all to have females attending classes. From the comments our male students have made, it's a positive improvement." This elicited another round of chuckles in the room. Again, Rae wasn't at all amused.

She scratched her head. *Could Dean Carter be schizophrenic? He hates having women here.* She huffed. The guy obviously wanted to put on a show for the parents.

"Ms. Kerrigan turned sixteen just a few weeks ago, around mid-November." He looked directly at Rae. "She's inked with a very unique tatù, one which is new to all of us." The lights dimmed as he spoke. "But she is her father's daughter. And, it appears, has his ability." The dean held up a small remote and pointed it at a projector set up in the back of the room.

Mortified, Rae saw her tatù appear on the big screen behind the dean. She wanted to crawl under the table to hide. *The ability to teleport would be really handy right about now.* The quiet murmurs of her father's name and the whispered remorse over her mother's tragic death burned into her brain, but the part she couldn't stand to hear were the questions of whether or not she was "dark" like her father had been. She wished Riley hadn't been touching her all night. She could use a disappearing tatù right now, not some hyped up cheetah. She felt trapped and needed to run.

Lanford moved in front of the podium, cutting off the Dean, and raised his hands. He shushed everyone with his words. "Thank you, Dean Carter. I'm sure the alumni are interested in Ms Kerrigan's tatù and are concerned with her well-being." He turned to the audience and slipped a hand into his pocket. "Rae has settled into Guilder with grace and a willingness to learn. She spent most of her first term at a disadvantage to the other students in her class, yet still managed to maintain a perfect 4.0 GPA, without the use of her tatù. She's a very talented student. There has only been praise from her professors. Well done, Ms Kerrigan!"

The headmaster began clapping. The audience, like sheep, reluctantly joined in.

Riley leaned over to Rae and whispered, "You should stand up."

Her face burning and her heart hammering away, Rae shyly rose. A sea of heads turned her way, making her instantly nauseous. She quickly sat back down and kept her eyes trained on her hands, refusing to look up again.

Thankfully, Headmaster Lanford changed the subject. "Now, shall we consider the new matters at hand? There has been keen interest in some upgrades to the school's grounds. I have hopes for building a new football pitch which includes heating pipes underground so the teams would be able to play on the field year round..."

Rae listened to the crazy suggestion. Only professional football teams did that sort of thing. Then again, at Guilder, ordinary just wouldn't do.

The remainder of the evening continued at a snail's pace for Rae. Thanks to Dean Carter, she felt like the main attraction at the freak show. Alumni came up to shake her hand again and offer words of encouragement and also words of criticism. Again her tatù made it nearly impossible to handle the contact. Riley continued to stand by her and lend his support -- emotionally and physically. By the end of the evening, Rae wasn't sure what she looked forward to most: getting away from the alumni, or from Riley. She swore she'd never drink caffeine again.

At half past eleven, Molly found her. "Hey, are you 'bout ready? My dad wants to get going. We've got a long drive to Wales and he wants to do it all tonight. I think he's had enough socializing. He's kind of the quiet type."

Rae had a moment to wonder how anyone related to

Molly could be "the quiet type". The party looked like it was just beginning to liven up for the old people and Rae could have hugged Molly for finding her. She felt more than ready to leave. If she could, she'd have used Riley's cheetah skills to peel out of there. "Heck yeah! Let's go get our stuff."

"I'll walk you ladies to the door." Riley stepped between the two of them and kept his arm around Rae's waist. Near the front door, he leaned down toward her. At the last moment, she realized what he planned to do and quickly turned her head. Riley's sloppy lips landed on her jawline. She had no intention of her first kiss being with him.

"Thanks for helping me out, tonight. Have a good winter break." After gushing the words out, she grabbed Molly's arm and dragged her outside, not caring that it was a less than graceful exit.

Molly laughed when they hit the sidewalk. "That was awesome!"

Rae glared at her. "I didn't think he'd ever leave my side."

Molly interlaced their arms. "Riley's got a huge crush on you."

"Ya think?" Rae wiped her cheek, making a sour face. It still felt wet.

"Don't be so grossed out. The guy's good-looking and smart. He's also got great family connections. You know," Molly said, elbowing Rae lightly in the ribs, "you could do a lot worse."

"Thanks, but no thanks. I think I have enough on my plate." Rae sighed. "I don't really want to deal with a relationship on top of everything else." *Except with this one, totally unattainable guy with the perfect dimple...*

Molly, for once, didn't say anything. She just shook her head.

Chapter 19

Friendly Advice

THE drive to Cardiff ended up taking about five hours. Not that Rae paid much attention. Her thoughts kept creeping back to Dean Carter blurting out her ability to everyone at the Alumni dinner. She stared at the back of Molly's head as she sat in front beside her father. Eventually, Rae had kicked her shoes off and stretched out across the back seat, using her bent arm to cushion her head against the side window.

The sound of the car downshifting and the flash of street lights on the back of her eyelids woke her. She yawned and shifted, cringing when she discovered the crick in her neck.

After rubbing her eyes, she stared silently at the city of Cardiff. She checked her watch, and realized that even at three am, the city didn't sleep. A few cars cruised the roads, either coming home or maybe heading out. Who knew? *Who really cares?* Rae thought, yawning again.

Molly leaned forward doing the "seatbelt sleep" - her head bounced with the motion of the car, the seat belt the only thing that kept her upright. They went over a bump and Molly's head bobbed up and down like a fishing bobber, making Rae giggle. Molly snorted, but didn't wake- up.

"We're almost thar," Molly's dad said in his thick Welsh accent. Rae wouldn't have understood him if she hadn't been living with Molly for the past few months. Molly's accent seemed barely noticeable to her now.

He flipped the turn signal on and turned right, down a street with row-on-row houses. Another turn and the houses became semi-attached and then increasing detached as they drove on, indicating a rise in home price. They finally pulled into a cul-de-sac with four large homes. He parked the car in the first driveway on the left and turned the ignition off.

"We home?" Molly croaked, popping her head up. "Thank goodness. I'm so tired."

"Yar, yer mum set up the spare room fer Rae." He hopped out of the car and opened the back passenger door, saying to Rae, "It's right by Molly's and you 'ave yer own bathroom." He slung Molly's bag over his shoulder and put his arm around Molly. "Nice t'ave you back fer a bit."

Rae leaned over and grabbed her bag and followed them in. She smiled when she heard Molly's dad whisper to his daughter. "Everything good wit yer ink?" He snapped his fingers and a few sparks flew out of them. "Able to do this yit?"

"No, but that's totally awesome." Molly perked up. "Can you teach me?"

"Sure, if yer mum gives us a bit of time on our own." He laughed, as if at some private joke. "She wan's ta take you two to the shops 'ommorrow."

Rae followed them inside, a small pang of jealousy filling her. Molly's dad seemed so sweet. Quiet and reserved, he had a kind and sincere quality about him. He obviously adored his daughter. Rae thought back to Molly's words when they'd first met. She'd said something about her dad telling her to be careful around Rae. He didn't seem the kind of person to be like that...maybe Molly had taken his words out of context.

Based on what she knew of her roomie, it seemed likely. Rae grinned involuntarily, thinking back on multiple instances where Molly had blown things out of proportion.

Rae took a moment to wonder how someone so loud and outgoing could come from someone so quiet and introverted. Maybe Molls' mom would be the pushier kind. Her dad wore very nice, labeled clothes, but maybe it was Molly and her mom who did the shopping.

They carried their stuff up the large staircase, giving Rae a glimpse of the house. Everything in the house was designer and classy, looking like it had jumped straight out of a high-priced magazine. It reminded Rae of Molly's wardrobe.

Her room, across from Molly's, looked like it'd been a photo-shoot backdrop in Vanity Fair: Polo sheets on a high poster bed, the walls and trim painted a brilliant white. The ensuite bathroom had a shower, separate bath and sink done in silvers and lilac. Rae brushed her teeth and crawled into bed, too tired to let her brain take in anything more beyond the luxurious softness of the sheets. She fell asleep immediately.

"Rae... Rae... You awake?" Molly whispered loudly, her weight dipping the mattress beside Rae on the large bed.

Rae felt Molly's finger touch her eyebrow a split second before her eyelid jerked open of its own accord.

Her eye rolled left to right, catching Molly dressed in pajamas covered in Chanel logos, before pulling her head back. "I am now." She considered tossing one of the five hundred thread count pillows at her friend, but it would be a shame to throw something so wonderfully soft. "What time is it?"

"'Bout eleven." Molly's fingers reached beside Rae's head and pulled at one of her curls. "You know, you would look fantastic if we lightened your hair. Hmm... maybe blonde?" She shook her head. "No, too much. Maybe some chunky highlights. Oh! You'd be like a modern day Tinkerbelle." She tilted her head, obviously visualizing it in her mind. "I can color your hair sometime if you want. I took a class a few summers ago."

"You took a hair class?" Rae couldn't picture it. Her flashy, designer-labeled roomie, a beauty school girl? *Maybe a dropout.* Rae grinned at the cheesy Grease-Lightening comparison.

"Aced it. Even the teacher was asking me to do her hair. She said I had some natural talent for finding the right colors for people. Whatever." She shrugged. "I thought I might be a stylist, and wanted to make sure I knew how to do people up from head to toe." She looked around the room. "Sorry this room's so boring. The antique bookcase, over there by the window, has a section which drops down and turns into a desk. You can set your computer up there and we've got wireless. Password is "tricity" with no caps or anything. Like elec*tricity*" She began snapping her fingers, staring intently at them.

Rae sat up, fluffing a pillow behind her back and leaning against the headboard as she drew her knees up. "What're you doing?"

"My dad showed me this cool sparkly-trick, but I can't figure out how he did it."

"Let me try." The words were out before Rae realized. Her eyes grew wide as she waited for Molly's response.

"You can't, silly." Molly patted Rae's hand. "My dad and I almost have the same ink." She snapped her finger again. "I almost forgot the whole reason I came in here. My mom wants to go shopping. She's dying to buy me some new outfits for school." She hopped off the bed. "First we eat, then we shop."

Rae had a bit of money her aunt and uncle sent as her Christmas present. Maybe she'd buy a new outfit as well. She also wondered if the dean's words had sunk in for Molly. *Did she get that I can copy her ability? Or was she purposely ignoring it?* "I just need a shower."

"No probs. I'll meet you downstairs." Molly disappeared around the door, still snapping her fingers.

Rae sat a moment longer staring at her hands. Then she got up and peered into the hallway before she quickly, and as quietly as possible, closed the door. Leaning her back against it, she tried snapping her fingers. Nothing happened. Focusing on Molly's tatù hum, she intently watched her fingers and palm, rotating her wrist. Eyebrows pushed together, she tried to imagine the electricity flowing through her veins from her forearm and up her wrist to the tips of her fingers.

Instead of snapping her fingers, she felt the urge to flick them, and jumped when tiny little sparks flew out. She stepped away from the door and headed toward the bathroom, still practicing her finger sparklers. *Cool trick! I gotta show Molls....oh wait...shoot.* She didn't know if Molly knew and the only way to find out would be to ask her. *Hmmm... or maybe show her!* Molly had been so nice to invite her here, and what if Molly didn't get what the loser-dean had said and she heard it from someone when she got back from school? Rae though it might break her heart if Molly turned her back on her.

They shopped all afternoon. Molly's mom turned out to be an older, more mature version of Molly. It made Rae giggle. The two of them headed to every shop where nothing seemed priced below a hundred pounds. It was way above Rae's comfort zone.

The next day they shopped again, even with all the crazy holiday rush of shoppers. Molly and her mom didn't mind. They still came home with presents for others and themselves. Rae thought it'd be nice to have that kind of money, but she didn't think she'd bother with the crazy priced clothes. She did buy a scarf and matching gloves from Burberry and it kept Molly quiet for about half an hour.

Molly and her Mom couldn't wait to go shopping for the Boxing Day sales. After a quiet, but fancy Christmas dinner with presents, including presents for her, Rae had no desire to shop more. The next morning, she sat at the little antique bookcase, her laptop loading. Molly stood, flipping through some fashion magazine.

"Would you mind if I just stayed in?" Rae asked.

"You're kidding! You don't want to go?" Molly looked confused.

"I, uh, I'd like to give my Uncle Argyle and Aunt Linda a call and just take it easy. Is that okay?"

Molly, still looking like she couldn't figure out why in the world staying in would be more exciting than buying clothes, finally nodded. "My mom and I can get a bit of one on one time." She turned to go, at the door, she paused. "Hey, can you do me a favor?"

"Sure."

"Do you mind hanging out with my Dad for a bit. I meant to do something all week and haven't gotten around to it. Maybe just have lunch with him or something?"

Rae liked Molly's dad. He didn't seem to care about who her parents were. Plus, she wanted to do this for Molly, for having been so nice to her. "I can do that."

"Hey Molls?"

"Yeah?"

"Did you... um... did you get what the dean said about my tatù at the dinner?"

"What part? That the guy's a complete dufus?"

"Well, that's a given." She grinned, her stomach fluttering with nervousness. "That he figured out my ability's kind of like my dad's?" She waited for a reaction, dreading what she might hear.

"I kinda figured your ink was something bigger, but who cares if you can't figure it all out now. It'll come." She headed toward the door and turned back just before exiting. "Look at what's changed since I got inked in September. Watch this." She flicked her fingers and sparks flew and fizzled out. "Maybe I can teach you sometime." She waved her hand, sparks still flying and leaving small brown burn holes in the white carpet.

Rae sat stunned, staring at the carpet. *Wow, she didn't even need me. At least she isn't mad at me. But I wonder if she really understands?* Rae didn't know what to think. She only knew that she felt unbelievably grateful that Molly hadn't turned on her.

When Molly left, Rae called her aunt and uncle. She spoke with them for a bit, glad to hear that they had a white Christmas, something her Aunt adored, but didn't always get to see. Her uncle never mentioned anything about her tatù. The way Aunt Linda kept chatting over him in the background gave him a good excuse, so she couldn't blame him...much.

After hanging up, Rae glanced at the clock and realized it was half past twelve. She headed downstairs and into the kitchen. She could hear Molly's dad tinkering around in the garage connected to the kitchen. Rae went to the fridge and made the two of them some sandwiches and grabbed a couple of bags of crisps and some drinks.

She carried them into the garage. Molly's dad stood bent over the hood of a perfect looking Porsche.

"Hi, Mr. Skye. I made you some lunch."

Mr. Skye popped his head up and smiled. "Well, arn't you a dear!" He walked over to the small sink beside the table Rae had set the sandwiches on. He turned the taps on and washed his hands, which already looked clean. He pulled two stools out from under table and indicated she should sit on one.

They sat in companionable silence for a few minutes, munching on their lunch. Eventually, feeling the need to fill the quiet void, Mr. Skye cleared his throat and said, "Har you enjoyin' yer year wit Molly?"

Rae smiled, catching the teasing glimmer in his eye. The man obviously knew his daugther's effect on people. "She keeps things interesting."

"Oi! That she does. She's always been interested on the outside stuff, but she's got a big heart." He patted the left side of his chest. "An' if you haven't seen it yet, give er time and it'll come through." He fiddled with a lose thread on his shirt. "Now fer you."

"Fer – For me?" Rae's head started pounding. *Now it comes. He's going to bring up my folks and tell me to stay clear of trouble. Tell me to not tempt his daughter with evil.*

"Don't you be frettin' about the past. It'll catch up with yer soon enough – when yer ready. You've got yer hands full wit yer future. That's what's important." He smiled and winked at her.

All the panic drained out of her with a rush. She had the oddest sense of calm acceptance.

"Uh, thank-you." Rae didn't know what else to say. That had probably been the nicest thing an adult, besides the headmaster, had said to her regarding her ability.

"How're the boys? Arr they causing you an' me Molly trouble?"

Rae giggled. He wanted to have *that* talk with her. *Of course he does!* Molly probably had strategically told her dad just enough to not be lying and as a good father, he was hoping for more info from another source. *Like my father...like a father should.* She stopped giggling; she kind of needed the talk.

"There's a few boys. None of them cause trouble." She sighed, not sure how to say anything the right way. She had questions, and she needed guidance, a father's guidance. She knew she wouldn't get it from Uncle Argyle or the headmaster. She couldn't even picture asking anyone else. The pressure and uncertainty built up inside her. Finally, when she realized she couldn't keep it inside anymore, she blurted, "Mr. Skye what do you think of tatù people dating?" Her faced burned and she wished she could take the words back.

He stood and walked over the Porches and dropped the hood with a resounding bang, making Rae jump and regret that she had said anything. *I don't know this man, he doesn't know me. Why didn't I keep my mouth shut?* But his words, once he spoke, gave her hope.

"You girls 'ave it 'arder than we did. They don't want you ta be together, an' yet they stick adolescents in the 'ame room." He tsked.

He went around to the driver's side and sat in the seat, turning the key. Nothing happened. He stood and leaned over the door, flicking his finger at the engine. A thin white and blue line escaped his fingers.

"Jus' be careful. As I sorta said before, you don' want yer past to predict yer future. Stay clear of gray areas fer a wee while."

He wrinkled his nose and sat back down in the driver's seat to try the key again. This time is purred like a kitten. He shut it off and closed the door.

"Yer young. Have fun an' just make sure a boy's interested fer the right reason. Tatù or not."

Rae decided to take his advice and leave before this happy interlude went south. She picked up the dirty dishes to take back into the house, but paused on the bottom step. "Thanks, Mr. Skye. Molly's lucky to have a dad like you."

He chuckled. "I didn' choose to do something big with my ability. I choose a simple life, but wit a wife who likes to go big. Me girls, Molly and her mum, deserve their castle. I'm the one who's lucky to 'ave them. Jus' do me a favor an' keep me Molls outta trouble." Then he added, as if having an afterthought, "An' keep 'er away from them boys."

Rae giggled as she went back into the house, thinking to herself that Molly's father knew his daughter to the bone.

Chapter 20

Personal Demons

THE rest of the Winter break passed slowly with Molly and her mother taking every possible opportunity to drag Rae out shopping to stores which were so far outside of her price range, it felt ludicrous to even walk in the shop's door. It took some time for Rae to give in, and just enjoy the company.

There were moments when Rae felt like she was looking at a Norman Rockwell painting, watching Molly with her parents. They were disparate parts of the same whole, like puzzle pieces that seemed so different, yet fit together perfectly to make a beautiful picture.

They were so perfect together, and sometimes Rae longed to have that so much it hurt. Molly always seemed to know when Rae fell into a dark mood. She would come and drag her back into the fray, until Rae felt she was no longer on the outside, that she kind of became part of their family. It was an idyllic time, a welcome respite from the stress and pressure of school. Part of her wished it would last forever; the other part couldn't wait to go back to Guilder, to see Devon, the headmaster and to face the other students.

Eventually, Rae found herself and Molly on a train, heading back to Guilder, the golden times ended. But even with the grim and dreary environment of school, teachers, expectations and the ever -watchful eye of the dean, the one thing life at Guilder wasn't, was slow.

The first week back at school seemed to pass faster than all three weeks of the Christmas break combined. While on vacation, she had enjoyed the privacy of not having to talk about her tatù. In fact, after having flashed through inks like a cartoon flip book at the Alumni Dinner, Rae realized having had only Molly's ability for three weeks had been heaven.

In no time, everyone fell back in the swing of things and gossip was abundant. On campus, everywhere she went, Rae heard students talking about her tatù and the alumni dinner. She ignored the whispers, figuring she'd show them what she needed to in the Oratory.

Monday evening, Rae headed down the marble steps and into the library a few minutes ahead of eight. She passed a few seniors sitting at the front of the room. She settled at her usual table with Devon near the back.

She hadn't chatted with him since before Christmas. Her knees bounced against the underside of the table making it shake noisily, and earning her dark looks from Madame Elpis. She got up and began pacing around the aisles at the back of the room. Rows of books lining the shelves looked like walls.

Rae dropped her head sideways to get a better view of the titles. Most of the books were old leather -bound tomes with gilt printing on the bindings. She touched one, pulling her hand back in surprise. She felt power from the book shift into her. *Well that's new. How could a book have ink power?* Well, there was only one way to proceed.

Dropping her hands to her sides, and standing perfectly still, she waited for her gift to show her what power she'd just absorbed. Eyes closed, she focused on the inner hum of her body.

The library grew completely silent -- aside from the steady noise of the old ceiling lights and the computers.

The urge to wrinkle and twitch her nose grew strong inside of her. Rae knew the ability she'd just absorbed belonged to a shape-shifter and immediately following the realization, came the knowledge of whose it was. She opened her eyes and sighed. "Gale, I know it's you." She tried to peek over top of the books. In her best sing-song voice impersonation of the Shinning, she said, "Come out, come out, wherever you are."

Laughter erupted from the front of the room. A tiny mouse crawled between two books, one of which Rae had touched. It jumped to the floor.

Within seconds, Gale stood beside her, a sheepish look on her face. "Sorry," she whispered. "The girls dared me to try it. I hope you're not mad." She looked frightened enough to turn back into a mouse.

Rae smiled and laughed, trying her best to show that she was nothing to be scared of. "Here I was thinking some book might actually be a human stuck in the library stacks. I was about to pull the book out to try to free it!"

A small, squeaky laugh erupted from Gale and she hurried back to her friends, giggling the whole way.

"What am I missin' out on?" Devon's voice came through the other side of the aisle, behind the books.

Rae peeked through the stacks, disappointed not to sneak a glimpse of the sexy body the voice belonged to.

"Just playing a joke on Kerrigan," Nadia, one of the twins, called from across the room

"Except she didn't fall for it," Gale added. "Figured it out in about five seconds."

Aidan appeared in the aisle. "I got her once already."

She grinned triumphantly.

"What?" Rae asked, furrowing her brow. "When?"

"The night of your birthday. In the Infirmary." Aidan's eyes sparkled. "I snuck outside your window and tossed you some crazy dreams."

"That was you?"

"Yeah, 'til you rolled out of bed faster than the wind and stared right at me. I took off running, positive you had caught me." She giggled. "You never ratted me out. I thought that was cool of you."

Rae thought back to the night. All of it had been strange. "I remember waking and jumping out of bed. I freaked at my own reflection. Never saw you."

Aidan winked. "Gotchya."

Devon leaned over Rae's shoulder, his hand wonderfully warm on her arm. "I'd watch it. From what I've heard, payback's a bitch." His smug smile backed up his words, making Rae wonder what he was thinking.

That wiped the silly smirk off Aidan's face. Worried eyes glanced at Rae. "Sorry. I won't ever do it again."

Rae couldn't help grinning, even though she hated the nervous tension in Aidan's voice. "No worries."

"I-I'll leave you guys to get some work done. We won't bug you again."

"Happy New Year," Rae called out as they headed to their table, hoping she could do a tiny bit of damage control.

The girls mumbled a reply and turned back to their books.

"Sorry I haven't had a chance to catch up with you." Devon sat down across from her. "Things were just really busy at home. Now, it seems, just as busy here."

"Is it your mom?"

"Nah, Mom's doing great. Her cast came off last week. She's wearing one of those air casts now which she can walk on and take off to shower. She's in heaven." Devon let out a long breath. "My father's putting me through hell. He's hounding me to get my applications in order for university."

Rae's heart stopped. She'd never considered Devon wouldn't be here next year. She'd kind of hoped he might stick around and, if she had the courage to ask, maybe mentor her more.

"Where's your dad pushing you to go?" *Hopefully really close by.*

"Cambridge. It's his alma mater. For having a tatù, it isn't much help in deciding what to do. I was sort of thinking about some kind of spy work for the government, maybe the Privy Council. My dad disagrees. He seems to think I don't have what it takes." Devon looked dejected for a moment, but quickly cleared the expression from his face. "It was just a long holiday break, and I'm happy to be back again."

"Me, too." Rae blushed realizing how it sounded. "I didn't mean I was happy to have you back, I just meant it felt like a long break, and I was happy. To be back. At school." She shook her head, wishing she had Molly's mouth at the moment. *Because I sound lame.* "How's Beth?"

"Beth?" Devon looked like he'd forgotten his girlfriend for a moment. "Oh, Beth! She's good, I think. I haven't spoken to her since the first week of Christmas break." He reached over and grabbed a couple of books from the stack and flipped through one. "We broke up."

He said it so quietly, Rae wasn't sure she'd heard him correctly. "Oh." Maybe he broke up with her? *Yay!* Or did she dump him and he was totally depressed? *Poor Devon!* Rae didn't say anything else, but she harbored a tiny twinge of guilt when she realized she was suddenly in an awesome mood.

"My dad said you were the talk of the alumni dinner." Devon's soft brown eyes met hers. "Seems Dean Carter put you center stage."

Rae cringed at the memory. The entire night seemed like a bad dream now -- from Dean Carter to Riley's attempted kiss. In fact, she wished it had all been one of Aidan's creations. But, lucky her, it had all been real.

"Let's just say I've no plans to attend next year," Rae said firmly. "I've done my time."

Devon laughed and held his hands up front of him. "I won't bring it up again! I promise! Let's try and get some work done then, shall we?"

He pulled a folder from his bag. Inside were newspaper clippings. He slid the file to her and opened the cover.

Rae looked at the black and white photo on the first page, instantly realizing it was of the fire that had burned her house down and killed her parents. She read the caption: FIRE KILLS TWO. MIRACLE CHILD SAVED.

Leaning forward, she read the article.

> A combustible, deadly fire took the lives of two people: Simon and Bethney Kerrigan. Their remains were found inside their smoldering house. The cause of the fire has yet to be determined; firefighters are not ruling out foul play. Miraculously, their six-year-old daughter was found unharmed in the tree house in the yard. All trees surrounding were singed. However, the tree house mysteriously had no fire damage. Investigators are still trying to determine if she was inside the house when the fire began or if she may have seen anything that might explain the cause of the fire. The fire did not spread to any neighboring houses. The investigation continues.

Rae glanced at Devon. He nodded and turned the page to the next clipping.

SIMON KERRIGAN killed. Murder or Mistake? The man that many have come to fear and believed to be invincible is gone. His remains were located among the fire debris of his house. His wife, Bethney Kerrigan, who also died, was discovered beside him. Their daughter was found unharmed. Investigators are trying to determine the cause of the fire – possibly a mistake made by Simon or by another source outside the home.

Simon's business associates are devastated. For this reporter, I will sleep better at night knowing Simon Kerrigan is gone. He will no longer be a threat to any of our kind or the rest of the world. Many of our readers will feel the same as I do. Let's all hope the Kerrigan daughter has the gift of her mother, not the malevolence of her father. The six -year -old's only living relative is Argyle McBane; his whereabouts are currently unknown.

Rae looked up, slightly confused. The second article didn't come from a typical newspaper. It seemed pretty bold to think, let alone put down on paper that her father was the boogieman. Yet, it told her little more than what she already knew. The difference here, was that it made her feel protective about her family, flawed as it was. It still felt like her personal loss, no one else's, she greatly disliked having anyone else comment on it, especially with the tone this article had projected. Devon seemed to read some of her thoughts. "The first article's from the local paper. The second article is from *our* newspaper."

"You mean, those who are inked?" She blinked several times, trying to absorb what Devon meant. It was difficult to accept, even though she knew it was true. People had actually feared or hated her father, and even after his death, they didn't put much confidence in her future. They were passing the gauntlet from him straight down to her, had done so in fact, before she was ever inked. Her need to defend herself, her life, her family, both dead and alive, and her tatù grew stronger. *Just a reflex,* she told herself, but felt like she'd still been actively attacked. It had felt that way for a long time, and had only been growing worse. *I've been naïve all this time to think I'd ever fit in here.* She might be one of them, but she would never belong. *They'll never accept me.*

She played with the zipper on her backpack. "You know, I wish I hadn't been born. Or maybe had a brother to carry this load instead of me. It would've been better if it just skipped over me."

"You don't mean that." Devon looked horrified. He took her hand in both of his.

"When Lanford told me you were coming, know what he said?" He squeezed her hand before releasing it. "He said you were coming to this school because of how special you are. He said you were going to need this tatù like the river needs the sea. And it would need you like the sea needs the river to survive."

"Sounds like Lanford's been having conversations with my uncle." Rae couldn't keep the sarcasm out of her voice.

Devon pressed on. "You can't bury it deep inside and pretend it doesn't exist. The sooner you realize that and accept it, the easier life will be."

Rae scoffed. "Easier? You've no idea what it's like to be me! Did you have newspaper articles written about you? Or an entire school and fraternity of gifted people leery of your tatù, watching your every step, suspicious of everything about you waiting for you to turn into a monster?" She ticked each point off on her fingers, her voice rising with each point. "I don't know who my real friends are. I have an uncle who never told me the truth and a mother who wrote me a letter before she killed my father! Don't even let me get started on my evil so-called evil father. I don't even know if the school has me here to help me, or so they can try to protect their own asses from what I might become!" She rolled her eyes.

"Sure, this ink's awesome. I can do such *wonderful* things. All I need is a little group of adoring psychopaths following me around so I can mimic their abilities." She stood, tossing the articles back at him. "How would you feel if people shrank away in fear of you and you'd done nothing wrong? Don't give me some river-sea metaphor and try to make me feel all better -- it isn't going to change anything!"

Rae grabbed her bag and threw it over her shoulder, storming out of the library, not caring that four senior girls were staring at her, mouths hanging open. If she'd given it a second thought, she'd have given them all the bird. Too bad she didn't notice anything outside of her inner pain.

A big part of her hoped Devon would come running after her to tell her everything was going to be all right. Rae snorted. Devon compared her to a river yet she was bloody drowning.

She stomped up the marble stairs, pissed that the marble absorbed her heavy stomps instead of making loud echoes. She wanted her angry stomps to boom like thunder through the air, because it would match her anger and her pain. She headed straight for her room, slammed the door and dropped onto her bed, punching the wall in anger. The lights flickered out.

After that night, Rae avoided Devon. It started out with her just wanting some space for a couple of days, but turned into a few weeks. Devon made no effort to try to talk to her, not even to set up further tutoring sessions, which adversely made her more determined to avoid him.

She spent a month being angry, not just at him, but at herself and the situation she'd been born into. If her stupid dad hadn't married her mom, or if they'd had a boy first or even after her, she might never have been put in this position. Nobody would be mean, nobody would blame her for her father's screwed up mind, she'd be...normal; an average teenager, concerned with nothing but school and boys.

She wore her self-pity like a cloak, refusing to admit it to anyone. It was easier to pretend to be hard, pretend she didn't notice the other students avoiding her or moving out of her reach so she couldn't touch them.

Some of the guys didn't seem to mind this tough, wild Rae. In fact, she constantly got asked out for lunch, or for a drive, or to the movies. She said yes to everyone. It was better than sitting in her dorm room feeling sorry for herself. Since she couldn't avoid it, she might as well enjoy the popularity of being *the freak*.

Her grades started slipping, but she didn't care. She was tired of trying so hard. What good was a 4.0 GPA if people judged her by her family's past without getting to know her at all? Things were spiraling out of control. She knew it, but had nothing to reach for to save herself.

After Oratory class near the end of March, Lanford asked her to stay behind.

"I'll meet you in the room," Rae said to Molly and rolled her eyes toward the headmaster.

"Sounds good. I'll get one of the guys to drive us into town for dinner." Molly headed out the door.

Rae turned, tapping her foot so it squeaked against the

marble floor.

"How are things going?" Lanford pulled on his earlobe and then patted his awful hair.

"Fine. Things are grand." *How're things for you, Headmaster Lanford? Having problems now that your star pupil isn't so shiny?*

"Are you sure?" He squinted at her. "Your grades aren't looking so *grand*."

Figures he'd feel the need to sit down and have a fatherly talk. She shifted her weight to her other foot and began putting her coat on. "The courses are harder this term. I'm trying to focus on learning more about my ink."

He scrunched his nose and lifted his head to stare at her from his bifocals. "You're a bright girl. I don't understand what you're trying to do to yourself." He took his glasses off and began to clean them. "Being like this isn't going to make your tatù go away. Nothing can do that."

Rae stopped zipping her jacket. He'd hit the nail on the head, something no one else had even tried to do. It didn't mean that she was ready to go all mushy and have a heart -to -heart though.

She sighed and crossed her arms. "I don't want it to go away. I'd like to learn how to use it more effectively. You know, for the good of the school and the good of mankind." *Blah, blah, blah and blah.*

"My dear," Lanford put his glasses back on their perch. "You can't undo the past."

Rae's breath caught. She finished the phrase inside her head: *the sins of the father are the sins of the son, or in this case, the daughter.*

"Are you listening to me?"

Eyes wide, she stared at the headmaster. All the anger and bitterness suddenly drained out of her, and the only emotion left behind was defeat. She started to cry. Embarrassed, she hid her face in her hands. "I-I'm s-sorry," she gulped.

"You don't need to be sorry," he said kindly. "I think you just need to let it out." He looked at her so kindly, without pity. She knew this man meant her no harm. He deserved better than just silence from her.

Rae took several slow, deep breathes and then let her thoughts out. "My mom warned me about my dad's demons. I...I wish I could change the past. Go back and make things right...fix my dad's mistakes. Make people stop looking at me like I'm a freak. That's what I'd hoped to do with my tatù, when I realized what I could do. I'd hoped to erase the fear and suspicion, to make everyone forget about my parents."

Lanford put his hands on Rae's shoulders and forced her to face him. "Don't ever be sorry for who you are, or who your parents were. Your father was brilliant and talented, despite his dark ways and your mother was a wonderful woman who sacrificed everything so you could have a better life, a better chance. That's an amazing gift."

"Yeah, and I'm screwing it all up!"

Lanford shook his head. "You've all this talent, and trust me, my dear, you haven't even begun to scratch the surface of it. After this term, you've another year at Guilder. Think about what you're going to learn and be able to do. Look at the students in class with you. Think how talented the senior boys seem by comparison. You can already do more than them. I look forward to watching you grow." He paused then gave her a hug, his goofy combover falling across his forehead. "Get rid of the baggage in your head and start concentrating on your classes. And, in this room, show everyone you are Rae Kerrigan, more than just a madman's legacy!"

Rae wiped the remaining tears from her cheeks and smiled at the headmaster. She didn't want to be constantly compared to her dad. She knew Lanford was right, she needed to let it go in order to be what she was meant to be, and she desperately wanted to be rid of her father's dark shadow. She whispered, "I'd like that."

He patted her on the shoulder, pushing her toward the door. "Oh, and ask Devon to start tutoring you again." He shook a finger at her. "I told you at the beginning of the year you'd do well to stick by that boy."

Rae nodded, but said nothing. Apologizing to Devon was going to take some serious groveling and she didn't quite know where to start. She headed out of the Oratory to meet Molly, who was waiting, impatiently, outside the dorm.

"What took so long? Lanford ask you to teach him something?" Molly stood, hands on her hips. .

"Something like that." Rae smiled a real smile, realizing how wonderful it felt to do so after being angry and hurt for so long.

The two girls walked over to Joist House. They headed up the marble stairs, and as they reached the top, Rae made a quick decision.

"Molls, can you get Julian? I need to ask Devon something."

Molly raised her eyebrows, but didn't say anything. She nodded and headed down the hall. Rae wiped sweaty palms on her jeans and lightly tapped Devon's door.

"Andy, I already told you I'm not going with you guys." Devon shouted from behind the door. "Leave me alone!"

She wasn't sure he'd be any happier to see she wasn't Andy, but Rae knocked harder anyway. She jumped back when Devon swung the door open, looking ready to cuss her out.

His eyes widened and his body language changed completely when he saw her. "What're you doing here?"

Rae froze. She hadn't planned any of this. It'd all been spur of the moment. She knew she needed to say the right words, to truly apologize to him, but at the moment she had nothing but scattered thoughts banging around her head. So she said the first thing that came to mind. "I was wondering if you wanted to head into town for dinner with me, Molly and Julian." She tried to swallow, but her mouth had turned completely dry.

"Dinner?" He sounded and looked dumbfounded, as if the word itself didn't make any sense coming from her.

"You know, we go to a restaurant, we order some food, the waitress brings it out, we eat it and then we pay the bill?" She realized sounded exactly like Molly. "Crap, that's not what I meant!" She stomped her foot. "I'm trying to apologize. I'm just really lousy at it."

Devon laughed. She wondered how much he enjoyed seeing her at odds with herself, but in the end, he must have decided to put her out of her misery. "Friends?" He smiled, his dimple winking at her from his cheek.

Rae's heart melted, like it always did when his dimple made an appearance. "Hard as this is, I'm offering a free dinner to show how sincere I am."

"FREE dinner?" He leaned behind his door. "Heck yeah! Let me grab my coat! I can hear Molly at the stairs complaining you're taking too long."

She reached out and grabbed his hand, mimicking his ink. He stared at her, surprised by the contact.

"Sorry, just need to borrow that great hearing of yours for a moment so I can hear what Molly's saying." She smiled mischievously, squeezing his hand before releasing it. "Then I can call her on it later."

Devon's smile widened slowly, as if he enjoyed soaking- in the playful mood in the air. "Sounds good." He shut his door. "I'm suddenly starving."

Rae knew him better than that. "Starving because dinner's on me?"

"You got it, fairy-girl."

Chapter 21

Deceived

RAE laughed so hard through dinner her cheeks and stomach muscles hurt. It felt good to let go of the cloud that had been hanging over her. Dinner and ice cream dessert were both a riot, and the evening was over way before Rae wanted to head back to Guilder.

Julian pulled his Jaguar into the student parking lot, and the four of them walked toward Aumbry House together.

"I hate to call it a night," Rae moaned, sandwiched between Molly and Devon, "but I've some major catching up to do. If I don't start studying, I'm going to need a real tutor." She elbowed Devon.

"We still up for a session this week?" Devon shoved his hands into his coat pockets.

"Definitely," Rae replied.

Molly shouldered Rae. "Let's go in. It's freezing."

As they turned to go, Julian touched Rae's arm. "Do you have an extra moment? Can I show you something?"

"Sure. Anything wrong?" Rae watched Molly head to the warmth inside.

"I don't think so, but I had a vision the other day. I've been trying to figure it out. As usual, I'm lousy at it." He paused then quickly added, "I think it has something to do with you." He pulled a sheet of folded paper out of his coat and handed it to her.

Rae opened it, her body shaking from the cool evening air.

The picture had been drawn in some type of charcoal or pencil. A circle lay in the center with a fairy sketched inside. Dark ghost-like figures were around the circle with an eye looking down on the sketch. The detail and tone reeked of something dark and scary.

She studied the paper for a few moments. Then realization hit her and she grinned. "When did you say you drew this?"

"Two mornings ago." Julian pulled on his ponytail. "Does it make sense to you? It's so freakin' frustrating when I can't figure out my own visions. I feel like a flippin' book sometimes: my drawings are foreshadowing bits and the reader doesn't realize it until they finish the rest of the story, only...I'm the reader!" He shook his head. "I figured if I showed you and maybe touched you so you could mimic my ink...well, maybe you could read into it somehow, figure it out."

"Oh, I know what it means." She blushed, despite the cold. "I've been going through a bit of a rough patch. I had a little -- well, more like a lot -- of self-pity. Angry at myself, at my tatù and at my family's past." She pointed at the picture. "This shows me fighting my own personal demons. The eye is probably Lanford. We talked today after class in the Oratory, and he kind of straightened me out. Maybe this vision came from Headmaster Lanford. You know, him seeing me and being worried about what was happening to me?"

Relief flooded Julian's face. "My ability's pretty difficult to read. I get these visions, and sometimes they're insignificant and other times they're huge. I'm still learning how to read them. Guilder and the Privy Council really want to work with me to learn to figure them out." He zipped his coat tighter. "Originally, I'd draw stuff that was going to happen, but things now seem to be evolving and my head's flooded with stuff."

"It sounds very challenging." Rae felt bad for him, but also glad she wasn't alone in her own personal frustrations.

He gave her a quick, friendly hug. "I'm just dumping my problems on you. Everyone here has them. None of us are perfect."

She grinned. "I'm glad you might come back next year. Maybe I can help you a bit with your ability." She shrugged, totally embarrassed by her own words. *Like this guy needs my help. You're such and idiot sometimes, Rae!* "I doubt I'll figure out anything, but if I tried to mimic your tatù, maybe we could figure out some stuff together."

"Great idea. It's definitely worth a try. It's not like I have anything to lose."

"Let's get together sometime after the spring dance. Like, when it's warmer." She stomped her feet, trying to stop the chills.

"Sounds good." He turned to go. "Thanks again for helping me with this vision. I'm glad it didn't turn out to be something terrible."

"Me, too. Have a good night." Rae folded and handed the charcoal drawing back to Julian.

He waved his hand. "Keep it. Hang it on your bulletin board beside the other one." He winked. "As a reminder you need to stay away from demons." He laughed and headed toward Joist House.

The next few weeks, Rae felt like a squirrel that'd been holed up for the winter, coming out for spring with a to-do list. She spent the time leading up to the dance working on incomplete assignments, studying and catching up. Thank goodness all her teachers were willing to work with her and she took advantage of the sympathetic looks, promising to hand in reports and labs as soon as she could. She continued meeting with Devon and focused on strengthening their friendship. With the back-log of work and keeping up with current class homework, she didn't have much time for distractions, but her time with Devon was something she wasn't willing to give up.

For the spring dance, Rae asked Molly to help her find something to wear. Molly spent an entire weekend dragging Rae through endless shops until she found the perfect one. It was a two-piece dress in a lovely pastel, and in different shades of green ranging from light to emerald. The skirt was silk with layers of chiffon. It rested just above her knees. The matching top had been designed a few shades lighter, with simple straps.

"The best part," Molly said, holding the two pieces together against Rae, "is if you lean forward, your tatù is going to show."

Hopefully Beth will see it then. Rae snorted, surprised at her own thoughts.

Molly hit her on the back. "You okay?"

Rae pretended to cough. "F-Fine."

Rae finally asked Lanford to help her figure out how she could mimic abilities. He didn't seem surprised by her request but actually, quite pleased. Everyone at the school knew what she could do now, but no one had approached her or asked for help. Lanford promised to make things interesting.

Classes in the Oratory took on a new twist – He would instruct Rae to touch a student and mimic their ability. Together, they would try to see if there was a hidden part of the tatù that the other student might not have realized yet. Each tatù seemed molded to the personality and physical attributes of the person possessing it. Most often, Rae could pick up a small talent or ability the other hadn't noticed, or vice versa. Rae loved the challenges, and some of the students who'd been shy around her began to warm up to her and feel more comfortable. There were still students who refused to touch Rae. She would occasionally catch Headmaster Lanford looking frustrated by the unwillingness of the students to cooperate, but he never pushed or forced any student to work with her. She and the other students respected him for it.

Dean Carter stood in during several of their classes, watching all the students intently, taking notes in a black leather journal he carried with him. Rae tried her best to ignore him when he came around and then avoided him after class. Ironically, he seemed to be staying away from her now, as well.

However, she knew from experience that Dean Carter was anything but predictable. So she wasn't entirely surprised when after Friday's class while she zipped shut her backpack, Carter came to speak to her.

"Ms Kerrigan, nice job again today. It's interesting to see how you're able to teach others to use their abilities more precisely. Your father was never able to show others how to improve their skills. He kept the advancements to himself." He made a note in his little black book and turned on his heel.

Rae watched him leave, her mouth gaping open. Had he actually just paid her a compliment? And what did he know about her father? He acted as if he'd personally been with her father and shared his skill, despite the fact that she and Devon had found no connection in their research. But then, so much was secret and unknown. No one could really say who had been a part of it and who hadn't. The thought made her stomach turn. The loser probably was her dad's biggest fan. Like the kind of groupie that kept scrapbooks and freaky stuff from serial killers in prison. Rae shuddered at the thought. Thankfully, Molly yelled for her to hurry up and all thoughts of the dean were pushed aside.

Molly said she needed Maria's help to get Rae's hair done for Saturday evening, which made her curious. But it wasn't until the morning of the dance, when Molly pinned a poster of Tinker Bell beside the mirror, determined to create an exact copy that Rae began to get nervous.

"I'm jumping in the shower before you get to work," Rae said after they'd come back from breakfast. She ran out the door before Molly could stop her.

She needed a moment to herself, knowing that having both Molly and Maria touching her at the same time was going to be chaotic at best. The few minutes of peace with the running shower faucet turned out to be short lived.

"Rae Kerrigan!" Molly shouted, the heavy wooden bathroom door slamming shut perfectly timed against her yell. The noise echoed off the tiled bathroom walls. "Get out of the shower! I have the perfect idea for your hair tonight. Are you willing to walk to on the wild side?"

Rae shut the taps off and peered around the curtain. "What do you have in mind?" She did feel a bit edgy this morning. Maybe she could be up for whatever Molly had in store.

Molly held up a hair coloring kit and pointed at it. "I'm going to give you blond highlights."

Rae stared at her roommate and played with a wet, dark lock. *Would Devon notice? Wait… would BETH notice?* Rae grinned, unable to contain her glee at the possibility of making Devon's ex jealous. Her face took on a wicked and playful expression. "I'm in."

Molly blow dried Rae's hair and then went to work. They sang along to Molly's iPod and Maria came in to help and speed the process up. After jumping in the shower again to wash everything, Rae patiently let Molly blow dry her hair. The large chunks of blonde blended almost magically with her dark, curly hair. Molly had left the bottom back part dark, saying it would look totally awesome when Rae put her hair in a ponytail.

"It's amazing, Molls." Rae couldn't stop staring at herself in the mirror, loving what she saw.

"I told you it would totally suit you." Molly grinned before bending over and grabbing a bunch of stuff out of her bag. She dumped hundreds of different bits and pieces of hair things and ordered Maria to grab the Tinkerbelle poster and hang it up in the bathroom instead. Maria winked at Rae and then disappeared down the hall to their room. She was back moments later and waited for Molly's next command. Rae heard Maria giggling inside her head and had to avert to her eyes to avoid bursting out laughing. Molly had done a fantastic job coloring but didn't, for one moment, stop talking.

"You planned this all, didn't you?" Rae asked two hours later, trying to sit still as a pin poked her scalp. They'd all dressed and were just finishing up with their hair.

"Ob coursthe." Molly said with a mouth full of hair pins.

Rae grinned, actually excited about going to the dance. "You're one very imaginative girl, Molly Skye, and I'm glad we got to room together this year."

"Me, too, but I have to admit I'm looking forward to moving upstairs next year and having my own room. You talk a lot in your sleep."

"You snore like a wood chipper."

"I do not." Molly put her hands on her hips. "...Do I?"

Before Rae could answer back, Madame Elpis shouted up the stairs that it was time to get moving. The guys' bus had already left ten minutes ago and many of the seniors were driving their own cars. Molly added a few more pins to Rae's head and gave a single sweep to her always perfect looking hair. Then the girls headed down the marble stairs.

The drive to Roe Hampton took about twenty minutes. The girls were giddy by the time they arrived, and were giggling when they walked into Roe Hampton's gymnasium.

"Ladies, you arrive at last." Andy spread his arms out to greet them. All the senior boys had dressed in tuxedos. Andy wore a polka-dot bow-tie.

"Nice dickiebow," Haley snorted.

Rae glanced around the room for Devon. She spotted him talking to Beth, and her light mood of the moment before was instantly dark. She strained to hear what they were talking about, but could barely make out their conversation over the music. Beth looked beautiful and mature, in a Victorian-style dress. Rae suddenly felt very childish in her Tinker Bell outfit. It felt more like a silly costume now.

"Why the long face?" Riley stood beside her. "Dance with me and let me put a smile there." He took Rae's arm and, without waiting for a response, led her to the dance floor. "You're gorgeous tonight, as you are every night. But I really like the hair." He pulled a blonde curl and watched it bounce back into place.

"Thanks," Rae muttered when they started to dance. Her plan had been to make Devon see her differently, but he couldn't be bothered to even glance her way. She remained quiet for the rest of the song and let Riley ramble on, barely paying attention to what he said. She did refocus when she heard Riley mention Devon's name.

"Crazy Dev...Hard to believe, isn't it?" Riley quipped.

"Pardon? What did you say?"

"I said, It's nice to see Devon and Beth together again. They're on the dance floor all cozy and lost in each other's eyes. It's hard to believe, isn't it?"

"I hadn't heard they were back together." Rae felt sick to her stomach. After the past few months of her rebel phase, she hadn't paid any attention to what was going on with Devon. If it didn't involve her grades, assignments or the two of them together, she hadn't bothered to ask or care. Why had she focused so hard on their friendship? She really liked the guy but had never stood a chance with him romantically and she hated herself for not realizing it sooner. The bitterness of disappointment churned in her stomach and the blood drained from her head.

"You all right?" Riley stopped dancing and stared at her with concern. His cheetah tatù making her feel even dizzier. "You look a little green. Do you feel sick?" He took a slight step back, but held onto her wrists.

"A little..." She suddenly felt like this was the last place on earth she wanted to be. *What a stupid idea this was.*

"Do you need some punch?" He glanced over at Devon then back at her. "Or do you want to go back to Guilder? I have my car and can drive you home."

"I don't want you to miss the dance," she argued weakly.

"Don't worry. Let me drive you back, and I can head back here after I know you're all right. Just say the word." Riley squeezed her wrist.

Going back to the dorm sounded better than staying here watching Devon and Beth fall back in love. She'd vomit all over the dance floor if she had to watch that.

She stared across the room one last time, silently begging Devon to turn her way. Instead, she felt the bracelet he'd given her slip off her wrist, like a sign telling her to give up. She bent down to pick it up, and heard gasps behind her. Remembering her outfit had been designed to show off her tatù if she bent over, she straightened as fast as she could and pulled the back of her top down with lightning speed. She could hear the whispers from the Roe Hampton girls and saw Beth, a smug look on her face, lean over to whisper to a surprised Devon. Rae grabbed Riley's arm, not paying any attention to the smirk on his face.

"Let's go." She pulled him toward the exit.

"Hold up." Riley stopped just outside. "I gotta tell Molly I'm bringing you back. If any of the professors ask, Molly can explain."

The fresh air offered nothing to cool her burning face. She could feel a headache starting at the back of her head, creeping its way to the front. Riley raced back out of the large metal doors and helped her into his car. She sat in the passenger seat and covered her face with her hands as he drove.

Rae didn't glance up until she felt the car roll to a stop and felt the car rock when Riley got out. She lifted her head, and had to blink, surprised to see they were parked in front of the Main Building. Riley opened her door to help her out.

"What're we doing here? Are the gates locked or something?" Rae tried to focus, the headache putting dots in front of her vision.

"No. Dean Carter asked me to bring you here." Riley's answer came out curt.

"Carter?" *Just freakin' great! What a topper to a screwed up evening.*

Riley grabbed her hand and pulled her toward the building door, kicking it open with his foot.

"Let go!" She tried to shaking her arm free. "Riley, you're hurting me. I don't want to see Dean Carter tonight. I just want to go back to my room."

"Sorry, but you need to see the dean. Right now." Riley continued to pull her up the stairs.

Too ticked to resist him, she jerked her arm free. "Fine, but this had better be quick." She stomped up the stairs, passing Riley and barging into the dean's office. She didn't even bother to knock. She was too angry to worry about being polite.

Dean Carter stood leaning against his desk. He'd been checking his watch. He smiled when he saw Rae and Riley come into the room.

"Well done," he said, clapping his hands slowly, making her head ache with each loud, percussive clap.

Rae opened her mouth and then glanced at Riley.

"Thanks." Riley puffed his chest. "It was easy. I just told Kerrigan the Wardell boy was back with his old Roe Hampton bit-girl. Kerrigan fell for it." He snickered. "She hesitated, but I slipped the stupid bracelet he bought her off her wrist. Suddenly, she was more determined than me to leave. She feigned being sick, and now the entire school thinks I'm taking her back to her dorm room." His face and shoulders bunched in excitement. Rae felt nauseous when she realized how easily she had been tricked.

"Fine." Carter flipped his wrist to dismiss Riley. "Go to Rae's dorm room. Make her bed look like it's been slept in and then grab her backpack and throw some clothes in it. Make it look like she's gone somewhere purposely. Then go back to the dance and let everyone know, especially Lanford, that she's resting."

"Yes, sir." Riley turned and headed out of the room, closing the door behind him.

Rae watched Riley leave. She was completely shocked at what had just occurred, but the pieces all slid into place in her mind. This had been planned. Dean Carter wanted to be alone with her. For what reason?

She turned to eye him cautiously, jerking back in surprise when she found his face hovered only inches away from hers.

Great...what do I do now?

Chapter 22

Destiny

"WHAT DO YOU WANT FROM ME?" Rae whispered, taking another step back.

Dean Carter grabbed Rae's arm. Instantly visions of his life began appearing behind her eyelids as if she were watching them live. She stood frozen. She couldn't have moved if she wanted to.

She saw a younger version of the dean, in this very room, standing with her father, making a pact to screw the greater good of mankind. Another vision popped in to show Dean Carter and her father, a few years older, arguing. It became clear that Simon intended to use his ability to make them more than just powerful-- to run the British government and let the world know about the abilities their tatùs gave them. They were going to terrify the world; force everyone to follow them, for their own safety and protection, they mocked.

The visions stopped. Shocked, Rae stared, open

mouthed, at Dean Carter. "You worked with *my* father?"

The Dean straightened as if he'd been slapped. "I was once your father's friend. Things changed."

"Whatever." Rae let her eyes slide toward the closed door and took a step toward it.

"No, my dear," Dean Carter said. "You aren't going anywhere for a bit." He moved around her and blocked the entrance.

Rae shook her head. *This can't be happening.*

The dean leaned in closer, his breath hot against her face, making her shudder. "You know, I'm not the bad guy. I'm the one actually on your side. We need to get you somewhere safe."

"Out of this room and away from you seems my safest option." Rae clenched her teeth, thinking back over the evening. "You had Riley trick and drag me out of the dance and –"

"Something's going to happen tonight. The Privy Council believes you are in danger. Riley wants a job, so he's willing to do anything it takes."

"Riley's an idiot." *And so are you if you think I'm going to believe you.*

"I'll explain things better once we get you away from here. My car's in the parking lot." He opened the door and turned around to motion at Rae with his hand. "Come on now. We haven't much time."

Rae opened her mouth to protest but not got further than the "O" shape of her mouth. A large piece of wood rose above the dean's head and came crashing down on the top of it. He crumpled to the ground and slumped forward.

With wide eyes, Rae watched a familiar looking cane push the dean's arm out of the way. Headmaster Lanford appeared in the door way, out of breath.

"A-Are you a-alright?" He took one look at her and tapped his cane against the ground. "What did he say to you?"

Rae glanced from the motionless dean to the headmaster and back down again. "Nothing. But I think you need to call the cops." She scurried around to his side, avoiding all contact with the dean's prone form.

Lanford slipped his arm around her and with an iron grip, pulled her across the waiting area. "I'm glad I got here in time."

"Thank goodness." Rae reached for the handle of the exit door when they came to it.

"No, dear." The headmaster pulled her closer to him, his hand covered in the material of his jacket. He didn't seem to want to touch her. "We need to let them think you've left but the safest place is through that door." He pointed to an ancient looking oak door that obviously led to the other tower room. "Let's get you in there and I'll explain everything."

He opened the door and led Rae through. The room was round like the dean's office, but about four stories high with no windows except near the top. Round with nothing in it but a flat screen TV hooked up to a laptop on a very small table.

Rae walked over the rough, cobbled floor to the laptop. "What's this for?"

"Move back a bit and I'll show you." The headmaster stood behind her.

Rae pressed back against the wall so Lanford could get by. He stood in front, facing her. "Let's get this sorted." He lifted his arm and flicked his hand.

Rae jumped when a pair of cold clamps locked around her wrist. She started down in surprise. "What the --?"

Confused, Rae watched as an evil grin split Lanford's face, transforming him completely from the kind and protective man she thought she had come to know, into a total stranger. This scary figure made her heart race with fear. It reminded her of... her father. Before she had the chance to even raise her arms to protect herself, Lanford used his tatù to slam her back against the wall, cracking her head against the rough, ancient brick. She blacked out.

When she came to, her head throbbing like a bass drum, she reached to rub the back of her head, only to realize her hand couldn't get her arms that far. She'd been shackled with metal chains screwed into the wall on the other side of the room. Lanford sat close by, doing his typical invisible chair routine.

"What're you doing?" Rae blinked trying to clear her head. "You're on my side. The dean's the one..." She paused remembering him saying that he wasn't the bad guy. Her brain rushed to bring back all the encounters she'd had with the dean and Lanford, seeing everything in a new light. Her head felt as if it were spinning, and not from the lump on the back of her head.

Something inside the headmaster changed. His face scrunched and he glared at her. "I've been at this bloody school longer than one man should have to. I helped your father as a student and what does he do? He turns his back on me. Leaves me here to rot with promises that he'll come back." Lanford's mouth pressed tight and he shook his head. "We devised a plan and what happens? He goes and gets himself killed."

"My mother –"

Lanford lunged forward off his perch shouting "Your mother ruined everything!" He took a deep breath, then two, calming himself and patting his riotous combover. Lanford carefully straightened his waistcoat and said with incongruent calm, "But now I have you...someone with your father's ability."

Rae couldn't wrap her head around the idea that this man she had trusted had been deceiving her all this time, yet it was true. The cold metal chains were irrefutable truth. "You can't keep me locked up in here. People are looking for me."

The headmaster tsked. "No one's going to look tonight. Your roommate will think you're with Riley and, by tomorrow, it won't matter as I'll have you convinced to work with me." He smiled wickedly, his combover falling out of place. He looked like he'd gone mad. *From Dr. Jekyll to Mr. Hyde...*

"Your father and I devised this intriguing plan before he died. Now, you will help me complete HOC."

"HOC? What, is that some file or something?" Rae shook her head. "I'll never help you finish something my father started." Rae pulled herself from off the ground. "You can go screw yourself!"

The headmaster slapped her face with a gust of air, not touching her with his hand. He smirked and stayed out of her reach, making it impossible for her to fight back or protect herself. In an oddly sing-song voice, Lanford continued talking as if they were politely discussing the weather. "You have your father's impatience. He killed many good men too quickly because of that little angry streak of his. That's something we'll have to remedy in you." Lanford checked his watch and then straightened his jacket and tie.

"I need to make an appearance at the dance, so I'll leave you." Rae started to retort, but Lanford held up a hand, pushing air directly at her face, causing her body to instinctively react, closing off her airways. She doubled over trying to force her lungs to take in oxygen. He continued talking as if they were having a normal conversation. "Don't worry. I shall return in a short while. In the meantime, watch the videos and take mental notes. These are skills I'll be requiring of you. Watch it, *and* listen closely."

Frustration and anger roiled inside of her. She felt guilty, for having suspected the dean all this time, when really the danger had been much closer to her. She remembered her meeting with the dean in his tower office at the beginning of the school year. "I'll get out of here. These rooms are round and you're...the devil. You can't trap me in a corner," she hissed.

Lanford laughed at her. "Kerrigan, you're already trapped. What're you doing to do? Vision your way out of the room? You've got Carter's tatù and it's useless. You have no 'fuel' to use. It was your father's one weakness, one I plan to liberally exploit in you." He paused, pointing to the floor. "There are a few bottles of water within reach for you. Don't overdo it as you'll have to wet yourself if you need to go. That's always the first thing to go with you females and I'm not cleaning up any mess." He gave her a fond, almost fatherly smile, causing her stomach to turn. *He's insane...he's got to be insane...and I've trusted him all this time!*

Rae glanced to where he'd pointed and heard the dull click of the door as it locked. He'd moved and disappeared faster than she thought he could. She wondered if anyone knew he could move so quickly. *Probably not. He seems to be great at hiding things. Jerk.*

She stayed where she was, propped up against the cool wall, waiting to see if the headmaster would come back. She jerked when the laptop monitor flickered and the flat screen turned the semi-dark room an eerie blue color. A video began to play. She listened as the narrator explained that it was an instructional video.

A lifespan is spent seeking success and happiness. One chases after dreams, careers, ambitions, faith, partners and money; all in the hope of finding the success and contentment they so long for. The only place we need to search is within ourselves. Our inner powers will move us forward - we must show the world our tatùs. Our capabilities and potential are far greater than anything man has ever done, or will do. We are above mankind -- above the law which rules over them.

That voice...something about that voice. What was it?

Why did it tickle her memory? Her heart stopped when she realized the narrator was her father. Rae dropped the floor in the middle of the room and hugged her knees to her chest, trying to protect herself from the memories. His voice reminded her only of the time he'd been so mean and scared her as a child. She'd trusted him, because he was her father, but he'd turned on her that night. She began to cry. She'd trusted the headmaster completely and he... he... she couldn't even finish her train of thought. She'd never suspected any of this.

She felt so lost, so afraid and bloody cold. She had iron shackles on her wrists and the ancient, heavy metal chains felt like ice as they rubbed against her legs and arms. The entire room was cold, and her Tinker Bell outfit wasn't made to promote warmth. Her thin jacket didn't help much, either. Her teeth chattered as tears coursed down her cheeks.

How did she get into this mess? Her uncle's words screamed back at her: *the sins of the father are the sins of the son. You can't undo the past, Rae.*

She curled into the fetal position on the cold marble. Her foot bumped against something, and with dismay, Rae realized she'd knocked over one of the bottles of water. She felt wetness against her shoe and quickly realized the marble floor wouldn't absorb any of the liquid.

Swearing, she scooted over as much as the shackles would allow. She was already shivering. The last thing she needed was to slip into hypothermia too. She could hear the video with her father's voice telling her she could be part of a bigger picture, a new dream for the world with endless opportunities, yet she saw no great potential in this situation. *How freakin' ironic.*

Her uncle had been right; no one was going to come save her. Her only freedom would be death, the same choice her mother had made. She'd sacrificed everything to stop her father. Rae wondered if maybe she'd need to do the same thing in order to stop Lanford.

What can I do? Her ability was useless right now. Mimicking Carter wasn't going to help her escape. Rae banged her head on the floor, trying to come up with something – *anything* that would give her a glimmer of hope. The ache in her heard made her gasp, but it was preferable to her inner pain. At least it was real and tangible. She thought about her friends and immediately Devon came to mind. *I'm such an IDIOT for believing Riley. Devon's not back with Beth.* She'd been such a dummy. She needed to find a way to protect him.

Rae cringed as she remembered the picture Julian had shown her. He'd been convinced the vision meant she'd been in danger. The sketch was about right now, not about her chasing after her own personal demons. *Wait...it was about now...right now...* She shuddered at a realization. *Those were real demons, the ghost of her father, in a round room... What was with the eye of Carter watching me?* He actually had said he was on her side.

She abruptly sat up. *The eye...watching me...* She looked up, squinting trying to see if there were any video cameras watching her every move. She was pretty sure there would be. She strained, trying to force her eyes to focus on the dimly lit ceiling. It felt like she was trapped in the tower of London, with King Henry VIII about to execute her. She wished she had Devon's tatù right then. His night-vision would allow him to clearly see that high up in the dark. She squinted again and began to pick out a small, flashing red light. She knew immediately it was a camera, and it was recording her every move. The knowledge brought her no comfort.

How long before Lanford comes back? She thought about how disappointed her mother would have been with this end, how brief her life was and how little she had done with it. That thought brought fresh tears to her eyes. *Oh Mom...it's not fair! Why should we have to sacrifice ourselves to stop the bad people? I grew up without you and now I have to die to save the freakin' world?* But what choice did she have? She was all alone, and no one was going to save her. She'd never finish her father's work like Lanford wanted, she refused to even consider it. What she'd seen in his visions of her father was enough to show her that she was nothing like him.

She cued back into reality in when the voice on the screen stopped. The video was over, but the bloody thing had automatic playback, she could hear it resetting itself, all the little bits and chips in the laptop were zipping and whirring, doing their jobs.

She didn't want to watch it again, but how could she possibly stop it? She closed her eyes, leaning her head against the stone wall, and tried to think of nothing. She tried to block out everything and bury all emotions.

I am totally, completely screwed, she thought with a snort. Suddenly, thoughts of Nicholas filled her mind. He would have known how to MacGyver his way out of these shackles with a paper clip and then opened the locked, ancient iron door. *Yep, Nicholas and his amazing paperclip!* Rae barked a laugh and wiped the tears from her eyes, trying to calm her crazed mind. She needed to focus on what she could do to stop this.

I could use the shackles to strangle myself. All I'd have to do is cross my arms and pull tight... She felt no fear of dying, she didn't mind killing herself, especially if it meant saving others. Her mother had made the same sacrifice, so she could be at least as brave as her mother had been. Except, deep down Rae didn't want to die. She wanted to live! To learn to use her gift for good, to right the wrongs, to finish school, fall in love and experience a first kiss. She was a sixteen-year-old girl, for goodness' sake! Rae rolled her head from side to side as the video began to play again, trying to deny the reality of it.

Her father's voice grated on her nerves like sandpaper.

She tried to tune it out, but it only made the humming inside of her louder, and her headache worse.

Tapping her foot against the marble floor to dispel the tension building inside, she tried to cover her ears, even the clanking of the chains couldn't block the sound out.

"Shut up!" she screamed, bellowing straight from her gut. She yelled it again and again. "Shut up! Shut up! You were never my father. You were just a monster. You told me monsters were real, and I believed you. How could I've ever known you were the worst monster of them all? What kind of father would want their child to grow up evil? What kind of man were you and how did my mom ever love you?"

She wished she had Molly's gift and, for a brief second, she pretended she did, knowing the exactly how Molly's ink felt inside her. She threw her arm in the direction of the laptop and flicked her fingers, as if to throw a bolt of electricity into the laptop and the screen to fry them.

Blue jagged lines erupted from her fingers and made a bee line for the laptop. It sparked and hissed, the smell of burnt plastic immediately filling the air. The screen blacked out. The sudden silence was deafening.

That silence screamed the truth to Rae.

Chapter 23

Your Destiny

UNABLE to stop staring at the now fried computer, Rae made a conscious effort to close her mouth. *Holy...! What...?* She stood and started to pace with the shackles on her arms. Two steps one way and then backward two steps was all the room she had, but it was her mind that needed the space and it was clearing faster by the second.

I used Molly's gift. I killed the laptop, but how? I haven't touched Molly in hours. I'm supposed to have Dean Carter's ability.

Rae suddenly froze on the spot as the enormity of what had just happened hit her full force.

Woah...I killed the laptop. I don't have Carter's ability...why not? Or do I?

Realizing she didn't have time for *why not*, Rae focused on how to use this new-found information to free herself. *Okay, what do I know for sure?*

I know I used someone's tatù without touching them. Or out of order.

Wait, Rae cocked her head to the side, trying to break

242

down the truth into its most basic form. Occam's Razor, "the simplest explanation is most likely the correct one." *Okay, if I thought I could only use the tatù of the last person I touched, yet I used Molly's ability out of order, I must be wrong. So then...*Rae swung her leg around in a partial semi-circle, dragging the sole of her shoe against the cobbled floor as she tried to consider what exactly the opposite of her wrong assumption would be. *Can I use anyone's tatù who I've touched, whenever I like?* An excited breath seized in her throat as she realized the only way to know would be to test the theory.

She tapped her foot, trying to think of someone else's ink she understood deeply. Healing – she could get rid of her headache and the goose egg on the back of her head. She closed her eyes and tried to find the slightly-unfamiliar hum inside of her. Once found, she fed it, nurtured it until it became more than just a memory in her veins. The hum spread through her body. Finally, she could think more clearly, without the murky cloud of pain hovering over her. She touched the back of her head and grinned. *No bump.* Rae resumed her pacing.

Devon's ink came to mind next, along with his image and she instantly felt nauseous all over again. *How could I be so stupid?* Taking a deep breathe to dispel the sick feeling in her stomach, she promised herself she would see him again. *But for now, I have work to do.* She forced him out of her mind so she could concentrate. She realized she must've used his ability when squinting to see the recording camera in the dim light. *Damn! The camera!* She stopped pacing and stared up at it. Lanford might be watching even now and would have seen what she'd just done.

But what exactly have I done? Maybe...maybe there's nothing to see on the camera but me acting crazy. Little bits of hope trickled through her as she tried to focus. *There's got to be something I can do without getting caught on camera.* She sorted through the classes she had in the Oratory this term -- thinking about everyone she had worked with. It was an uphill battle because everything reminded her of how much Lanford understood her ability and wanted to nurture it. *Nurture my ass. He wanted it working at full force for when he needed to use me to his benefit and no one else's, not even mine.*

A deep breath in and out helped fortify her. *Let it go,. Focus on the problem at hand.* She stood still, legs akimbo, pondering everything. She twirled a blonde strand of hair over and over through her fingers. Her ink was stronger than her father's, just like her mother had said. *I'm not my father, I'm nothing like him. I have to get out of here so I can prove it to the world.* "Now how am I going to do that?" she asked herself aloud.

She leaned back against the cold wall and slid down, bumping into another bottle of water, catching it before it fell. She was immediately reminded of Craig as she felt a few drops spill onto her hand. Craig was able to change water into different forms. Rae leaned forward and rolled the water bottle away from her, letting it leave a trail of liquid along the way. She did the same for the remaining bottle as well. Making sure it was toward the door, not near her. She closed her eyes and leaned back against the wall again, waiting for the hum to start. She remembered the feeling inside of her from Craig's tatù. She searched for it inside of herself. When she found it, she leaned forward and brought a finger toward the water. It instantly turned to ice. She could even hear the crackle as it froze against the marble. She didn't think it was going to help, but at least she was able to draw on another skill if she needed it. And with the color of the marble she thought it couldn't be visible to the camera.

She shivered with cold as she tried to think of a way to get the shackles off her wrists. She rubbed her hands together, trying to think of all the gifts she'd mimicked.

Nicholas' ink would be useful, but she had nothing to work with except the bracelet from Devon, and that was obviously going to be a last resort. She thought about shape-shifting, but being a wolf or a bird wasn't going to get her out of the room. She needed something smaller, something more petite, something which would allow her to slip through the shackles...GALE!

Just as Rae closed her eyes to catch Gale's ability, a heavy slamming muffled against the other side of the wall. A very angry, and apparently alive, Carter hollered at Lanford.

"You bugger! You've been playing her since day one!" Another loud crashing echoed through the door of her prison. Lanford was obviously using his ability against Carter. Rae pressed herself back against the wall. Nothing could come flying through the ancient brick walls but it still didn't stop her from flinching. Still feeling the hum of Gale's ability, she changed only her hands and feet, focusing until the shackles slipped off her wrists and clanged to the floor. She carefully slipped her misshapen feet out of their shackles and focused on changing both her hands and feet back to normal. When done, she let out a relived sigh, thankful that nothing had gone wrong in the process. At the same time another piece of furniture burst into a million pieces on the other side of the wall.

"You know nothing!" Lanford hissed. "You obviously have no idea what she is capable of or who she can hurt."

"She's not going to hurt anyone. Guilder's supposed to protect her, not use her!" Several grunts and scraping noises followed. "Now, where did you hide her, old man?"

Rae, avoiding the ice, ran to the door and began pounding on the heavy oak. Her fists barely made a sound on the dense, almost fossilized wood. "I'm in here! Help me! I'm here," she yelled.

More fighting and grunting ensued from the other side of the door. Rae knew they probably hadn't heard her.

Carter fought outmatched anyway. Even if he had heard her pounding on the door and calling out, Lanford's ability could toss the dean in the air like a rag doll. He didn't stand a chance.

Shoulders slumped, Rae edged back to the spot by the chains and slid to the floor, hugging her knees. Head tucked between her legs, she wished this was a bad dream and it would all just end.

The scraping sound of the rusty dead bolt brought her head up. She held her breath as it swung open.

Lanford, his combover now looking like a bad wig and his clothes completely ripped and covered in red smudges and dirt, looked furious. He glared at her, then the TV screen, then back at her. "The video obviously doesn't work." He didn't sound nearly as angry about it as she had expected he would, which surprised her.

Rae kept her eyes on him, wondering what the heck he was going to do, but tried to focus on an ink that could match his ability. *His own.* She let the hum fill her body and grow familiar inside her. Then she thought one ink better and had to fight to keep the triumphant smile from breaching her lips. *Oh yeah...Mr. Fluffy Bad-Hair is going down...*

He moved just inside the doorway.

Right where I want you... "Take one step closer and I'll burn you and this building down like my mother roasted Simon." Rae had no idea how her mother's ability worked, but she figured those words would be enough to stop him in his tracks and Lanford had no idea of what her capabilities truly were anyway. She was betting he didn't have the guts to call her bluff.

It worked, for a moment, at least until Lanford pulled a gun out of his jacket pocket and pointed it at her. "You may have some hidden talents, but I have five hidden friends inside of this." He jiggled the gun in his palm, just to make sure she didn't misunderstand his poorly chosen pun. "You move and I'll send all five of them out to meet you."

Seriously bad joke, but that gun isn't funny. What now? Rae hesitated. She couldn't think of any tatù that could stop one bullet, let alone the five that would fly in her direction if she pushed him. She knew she could heal relatively small and internal injuries, but she had no idea if it could save her from the damage caused by bullets, or if it would work fast enough. What if she went unconscious? Would the tatù still work? She didn't know. *Of all the questions I really should have asked in class...this is the one that comes back to bite me in the butt? Really?!?!_* Her internal turmoil aside, she knew now wasn't the time to test the far flung theory hoping she'd be alright.

Wow, kinda wish I'd thought this through a little more...

"Did you think you'd be able to get away, Kerrigan?"

Well, kinda...yeah. But she knew now wasn't the time for her smart mouth. She decided to let him keep talking. *The longer he yacks, the longer I live to try to get myself out of here.*

"For ten bloody years I served your father. For another ten years I had to wait for you to turn sixteen. You think I just sat and twiddled my thumbs while I waited? That I didn't take the time to think about what you might become or what monster you might turn into that would be different than your father?" Lanford paused for dramatic effect and Rae knew he was about to go on the attack, but she stood completely unprepared for it when it came. Physical blows she might have been able to deal with, but Lanford's chosen weapon was her own insecurities. Like a passive-aggressive parent, he dug into her psychological wounds with unerring accuracy.

"Everyone here is terrified of you."

No. Don't listen to him. He lies.

"You're never going to be accepted anywhere you go."

NO. I won't let him turn me inside out! Rae felt a curious sensation, a warmth and strength like fire-cured steel filled her up, blossoming from her heart to her fingers and down to her toes. She didn't know what it meant, but she knew it meant something good.

Lanford, ranted on, completely unaware of the change. "The sooner you realize that, the sooner you can see what I have to offer you is your freedom, and the power to make those fools serve you. Wake up and see your destiny!"

The crazed light in his eyes gave Rae pause. But she was done cowering from him. "I have a hard time believing you're my destiny. I don't follow assholes."

Rae heard someone's voice hollering from the stairwell. "They're up here!" Riley. Riley had called for help. Her heart leapt with joy. *Go Cheetah-boy!*

Lanford glanced over his shoulder and then took another step toward Rae, gun aimed at her heart. "Fight with me or die. You choose."

Rae lowered her head, glaring at him from under her lashes, and squared her shoulders. She spoke evenly, precisely, wanting to make sure there would be absolutely no misunderstanding. *If these are my last words, this asshat is going to* hear *them.*

"I would rather die, than be even one-tenth of what my father was." She shut her eyes and inhaled slowly, trying to focus on the waiting bullet. *Let it come, I have hope.*

The gun fired with a percussive boom, amplified by the acoustics in the round stone room, making her ears ring so loudly no other noise could have been heard.

Despite the noise, Rae was ready and she exhaled a breath, thinking of Haley and hoping the gust might curve the bullet away from her. She had the tatù's power zipping through her veins, had made sure she had it ready, but she had no idea if her crazy plan would work or not, until she felt the bullet's wind brush by her hair and the dull crushing sound against the old stone, an impact more felt than heard. Little bits of wall pelted her back and scattered to the floor. At the same time, she felt the vibration of something large hitting the floor hard and clumsily.

Then, there came a noise Rae had never heard before -- a very dull, but thick, cracking sound, heard even through the ringing in her ears. She peered through her half-closed eyes and saw Lanford on the ground. The scene made no sense at first. It took a moment or two for her understand what she was seeing.

He must have slipped on the ice. Rae's eyes opened wider when she saw a pool of blood begin forming around his head. He didn't move and the gun lay by the door.

She didn't know what to do. Part of her screamed that he was dead, another part told her to check to see if he might still be alive. *Fight or flight...Fight or flight...*played over and over inside her mind. *Just freakin' run!!* But she stood frozen in place, and everything seemed to move in slow motion, sounds coming to her as if from under water while her heart raced. Her ears rang like cymbals and her head pounded. *I must be in shock...is that what this is? Or am I dead? Dead, too?*

She heard and felt nothing, almost like she wasn't really there. Afterwards, she couldn't have said how long she'd stood there, acting a zombie; there but not there; her body a sort of place holder for something that had said "brb" and left.

Sound came back slowly, but it returned before anything else did. She heard something...something familiar, but her eyes were fixed on the body lying before her. Gradually, the sound became words, and then the words became a voice she could understand.

"Rae. Rae! Come here. Walk around the body but don't touch him. Come over here by me." Dean Carter's urgent voice beckoned her. The thought *why not* whispered through her foggy mind.

She let her eyes trail away slowly from the body to the dean, his face full of concern, but the pull to stare at Lanford won and she couldn't stop her gaze from fixing on him again. "Is he...dead?" she whispered, still afraid to move.

"I need to check his vitals, but I'm not doing anything until you're out of the room and safe."

Safe...he wants me safe. The dean? Wait, but he's bad, isn't he? Rae's mind continued to futilely trying to put coherent thought together. It took momentous effort on her part. A warning finally got through to her brain, telling her lungs they'd forgotten to breathe, and she sucked in a long, noisy breath. The rush of oxygen flowing into her body was just what she needed, so she did it again. But somehow, she lost control of it after that and began hyperventilating. She knew she had to slow her breathing, but the rush of oxygen felt like a welcome relief and at least her brain had started working again.

She forced words out between her heaving. "Wh-What about Riley? Is h-he outside?" Still unsure if leaving the room was her safest option, Rae's feet refused to budge.

"Riley's a good guy. He works for me. For the Privy Council." He beckoned her with his hand, gently but firmly, a perfect counter-balance to her terror. "Come now. Let's get you a blanket. Your teeth are chattering. You've got goose bumps the size of mountains."

Great. Hyperventilating, freezing my ass off, trying not to die...and the icky Dean is the hero? This has been a night I'll never forget. Rae edged toward the dean, small hesitant steps between gasps for air and violent shivers, keeping her back pressed against the circular stone wall until she reached the door. *Where's a freakin' paper bag when you need one?* Then the dean pushed her behind him into the reception area, slung a rescue blanket over her shoulders and forced her to look him in the eye.

"Stay here. Don't go anywhere. We need to talk." He turned and stepped into the room, slamming the door shut.

Chapter 24

Why me?

RAE stood in the middle of the reception room. Strangers bustled around, whispering and pointing to the closed door, and then to her. Someone had called 999 and an ambulance was en route. Riley been hovering nervously by her side for a while. She wasn't sure how she got there, but she ended up in front of the leaded windows. Resting her forehead against the cool glass, she stared out.

"Rae," Riley said, politely keeping his distance for once. "I'm sorry I had to be such a jerk before. It's just... It's just that I really want this job. I had to prove to Carter and... well, you know."

She glanced at him from the corner of her eye. "I know what? That you betrayed me? That you lied to get me here, where I almost died? That Lanford worked for my father? That he planned this whole stinkin' thing and wanted me here to finish some stupid file my dad started?" She paused when Riley's eyes grew as big as his open mouth. He obviously knew nothing either. She should care that she'd just given him information, considering she hadn't really decided for herself which side he was on, but then again... She shrugged and turned back to the window. "Whatever. Thanks for getting help, but it doesn't erase the rest. You're gone after this year and I hope I never have to see your stupid face again."

"For what it's worth, I'm sorry." Riley reached out and touched the blanket on her shoulder. "Not everything was an act."

He dropped his arm and straightened when the door to the prison tower room opened. Carter stepped through, spoke quietly to the paramedics and then came over to the window.

"That'll be all for now, Riley," he said. "Pack your stuff from the dorms and one of the drivers will take you to the training center."

Rae watched several professors and students crowd into a small area of the parking lot. Molly, Maria, Haley, Julian, Andy and Devon were down there waiting. *All my friends...* "How's Lanford?"

"He's in bad shape. Seems you had a slip of luck." He paused before speaking quietly, "Lanford cracked his head, and it looks like he's broken his neck."

Good. A twinge of guilt settled in Rae's stomach, but she quickly squelched it. *He's the monster, I do not have to feel sorry for him,* "Can we get out of here?" She felt trapped inside the reception room and wanted to get outside where her friends were.

"Of course." Carter pointed to two chairs in the corner. "But first, we need to talk."

Rae glanced longingly at the window to her friends below, but realized she had a few questions for two-faced Carter. She'd seen enough psycho-ness for one night, and she intended to get to the bottom of it. She led the way to the chairs and dropped into one.

"I guess I owe you an apology... and an explanation."

Carter smiled, actually smiled and he didn't seem so old when he did it. "I work for the Privy Council and they wanted me here. I didn't want to come."

Rae scoffed, unable to hold it back. "Yeah, that was a bit obvious. You're pretty miserable." The words slipped out before she realized.

Carter scratched the back of his head, looking sheepish, which weirded Rae out even more. "I deserve that. I didn't want to have you girls here. It was Lanford's idea and I seemed to be the only one who didn't trust him. He wanted you, not the other girls, but you, here, away from your family so he could swoop down to protect you and have you trust him."

Rae stared at the hem of her Tinkerbelle dress as the guilt she'd been denying rushed out of its hidden place and filled her up. "I did trust him. He was, or at least, he seemed to be sincere and genuinely concerned about me." Slow tears started dripping from her eyes.

"He needed to find out your ink. I knew that's what he was after, but I had no proof and it drove me mad. I finally had to resort to asking Riley for help. He's a candidate for joining the academy." Seeing the confused look on Rae's face, he added, "It's an intense training group of tatùs. Riley was more than eager to prove himself." Carter shook his head. "It drove me bonkers having to hang out with all you kids when I should be out in the field. I'm a man of action, not subterfuge. I'm terrible at having to wait. And having to watch you and wait for Lanford to reveal himself as the bad guy would make anyone cross. I'm sorry for giving you such a hard time. It's not your fault." Rae had a hard time picturing him as some British version of a G.I. Joe, but she figured maybe it was different with tatùs. He patted her knee. "You're a lot like your mom, you know? She had the same spunk, that inner fire which makes people want to be around you."

Rae's head felt as if it were spinning. *Now he knew her mother?* She had a million questions she wanted to ask him, but not tonight. "Will I have to leave the school now?"

"No. Now I think this is the safest place for you."

He didn't even hesitate when he replied. Rae let out a sigh of relief. She didn't want to go. "Are... are you coming back next year?"

Carter stood and crossed him arms over his chest. A small smile played on his face. "It seems Guilder is going to be in need of a new headmaster. Which is something I might be interested in. Especially when Rae Kerrigan has another year left and, as much as I hate to admit it, Guilder needs you girls here. It's good for everyone." He offered her his arm. "Shall we?"

They headed toward the stairs, moving aside to let the paramedics rush by. Alone on the staircase, Carter spoke again. "I'm sorry again about Lanford. I had no idea he was in league with your father." He shook his head. "Everything checked out. He'd been here ten years and nothing showed otherwise to mistrust him. It was only a gut feeling I had. I couldn't use my ink on him until tonight. Then I saw everything."

"It's not your fault, sir," Rae said woodenly. It came out an automatic response, with no feeling behind it. The truth was, Rae didn't know who was at fault and who wasn't. At the moment, all she knew was that she wanted to get out of the towers and never come back.

Carter sighed. "I've disappointed you and, most of all, I've disappointed your mother. I promised her a long time ago I'd keep you safe."

For a weird moment, Rae felt older than sixteen, her guilt, suspicion and hurt got pushed aside. "You can't protect me, and you can't undo the past. Lanford would've found a way to get to me one way or another. He said he'd been planning this for years."

RAE OF HOPE

Carter paused on the stairs. "Can I ask you a question?" He waited until she turned to face him. "How'd you get out of those shackles tonight?"

"M-my tatù." She felt like the wings were fluttering on her back, encouraging her to tell the truth. It was an odd sensation and caught her completely off-guard. "I-It's the same as my father's. But different. More." She didn't know how to explain it.

"Did you make the ice?"

Rae nodded, her mind picturing the prison room. If her tatù wanted her to tell Carter that much, then...what about the rest? "Sir, have you ever heard of something called 'H-O-C' or a hoc file?"

He shook his head slowly. "I've never heard of it."

"It's something my father and Lanford created." She went on to explain about the video in the laptop and what little detail the headmaster had provided, knowing in her heart that she needed to pass this information on to him.

"Interesting." The dean ran his fingers along his chin. "I've spent a lot of time working on your father's jobs and experiments. Most of his interests and agendas were very secretive. Only those close to him knew, and even then, it was always very little or bits and pieces, no one but Simon had the complete picture. I've...the Privy Council has spent years trying to find those who've worked for or with your father."

"I, uh, kinda fried the computer and there was a camera in there. I don't know how much it recorded..." Rae couldn't help but feel proud of the admission even knowing she may have destroyed vital clues.

"We'll see what we can salvage from the laptop and we'll check into the camera, too." Carter flashed a quick smile. "Your friends are waiting outside for you." He opened the door.

"Thanks." She looked at the dean, who beckoned her forward a few more steps.

"May I suggest we try and keep most of this quiet? You know which friends you can trust. The rest will know the truth soon enough. Or at least, what needs to be told."

"Yeah, I think I know what you mean." She started toward her friends. She glanced back. "Th-thanks…" But Carter had disappeared, "Sir," she whispered to the closed door. Maybe having him back next year might not be a bad thing.

As she turned to the parking lot, Molly came running, tears coursing down her cheeks. She enclosed Rae in a tight hug. "I can't believe it! You're okay! I'd have been a total mess. I'd have electrocuted everything in side, burned everything down and probably fried myself in the process." While she babbled on, Rae stared over her friend's shoulder and spotted Devon standing by Julian's car. She wanted to run and wrap her arms around him.

She never got a chance. Soon, everyone stood around her hugging, some crying and laughing, all at the same time.

"Rae, your outfit's ruined." Molly exclaimed as Rae threw the blanket onto the back of Julian's car.

"It's all right. I don't have any intension of ever wearing it again."

"Hey, watch the car." Julian's lips twitched.

She gave him the bird and laughed at the surprised look on his face.

"Uh… Rae?" Haley stood a few feet back from everyone else.

Rae's guard instantly came up. "What?"

"I'm, uh, I'm sorry I was kind of a bitch to you." Haley stuffed her hands into the oversized men's tux jacket she wore. "You know, the trying to hit you with the darts, the note in Professor Stockheed's class…all of it."

Molly leaned in front of Rae and pointed a finger at Haley, little sparks flying from it. "You're just apologizing 'cause you don't want to get screwed over by Rae's tatù."

256

Haley turned red and opened her mouth, but before she could say anything, Maria elbowed her. She glared at Molly, then Maria. "Look, I said I was sorry. I won't pester you anymore."

"How about we head back to Aumbry House?" Julian said, "I've had a vision Madame Elpis isn't going to mind if we all crash in the Game Room tonight."

Rae grabbed his hand. *Your vision turned out to be spot-on. Everything you drew was about tonight. I was the one who didn't look closely enough at it. I won't make that mistake again, I promise.* The eye had been the dean watching over and protecting her. She understood it now. She watched his eyes grow large, obviously shocked at hearing her voice in his own head and then he nodded in understanding. She let go and rubbed her hands along her arms. The cool night air made her shiver.

"I'm giving Rae a lift," Julian said. "You all can walk back."

Devon came over and hugged her tight. "I'm really glad you're okay."

Devon's warmth seeped into her core. He felt so good and everything suddenly didn't seem so awful. He slowly, almost reluctantly, pulled away.

Before she could react, Julian wrapped the blanket back around her and gently pushed her toward the passenger seat. "Race you back to the dorms, Dev."

He drove off to the student parking lot, leaving Devon behind.

.

Chapter 25

Hidden Wishes

THE next day, Dean Carter informed the entire school during dinner that Headmaster Lanford had suffered a heart attack the previous night after a fall and had passed away. The dean wouldn't go into details, but the look of shock on the faces of the students made Rae wish she could disappear. Only Julian, Devon and Molly knew the truth. At least, from her end of the story.

So Lanford was dead. She didn't care. She knew she should, but she really just wanted to forget. She needed something to help her do that, so she refocused on classes, and didn't even mind when the dean took over class in the Oratory. His attitude had changed dramatically, making it easy to engage him as a teacher and Rae began to enjoy class again. Carter never focused on or brought any extra attention to her, and she appreciated it.

The ten remaining weeks of the school year flew by. During one of the final dinners with the entire student body, Carter stood and walked to the podium. "I have a few announcements to make. First, I'd like to let everyone know I will not be returning as the dean of Guilder next year." He paused, then grinned. "I'll be returning as Headmaster. Someone needs to keep a good eye on you folks." He waited till the students quieted. "Devon's father, Randolph Wardell, will be the new dean of Guilder. All the professors are in full agreement he will do an excellent job."

Rae sat at a table a few rows away from Devon. She smiled and clapped with the other students.

Devon seemed slightly embarrassed, but stood. "My dad's pleased to have been offered the position." He smirked. "And I'm happy to be graduating."

Students erupted in laughter throughout the room, everyone but her. Rae didn't want to think about next year without Devon. Maybe, if he was gone, she'd get rid of the crush she had on him. But who was she going to talk to about her father? Or how frustrating her ink was? Or help her deal with all the baggage and crap that had come with Lanford's actions? She blinked rapidly, forcing the sudden tears away, and tried to push back down the anxiety that had tried to rise up and overtake her.

Carter clapped his hands for attention and everyone once again settled down. "I'd also like to mention Riley Johnson has been offered a job and is finishing the year at his current location."

Rae's eyes flitted around the room. The students didn't bat an eyelash with this news. *Seniors must leave quite often before the end of the year, probably secret jobs from top secret tatù businesses. No one cares that Riley left or why. No one really knows what happened that night.* Molly threw an arm over Rae's shoulder and gave her a quick squeeze, without saying a word. Rae smiled at her friend. Someone did care. She wasn't alone, and it was nice to be reminded of that every once in a while.

A few days later, Dean Carter asked Devon and Rae to meet him in his new office in the Oratory building. Carter sat behind the desk, hands interlaced casually across his stomach in a distinctly relaxed posture that Rae had never seen him in before. He spoke first to Devon. "I'm hoping you'll come back next year, as a paid employee of the college. I'd like you to continue helping Rae with tutoring and training with her abilities."

Devon's and Rae's mouths both dropped open.

"One of the reasons is that you know the whole story. Rae will need someone to work with and she's comfortable around you." He straightened and rested his large hands on top of the desk. "We'll offer you living accommodations, of course. There are two penthouse suites above the senior's floor on Joist Hall. One would be yours. You won't have to live by your father or answer to him -- just to me." He chuckled, like it was some kind of private joke. "You'll be paid a very fair salary and any university correspondence courses you take will be paid for by the school." Carter twiddled his thumbs and smiled pleasantly.

Devon glanced at Rae and then took a few moments before answering. "I'd be honored to help as best I can."

Rae wanted to jump up and down. *YES!* However, the feeling was short-lived when Carter spoke again.

"We've been working diligently, but haven't been able to find out anything more about Lanford or your father's connection to him." He nodded at Devon, but looked at Rae. "Devon's been caught up to speed completely with what happened the night of the dance. The laptop was unsalvageable. The Privy Council hasn't found any records or anything else regarding this so-called HOC file. Hopefully, the two of you may be able to uncover some information next term." He stared down his nose at the both of them.

"What about the camera on the ceiling?" Rae asked. Maybe Devon and she could get some extra correspondence out of it during the summer months. *And*

I'll, of course, focus completely on Devon – I mean on learning.
"It was wireless, connected to some kind of satellite we weren't able to trace." Carter leaned forward and shuffled a stack of papers against his desk. "If we learn any vital information over the summer, I'll let you know. If you are able to recall anything between now and the start of the new school year, write it down and let me know. The Privy Council will continue to search for anything connected to your father." He pointed to the door. "Now, get out of here and spend a bit of time with your friends before you fly back to New York for the summer. I'm here if you need me."

They walked down the hall and through the empty Oratory quietly together. Devon spoke once they got out into the sunshine. "I hope you don't mind if I stay on next year."

"No, no, not at all," she gushed. "I mean, I really appreciate you being willing to stay here. It won't be too bad with your dad? Doesn't he want you at Oxford or something?"

Devon grinned, his adorable dimple popping through. "Nah, I'll deal with him. It'll give me some time to figure out what I want to do with my life." He stopped talking but stared at her, as if he had something more to say.

When the silence began to get awkward, Rae shifted her weight and glanced toward the playing fields full of students. "I should probably get back to Molls. She gets a bit paranoid now when she doesn't know where I am."

"I have to ask Carter something, so I guess I'll see you later?" He didn't wait for her reply, but headed back towards the large Oratory doors. Just before disappearing, his hand shot out to keep the door open and his head popped around. "By the way, Rae." His dimple flashed again, "Tell Molly she did a cool job on your hair. It totally suits you." Then, he was gone, and Rae was left feeling vaguely let-down.

Chapter 26

The Letter

RAE finished packing her suitcases and checked her watch. She needed to hurry. Julian had probably fallen asleep waiting for her downstairs. She needed to be at the airport about two hours before her transatlantic flight took off. She did a final check around the room to make sure she had everything. When she came back in seven weeks, she'd be living in one of the rooms on the floor above and wouldn't be coming back to this room. *It's a bit of a shame...*

Part of her felt sad to leave, but she wanted to head back to America and spend some time with her aunt and uncle. Hopefully, Uncle Argyle would be willing to tell her about her mother and grandfather and even talk a bit about her father. She could get information out of him which she couldn't get from anyone else, *if* she could get him to talk.

Rae headed down the marble stairs with her new, larger suitcases, courtesy of Molly, and set them by the door. She ran back up to grab her duffle bag. She had already said good-bye to everyone except Devon. He'd seemed preoccupied when he popped by yesterday to say good bye to Molly. She'd wanted to give him a proper farewell, but he'd left before she had a chance. Plus, she wasn't quite sure how to handle him now...after their awkward conversation outside Carter's office.

Julian stood waiting in the foyer. He took her suitcases from her and set them by the door. He smiled his warm, friendly smile. "I have something for you." He handed her a white envelope.

"What's this?" The blank cover of the envelope gave away nothing.

He scratched behind his ear. "I had a vision early this morning and thought maybe you could help."

Rae opened the envelope with apprehension. The last time he'd handed her a vision it hadn't turned out so well. However, the reveal was anti-climactic. Inside was a piece of paper with nothing on it. She stared at Julian, confused.

"Rae, this is going to sound kind of corny but...pretend it's a letter. I know I didn't draw anything on it, but just work with me here for a moment." He paused and gave a small smile when Rae nodded. "That paper's trying to tell you something, you just need to open your mind to what it says."

She blinked, trying to make sense of what Julian was asking. She held the sheet with both hands and tried to pretend she was about to read a letter. She closed her eyes and exhaled a long, slow breath.

Julian started talking quietly. "There's this dope I know, who wanted to try and write you a letter. First he tried emailing, but that didn't work. He wanted tell you how he felt and ask you to forgive him. So, he thought that if he wrote it to you, it would be better. Except, this dummy doesn't know how to say it. He's all messed and confused in the head himself." Julian sighed, as if he understood the writer's frustration. "If this guy could just

263

realize his feelings would explain everything to you... Ahh, but his pen never moves. The idiot doesn't know how to start, or finish, the letter. He wanted to tell you how he'd made a mistake and he wished he'd never listened to those around him, or allowed himself to step back from you." Julian grunted. "He should've just followed his heart all along."

Julian stopped talking and Rae heard him move towards the door. She opened her eyes and stared at the blank paper. She gazed at the pretend letter for a long time and then back to Julian.

"Where is he? Do I still have time to see him before we have to go?"

Julian grinned and glanced at his watch. "You've about ten minutes. He's in his room packing." He grabbed both of Rae's suitcases. "I'll get these in the car for you in the meantime." He disappeared out the door with a smirk on his face.

Rae looked down one more time. *Go to him.* She heard her mother's voice and knew that was exactly what her mom would have told her to do. Rae dropped the letter and took off running through the front door toward Joist House.

She barreled through the entrance, and straight up the marble stairs to the top floor, not caring what kind of scene she made. Winded by the time she got to Devon's door, she took a few deep breaths. She knocked once before barging straight into the room. Devon stood behind the suitcase on his bed.

"Julian, I told you already I'm not --" he stopped short when he saw Rae standing in the room.

"Hi." All the self-confidence Rae'd felt a minute ago, disappeared. She tucked a curl behind her ear and tugged it behind again when it popped back immediately, refusing to obey. *Great, here I am, tongue-tied with my hair flying everywhere...What now?*

"Hey." Devon stared at her for a moment and then focused on refolding a shirt he'd already packed into his suitcase.

"Julian's taking me to the airport. He said he had a vision this morning." She swallowed nervously, not sure what to say. When Devon stayed silent and continued to gaze at his suitcase, Rae mustered what courage she could find. "He said you tried to write me a letter..."

Devon's head popped up in surprise. Rae could feel tears fill her eyes, so she glanced at the ceiling, begging them not to fall. She took a deep, shaky breath and glanced back toward Devon. She trembled as she watched him walk over to her. He put both of his hands gently on her face, his fingers silently brushing the tears from her cheeks.

"I'm so sorry...About...About --" His voice broke as he spoke. "I didn't know what to write then, or what to say now. I'm just so sorry."

"Don't be sorry. It's not your fault." She reached up and removed Devon's hands from her face, keeping them held inside of hers. "Nobody saw it coming. Everyone trusted Lanford. Carter said he went off a gut feeling and had to follow the hunch, hoping he might be right." She blew her bangs from her face. "Julian's taking me to the airport in about five minutes. I don't want to spend the summer worrying if you're never returning to Guilder because of me. I don't want to lose your friendship." *I don't want to lose you. I need you.*

"I'm coming back." He smiled and showed his adorable dimple. Worry lines appeared on his forehead as his brows mashed together. "I'm the idiot. In so many ways, I can't even begin to explain, or try to show you."

"Don't --" Rae started, but Devon cut off her words off with a kiss. He pressed his warm, soft lips against hers. The kiss felt like the flutter of a thousand wings from butterflies setting off into flight. It was like time stood still and nothing else mattered at that moment or was ever going to matter again if Devon wasn't with her. At the same moment her stole her breath away, he stole her heart. He slowly pulled away, but barely. As he spoke, his lips brushed lightly against hers. "I have, for a very long time, been very much in love with you. I'm just a fool who didn't know how to say it. I kept trying to follow the path everyone else instructed us to go down -- the one I'm expected to follow." Devon swallowed. "When, all along, I should've just followed my heart."

Wow! Can life get any better than this? She smiled, sure the corners of her mouth were close to touching her ears. "I've never really been one for doing what's expected." She shrugged nonchalantly, but couldn't stop the excitement coursing through her body. *This is ten times better than the morning of my sixteenth birthday.*

Devon grinned and rubbed his nose against hers. When a knock sounded on the door, and Rae and Devon jumped apart, suddenly conscious about how wrong this could be. Getting caught before anything had started could ruin everything, on so many different levels.

Julian popped his head inside the room. "I really hate to be the one to interrupt the two of you, but Rae needs to head to the airport or she's going to miss her flight." He tossed a balled up piece of paper at Devon. "The offer still stands. -- if you're interested."

"Offer?" Rae glanced back and forth between the two guys.

Devon chuckled and put his arm around her shoulders. "Julian made two offers to me this morning. I could come with him to bring you to the airport, and try to tell you how I felt. Or, use his car and take you myself. I think I'll take him up on the second offer."

"You don't mind?" she asked Julian.

"Silly girl with the super-ability. Do you think I could say no?" Julian tossed his car keys at Devon. "Just don't let her drive. She may be talented, but she's a bloody

American." He laughed and jumped back when Rae forced the door closed with a gust of wind.

Devon and Rae stared at each other, both smiling like lunatics. They walked down to the car in a companionable silence.

"Do you have plans for the summer?" Rae asked once they were on the motorway.

"I'm heading home for a week and then Carter wants me and Julian to come back, and apply to the Privy Council academy. Plus, my dad wants me to help set his office up." He rolled his eyes. "What about you?"

She touched his knee, still thinking this had to be a dream. "Not much. I'll work on my tatù, and I've got a hundred questions I want to ask my uncle."

"Let me know if you learn anything. Email or, if you're allowed, call me?"

"Of course." She glanced at his tight jaw line. "What's up?"

"Nothing, really," he said. "I...I just think we maybe shouldn't say anything... to anyone, you know, about us."

She should have felt guarded. A boy asking a girl to keep their relationship a secret couldn't be a good sign. But this was different. They were different. She knew they weren't any normal boy and girl. "I think you're right. After the year I've just had, and my parents' history...We'd give the professors, and my uncle, a massive coronary."

"We can figure stuff out when you get back next term." He winked at her. "I'm still mentoring you, and I've got my own place next year. Nobody'll suspect a thing."

"Yeah, it's almost as if Carter knew, when he set up the position for you." They both glanced at each other and after a moment, broke into laughter. *Fat chance!*

At the terminal, Devon gave Rae a tight hug and leaned in to kiss her. A voice announced on the speakers that her flight was now boarding.

Devon deepened the kiss. Again, the flutter of butterfly wings floated around Rae. She totally got what Molly had been talking about all year. This was how a first kiss was supposed to feel. She understood her tatù's wings gave her the fluttering wing-feeling and smiled at her deep, personal understanding.

"This summer's going to take forever." Devon rested his forehead against hers.

"I'll let you in on a little secret." Rae loved the wild abandonment feeling being with Devon gave her. "The first kiss is something a girl never forgets. This feeling, at this very moment, could carry me through a hundred summers," she whispered, lightly pulling on her bottom lip with her teeth.

Devon groaned. "One summer apart is enough for me."

Rae kissed his ear and whispered, "I'm glad we stopped hiding and told each other how we feel." *I can't wait till next year, and a lot more kisses.* "I guess we owe Julian."

Devon shook his head slightly. "He's never going to let me forget." He wrapped his arms tightly around her waist. "It's totally worth it." He kissed her again.

Slowly, she stepped back from him, and, after a few reluctant seconds, he let go of her hand. "See you in seven weeks," he said.

She laughed. "You're counting already?"

"You better believe it!"

Ω

Glossary Terms – Tudor comparison

Aumbry House ----A recess to hold sacred vessels, often found in castle chapels.
Aumbry House was considered very special to hold the female students – their sacred vessels (especially Rae Kerrigan).

Joist House ---- A timber stretched from wall-to-wall to support floorboards.
Joist House was considered a building of support where the male students could support and help each other.

Oratory ---- A private chapel in a house.
Private education room in the school where the students were able to practice their gifting and improve their skills. Also used as a banquet – dance hall when needed.

Oriel ---- A projecting window in a wall; originally a form of porch, often of wood. The original bay windows of the Tudor period. Guilder College majority of windows were oriel.
Rae often felt her life was being watching through one of these windows. Hence the constant reference to them.

Refectory ---- A communal dining hall. Same termed used in Tudor times.

Scriptorium ---- A Medieval writing room in which scrolls were also housed.
Used for English classes and still store some of the older books from the Tudor reign (regarding tatùs).

Privy Council ---- Secret council and "arm of the

government" similar to the CIA, etc... In Tudor times, the Privy Council was King Henry's board of advisors and helped run the country.

SONG LIST

Chapter 1 - Guilder Boarding School
Closer to the Edge by 30 seconds to Mars

Chapter 2 - Proverb of Truth
You make me feel by Cobra Starship

Chapter 3 - Headmaster Lanford
Hello by Martin Solveig

Chapter 4 - Unwanted Answers
Iridescent by Linkin Park

Chapter 5 - Friends?
Changing by Airborne Toxic Event

Chapter 6 - Lessons of the Past
Weight of time by Rise Against

Chapter 7 – Tatù
The Requiem by Linkin Park

Chapter 8 - Dean Carter
Country Song by Seether

Chapter 9 – Competition
Woo Boost by Rusko

Chapter 10 - Magic Class
What you want by Evanesence

Chapter 11 - American Cheeseburger in London
Howlin' for you by the Black Keys

Chapter 12 - The Dance

Stereo Hearts by Gym Class Heros and
Change by Taylor Swift

Chapter 13 – Mail
Sail by AWOLNation

Chapter 14 – Gifting
Walk by Foo Fighters
and
Shake Your Tail Feather by Nelly, P.Didy and Murphy Lee

Chapter 15 - November 13 + 14
Walking on Air by Kerli

Chapter 16 - November 15
Panic by Sublime with Rome

Chapter 17 - C-O-P
When they come for me by Linkin Park

Chapter 18 - Alumni Dinner
Make It Stop (September's Children) by Rise Against

Chapter 19 - Friendly Advice
Sunset in July by 311

Chapter 20 - Personal Demons
Blackout by Linkin Park

Chapter 21 – Deceived
Weight of time by Rise Against

Chapter 22 – Destiny
Vox Populi by 30 Seconds to Mars   and
What Do You Want From Me? by Adam Lambert

2

About The Author

W.J. May

W.J. May grew up in the fruit belt of Ontario, Canada - St. Catherines. Crazy- happy childhood, she always has a vivid imagination and loads of energy.

She attended the University of Toronto, and Kansas State University winning CIAU's and becoming All-American 6x-NCAA Indoors Runner Up.

In 2009, May began her writing career with her debut novel Rae of Hope.

Visit her website:
http://www.wanitamay.yolasite.com

Blog site: http://www.wanitajump.wordpress.com

Made in the USA
Lexington, KY
17 November 2011